J. J. Connington and The Murder Room

>>> This title is part of The Murder Room, our series dedicated to making available out-of-print or hard-to-find titles by classic crime writers.

Crime fiction has always held up a mirror to society. The Victorians were fascinated by sensational murder and the emerging science of detection; now we are obsessed with the forensic detail of violent death. And no other genre has so captivated and enthralled readers.

Vast troves of classic crime writing have for a long time been unavailable to all but the most dedicated frequenters of second-hand bookshops. The advent of digital publishing means that we are now able to bring you the backlists of a huge range of titles by classic and contemporary crime writers, some of which have been out of print for decades.

From the genteel amateur private eyes of the Golden Age and the femmes fatales of pulp fiction, to the morally ambiguous hard-boiled detectives of mid twentieth-century America and their descendants who walk our twenty-first century streets, The Murder Room has it all. **>>>**

The Murder Room
Where Criminal Minds Meet

themurderroom.com

T0345483

J. J. Connington (1880–1947)

Alfred Walter Stewart, who wrote under the pen name J. J. Connington, was born in Glasgow, the youngest of three sons of Reverend Dr Stewart. He graduated from Glasgow University and pursued an academic career as a chemistry professor, working for the Admiralty during the First World War. Known for his ingenious and carefully worked-out puzzles and in-depth character development, he was admired by a host of his better-known contemporaries, including Dorothy L. Sayers and John Dickson Carr, who both paid tribute to his influence on their work. He married Jessie Lily Courts in 1916 and they had one daughter.

By J. J. Connington

Sir Clinton Driffield Mysteries
Murder in the Maze (1927)
Tragedy at Ravensthorpe (1927)
The Case with Nine Solutions
(1928)
Mystery at Lynden Sands (1928)
Nemesis at Raynham Parva
(1929)
(a.k.a. Grim Vengenace)
The Boathouse Riddle (1931)
The Sweepstake Murders (1931)
The Castleford Conundrum
(1932)
The Ha-Ha Case (1934)
(a.k.a. The Brandon Case)
In Whose Dim Shadow (1935)
(a.k.a. The Tau Cross Mystery)
A Minor Operation (1937)
Murder Will Speak (1938)

Truth Comes Limping (1938)
The Twenty-One Clues (1941)
No Past is Dead (1942)
Jack-in-the-Box (1944)
Common Sense Is All You
Need (1947)

Supt Ross Mysteries
The Eye in the Museum (1929)
The Two Tickets Puzzle (1930)

Novels
Death at Swaythling Court
(1926)
The Dangerfield Talisman (1926)
Tom Tiddler's Island (1933)
(a.k.a. Gold Brick Island)
The Counsellor (1939)
The Four Defences (1940)

The Four Defences

J. J. Connington

An Orion book

Copyright © The Professor A. W. Stewart Deceased Trust 1940, 2013

The right of J. J. Connington to be identified as the author of this work has been asserted in accordance with the Copyright, Designs and Patents Act 1988.

This edition published by
The Orion Publishing Group Ltd
Orion House
5 Upper St Martin's Lane
London WC2H 9EA

An Hachette UK company
A CIP catalogue record for this book is available from the British Library

ISBN 978 1 4719 0639 8

www.orionbooks.co.uk

CONTENTS

CONTENTS

Introduction
by
Curtis Evans

During the Golden Age of the detective novel, in the 1920s and 1930s, J. J. Connington stood with fellow crime writers R. Austin Freeman, Cecil John Charles Street and Freeman Wills Crofts as the foremost practitioner in British mystery fiction of the science of pure detection. I use the word 'science' advisedly, for the man behind J. J. Connington, Alfred Walter Stewart, was an esteemed Scottish-born scientist. A 'small, unassuming, moustached polymath', Stewart was 'a strikingly effective lecturer with an excellent sense of humor, fertile imagination and fantastically retentive memory', qualities that also served him well in his fiction. He held the Chair of Chemistry at Queens University, Belfast for twenty-five years, from 1919 until his retirement in 1944.

During roughly this period, the busy Professor Stewart found time to author a remarkable apocalyptic science fiction tale, *Nordenholt's Million* (1923), a mainstream novel, *Almighty Gold* (1924), a collection of essays, *Alias J. J. Connington* (1947), and, between 1926 and 1947, twenty-four mysteries (all but one tales of detection), many of them sterling examples of the Golden Age puzzle-oriented detective novel at its considerable best. 'For those who ask first of all in a detective story for exact and mathematical accuracy in the construction of the plot', avowed a contemporary *London Daily Mail* reviewer, 'there is no author to equal the distinguished scientist who writes under the name of J. J. Connington.'[1]

Alfred Stewart's background as a man of science is reflected in his fiction, not only in the impressive puzzle plot mechanics he devised for his mysteries but in his choices of themes and depictions of characters. Along with Stanley Nordenholt of *Nordenholt's Million*, a novel about a plutocrat's pitiless efforts to preserve a ruthlessly remolded remnant of human life after a global environmental calamity, Stewart's most notable character is Chief Constable Sir Clinton Driffield, the detective in seventeen of the twenty-four Connington crime novels. Driffield is one of crime fiction's most highhanded investigators, occasionally taking on the functions of judge and jury as well as chief of police.

Absent from Stewart's fiction is the hail-fellow-well-met quality found in John Street's works or the religious ethos suffusing those of Freeman Wills Crofts, not to mention the effervescent novel-of-manners style of the British Golden Age Crime Queens Dorothy L. Sayers, Margery Allingham and Ngaio Marsh. Instead we see an often disdainful cynicism about the human animal and a marked admiration for detached supermen with superior intellects. For this reason, reading a Connington novel can be a challenging experience for modern readers inculcated in gentler social beliefs. Yet Alfred Stewart produced a classic apocalyptic science fiction tale in *Nordenholt's Million* (justly dubbed 'exciting and terrifying reading' by the *Spectator*) as well as superb detective novels boasting well-wrought puzzles, bracing characterization and an occasional leavening of dry humor. Not long after Stewart's death in 1947, the Connington novels fell entirely out of print. The recent embrace of Stewart's fiction by Orion's Murder Room imprint is a welcome event indeed, correcting as it does over sixty years of underserved neglect of an accomplished genre writer.

Born in Glasgow on 5 September 1880, Alfred Stewart had significant exposure to religion in his earlier life. His father was William Stewart, longtime Professor of Divinity and Biblical Criticism at Glasgow University, and he married Lily Coats, a daughter of the Reverend Jervis Coats and member of one of

Scotland's preeminent Baptist families. Religious sensibility is entirely absent from the Connington corpus, however. A confirmed secularist, Stewart once referred to one of his wife's brothers, the Reverend William Holms Coats (1881–1954), principal of the Scottish Baptist College, as his 'mental and spiritual antithesis', bemusedly adding: 'It's quite an education to see what one would look like if one were turned into one's mirror-image.'

Stewart's J. J. Connington pseudonym was derived from a nineteenth-century Oxford Professor of Latin and translator of Horace, indicating that Stewart's literary interests lay not in pietistic writing but rather in the pre-Christian classics ('I prefer the *Odyssey* to *Paradise Lost*,' the author once avowed). Possessing an inquisitive and expansive mind, Stewart was in fact an uncommonly well-read individual, freely ranging over a variety of literary genres. His deep immersion in French literature and supernatural horror fiction, for example, is documented in his lively correspondence with the noted horologist Rupert Thomas Gould.[2]

It thus is not surprising that in the 1920s the intellectually restless Stewart, having achieved a distinguished middle age as a highly regarded man of science, decided to apply his creative energy to a new endeavor, the writing of fiction. After several years he settled, like other gifted men and women of his generation, on the wildly popular mystery genre. Stewart was modest about his accomplishments in this particular field of light fiction, telling Rupert Gould later in life that 'I write these things [what Stewart called tec yarns] because they amuse me in parts when I am putting them together and because they are the only writings of mine that the public will look at. Also, in a minor degree, because I like to think some people get pleasure out of them.' No doubt Stewart's single most impressive literary accomplishment is *Nordenholt's Million*, yet in their time the two dozen J. J. Connington mysteries did indeed give readers in Great Britain, the United States and other countries much diversionary reading pleasure. Today these works constitute an estimable addition to British crime fiction.

After his 'prentice pastiche mystery, *Death at Swaythling Court* (1926), a rural English country-house tale set in the highly traditional village of Fernhurst Parva, Stewart published another, superior country-house affair, *The Dangerfield Talisman* (1926), a novel about the baffling theft of a precious family heirloom, an ancient, jewel-encrusted armlet. This clever, murderless tale, which likely is the one that the author told Rupert Gould he wrote in under six weeks, was praised in *The Bookman* as 'continuously exciting and interesting' and in the *New York Times Book Review* as 'ingeniously fitted together and, what is more, written with a deal of real literary charm'. Despite its virtues, however, *The Dangerfield Talisman* is not fully characteristic of mature Connington detective fiction. The author needed a memorable series sleuth, more representative of his own forceful personality.

It was the next year, 1927, that saw J. J. Connington make his break to the front of the murdermongerer's pack with a third country-house mystery, *Murder in the Maze*, wherein debuted as the author's great series detective the assertive and acerbic Sir Clinton Driffield, along with Sir Clinton's neighbor and 'Watson', the more genial (if much less astute) Squire Wendover. In this much-praised novel, Stewart's detective duo confronts some truly diabolical doings, including slayings by means of curare-tipped darts in the double-centered hedge maze at a country estate, Whistlefield. No less a fan of the genre than T. S. Eliot praised *Murder in the Maze* for its construction ('we are provided early in the story with all the clues which guide the detective') and its liveliness ('The very idea of murder in a box-hedge labyrinth does the author great credit, and he makes full use of its possibilities'). The delighted Eliot concluded that

Murder in the Maze was 'a really first-rate detective story'. For his part, the critic H. C. Harwood declared in *The Outlook* that with the publication of *Murder in the Maze* Connington demanded and deserved 'comparison with the masters'. 'Buy, borrow, or – anyhow – get hold of it', he amusingly advised. Two decades later, in his 1946 critical essay 'The Grandest Game in the World', the great locked-room detective novelist John Dickson Carr echoed Eliot's assessment of the novel's virtuoso setting, writing: 'These 1920s [. . .] thronged with sheer brains. What would be one of the best possible settings for violent death? J. J. Connington found the answer, with *Murder in the Maze*.' Certainly in retrospect *Murder in the Maze* stands as one of the finest English country-house mysteries of the 1920s, cleverly yet fairly clued, imaginatively detailed and often grimly suspenseful. As the great American true-crime writer Edmund Lester Pearson noted in his review of *Murder in the Maze* in *The Outlook*, this Connington novel had everything that one could desire in a detective story: 'A shrubbery maze, a hot day, and somebody potting at you with an air gun loaded with darts covered with a deadly South-American arrow-poison – *there* is a situation to wheedle two dollars out of anybody's pocket.'[3]

Staying with what had worked so well for him to date, Stewart the same year produced yet another country-house mystery, *Tragedy at Ravensthorpe*, an ingenious tale of murders and thefts at the ancestral home of the Chacewaters, old family friends of Sir Clinton Driffield. There is much clever matter in *Ravensthorpe*. Especially fascinating is the author's inspired integration of faerie folklore into his plot. Stewart, who had a lifelong – though skeptical – interest in paranormal phenomena, probably was inspired in this instance by the recent hubbub over the Cottingly Faeries photographs that in the early 1920s had famously duped, among other individuals, Arthur Conan Doyle.[4] As with *Murder in the Maze*, critics raved about this new Connington mystery. In the *Spectator*, for example, a reviewer hailed *Tragedy at Ravensthorpe* in the strongest terms, declaring of the novel: 'This is more than a good detective tale. Alike in plot, characterization, and literary style, it is a work of art.'

In 1928 there appeared two additional Sir Clinton Driffield detective novels, *Mystery at Lynden Sands* and *The Case with Nine Solutions*. Once again there was great praise for the latest Conningtons. H. C. Harwood, the critic who had so much admired *Murder in the Maze*, opined of *Mystery at Lynden Sands* that it 'may just fail of being the detective story of the century', while in the United States author and book reviewer Frederic F. Van de Water expressed nearly as high an opinion of *The Case with Nine Solutions*. 'This book is a thoroughbred of a distinguished lineage that runs back to "The Gold Bug" of [Edgar Allan] Poe,' he avowed. 'It represents the highest type of detective fiction.' In both of these Connington novels, Stewart moved away from his customary country-house milieu, setting *Lynden Sands* at a fashionable beach resort and *Nine Solutions* at a scientific research institute. *Nine Solutions* is of particular interest today, I think, for its relatively frank sexual subject matter and its modern urban setting among science professionals, which rather resembles the locales found in P. D. James' classic detective novels *A Mind to Murder* (1963) and *Shroud for a Nightingale* (1971).

By the end of the 1920s, J. J. Connington's critical reputation had achieved enviable heights indeed. At this time Stewart became one of the charter members of the Detection Club, an assemblage of the finest writers of British detective fiction that included, among other distinguished individuals, Agatha Christie, Dorothy L. Sayers and G. K. Chesterton. Certainly Victor Gollancz, the British publisher of the J. J. Connington mysteries, did not stint praise for the author, informing readers that 'J. J. Connington is now established as, in the opinion of many, the greatest living master of the story of pure detection. He is one of those who, discarding all the superfluities, has made of deductive fiction a genuine minor art, with its own laws and its own conventions.'

Such warm praise for J. J. Connington makes it all the more surprising that at this juncture the esteemed author tinkered with his successful formula by dispensing with his original series detective. In the fifth Clinton Driffield detective novel, *Nemesis at Raynham Parva* (1929), Alfred Walter Stewart, rather like Arthur Conan Doyle before him, seemed with a dramatic dénouement to have devised his popular series detective's permanent exit from the fictional stage (read it and see for yourself). The next two Connington detective novels, *The Eye in the Museum* (1929) and *The Two Tickets Puzzle* (1930), have a different series detective, Superintendent Ross, a rather dull dog of a policeman. While both these mysteries are competently done – the railway material in *The Two Tickets Puzzle* is particularly effective and should have appeal today – the presence of Sir Clinton Driffield (no superfluity he!) is missed.

Probably Stewart detected that the public minded the absence of the brilliant and biting Sir Clinton, for the Chief Constable – accompanied, naturally, by his friend Squire Wendover – triumphantly returned in 1931 in *The Boathouse Riddle*, another well-constructed criminous country-house affair. Later in the year came *The Sweepstake Murders*, which boasts the perennially popular tontine multiple-murder plot, in this case a rapid succession of puzzling suspicious deaths afflicting the members of a sweepstake syndicate that has just won nearly £250,000.[5] Adding piquancy to this plot is the fact that Wendover is one of the imperiled syndicate members. Altogether the novel is, as the late Jacques Barzun and his colleague Wendell Hertig Taylor put it in *A Catalogue of Crime* (1971, 1989), their magisterial survey of detective fiction, 'one of Connington's best conceptions'.

Stewart's productivity as a fiction writer slowed in the 1930s, so that, barring the year 1938, at most only one new Connington appeared annually. However, in 1932 Stewart produced one of the best Connington mysteries, *The Castleford Conundrum*. A classic country-house detective novel, Castleford introduces to readers Stewart's most delightfully unpleasant set of greedy relations and one of his most deserving murderees, Winifred Castleford. Stewart also fashions a wonderfully rich puzzle plot, full of meaty material clues for the reader's delectation. *Castleford* presented critics with no conundrum over its quality. 'In *The Castleford Conundrum* Mr Connington goes to work like an accomplished chess player. The moves in the games his detectives are called on to play are a delight to watch,' raved the reviewer for the *Sunday Times*, adding that 'the clues would have rejoiced Mr. Holmes' heart.' For its part, the *Spectator* concurred in the *Sunday Times'* assessment of the novel's masterfully constructed plot: 'Few detective stories show such sound reasoning as that by which the Chief Constable brings the crime home to the culprit.' Additionally, E. C. Bentley, much admired himself as the author of the landmark detective novel *Trent's Last Case*, took time to praise Connington's purely literary virtues, noting: 'Mr Connington has never written better, or drawn characters more full of life.'

With *Tom Tiddler's Island* in 1933 Stewart produced a different sort of Connington, a criminal-gang mystery in the rather more breathless style of such hugely popular English thriller writers as Sapper, Sax Rohmer, John Buchan and Edgar Wallace (in violation of the strict detective fiction rules of Ronald Knox, there is even a secret passage in the novel). Detailing the startling discoveries made by a newlywed couple honeymooning on a remote Scottish island, *Tom Tiddler's Island* is an atmospheric and entertaining tale, though it is not as mentally stimulating for armchair sleuths as Stewart's true detective novels. The title, incidentally, refers to an ancient British children's game, 'Tom Tiddler's Ground', in which one child tries to hold a height against other children.

After his fictional Scottish excursion into thrillerdom, Stewart returned the next year to his English country-house roots with *The Ha-Ha Case* (1934), his last masterwork in this classic mystery setting (for elucidation of non-British readers, a ha-ha is a sunken wall, placed so as to delineate property boundaries while not obstructing views). Although *The Ha-Ha Case* is not set in Scotland, Stewart drew inspiration for the novel from a notorious Scottish true crime, the 1893 Ardlamont murder case. From the facts of the Ardlamont affair Stewart drew several of the key characters in *The Ha-Ha Case*, as well as the circumstances of the novel's murder (a shooting 'accident' while hunting), though he added complications that take the tale in a new direction.[6]

In newspaper reviews both Dorothy L. Sayers and 'Francis Iles' (crime novelist Anthony Berkeley Cox) highly praised this latest mystery by 'The Clever Mr Connington', as he was now dubbed on book jackets by his new English publisher, Hodder & Stoughton. Sayers particularly noted the effective characterisation in *The Ha-Ha Case*: 'There is no need to say that Mr Connington has given us a sound and interesting plot, very carefully and ingeniously worked out. In addition, there are the three portraits of the three brothers, cleverly and rather subtly characterised, of the [governess], and of Inspector Hinton, whose admirable qualities are counteracted by that besetting sin of the man who has made his own way: a jealousy of delegating responsibility.' The reviewer for the *Times Literary Supplement* detected signs that the sardonic Sir Clinton Driffield had begun mellowing with age: 'Those who have never really liked Sir Clinton's perhaps excessively soldierly manner will be surprised to find that he makes his discovery not only by the pure light of intelligence, but partly as a reward for amiability and tact, qualities in which the Inspector [Hinton] was strikingly deficient.' This is true enough, although the classic Sir Clinton emerges a number of times in the novel, as in his subtly sarcastic recurrent backhanded praise of Inspector Hinton: 'He writes a first class report.'

Clinton Driffield returned the next year in the detective novel *In Whose Dim Shadow* (1935), a tale set in a recently erected English suburb, the denizens of which seem to have committed an impressive number of indiscretions, including sexual ones. The intriguing title of the British edition of the novel is drawn from a poem by the British historian Thomas Babington Macaulay: 'Those trees in whose dim shadow/The ghastly priest doth reign/The priest who slew the slayer/And shall himself be slain.' Stewart's puzzle plot in *In Whose Dim Shadow* is well clued and compelling, the kicker of a closing paragraph is a classic of its kind and, additionally, the author paints some excellent character portraits. I fully concur with the *Sunday Times'* assessment of the tale: 'Quiet domestic murder, full of the neatest detective points [. . .] These are not the detective's stock figures, but fully realised human beings.'[7]

Uncharacteristically for Stewart, nearly twenty months elapsed between the publication of *In Whose Dim Shadow* and his next book, *A Minor Operation* (1937). The reason for the author's delay in production was the onset in 1935–36 of the afflictions of cataracts and heart disease (Stewart ultimately succumbed to heart disease in 1947). Despite these grave health complications, Stewart in late 1936 was able to complete *A Minor Operation*, a first-rate Clinton Driffield story of murder and a most baffling disappearance. A *Times Literary Supplement* reviewer found that *A Minor Operation* treated the reader 'to exactly the right mixture of mystification and clue' and that, in addition to its impressive construction, the novel boasted 'character-drawing above the average' for a detective novel.

Alfred Stewart's final eight mysteries, which appeared between 1938 and 1947, the year of the author's death, are, on the whole, a somewhat weaker group of tales than the sixteen that appeared between 1926 and 1937, yet they are not without interest. In 1938 Stewart for the last time managed to publish two detective novels, *Truth Comes Limping* and *For Murder Will Speak* (also published as *Murder Will Speak*). The latter tale is much the superior of the two, having an interesting suburban setting and a bevy of female characters found to have motives when a contemptible philandering businessman meets with foul play. Sexual neurosis plays a major role in *For Murder Will Speak*, the ever-thorough Stewart obviously having made a study of the subject when writing the novel. The somewhat squeamish reviewer for *Scribner's Magazine* considered the subject matter of *For Murder Will Speak* 'rather unsavory at times', yet this individual conceded that the novel nevertheless made 'first-class reading for those who enjoy a good puzzle intricately worked out'. 'Judge Lynch' in the *Saturday Review* apparently had no such moral reservations about the latest Clinton Driffield murder case, avowing simply of the novel: 'They don't come any better'.

Over the next couple of years Stewart again sent Sir Clinton Driffield temporarily packing, replacing him with a new series detective, a brash radio personality named Mark Brand, in *The Counsellor* (1939) and *The Four Defences* (1940). The better of these two novels is *The Four Defences*, which Stewart based on another notorious British true-crime case, the Alfred Rouse blazing-car murder. (Rouse is believed to have fabricated his death by murdering an unknown man, placing the dead man's body in his car and setting the car on fire, in the hope that the murdered man's body would be taken for his.) Though admittedly a thinly characterised academic exercise in ratiocination, Stewart's *Four Defences* surely is also one of the most complexly plotted Golden Age detective novels and should delight devotees of classical detection. Taking the Rouse blazing-car affair as his theme, Stewart composes from it a stunning set of diabolically ingenious criminal variations. 'This is in the cold-blooded category which [. . .] excites a crossword puzzle kind of interest,' the reviewer for the *Times Literary Supplement* acutely noted of the novel. 'Nothing in the Rouse case would prepare you for these complications upon complications [. . .] What they prove is that Mr Connington has the power of penetrating into the puzzle-corner of the brain. He leaves it dazedly wondering whether in the records of actual crime there can be any dark deed to equal this in its planned convolutions.'

Sir Clinton Driffield returned to action in the remaining four detective novels in the Connington oeuvre, *The Twenty-One Clues* (1941), *No Past is Dead* (1942), *Jack-in-the-Box* (1944) and *Commonsense is All You Need* (1947), all of which were written as Stewart's heart disease steadily worsened and reflect to some extent his diminishing physical and mental energy. Although *The Twenty-One Clues* was inspired by the notorious Hall-Mills double murder case – probably the most publicised murder case in the United States in the 1920s – and the American critic and novelist Anthony Boucher commended *Jack-in-the-Box*, I believe the best of these later mysteries is *No Past Is Dead*, which Stewart partly based on a bizarre French true-crime affair, the 1891 Achet-Lepine murder case.[8] Besides providing an interesting background for the tale, the ailing author managed some virtuoso plot twists, of the sort most associated today with that ingenious Golden Age Queen of Crime, Agatha Christie.

What Stewart with characteristic bluntness referred to as 'my complete crack-up' forced his retirement from Queen's University in 1944. 'I am afraid,' Stewart wrote a friend, the chemist and forensic scientist F. Gerald Tryhorn, in August 1946, eleven months before his death, 'that I shall never be much use again. Very stupidly, I tried for a session to combine a full course of lecturing with angina pectoris; and ended up by establishing that the two are immiscible.' He added that since retiring in 1944, he had been physically 'limited to my house, since even a fifty-yard crawl brings on the usual cramps'. Stewart completed his essay collection and a final novel before he died at his study desk in his Belfast home on 1 July 1947, at the age of sixty-six. When death came to the author he was busy at work, writing.

More than six decades after Alfred Walter Stewart's death, his J. J. Connington fiction is again available to a wider audience of classic-mystery fans, rather than strictly limited to a select company of rare-book collectors with deep pockets. This is fitting for an individual who was one of the finest writers of British genre fiction between the two world wars. 'Heaven forfend that you should imagine I take myself for anything out of the common in the tec yarn stuff,' Stewart once self-deprecatingly declared in a letter to Rupert Gould. Yet, as contemporary critics recognised, as a writer of detective and science fiction Stewart indeed was something out of the common. Now more modern readers can find this out for themselves. They have much good sleuthing in store.

1. For more on Street, Crofts and particularly Stewart, see Curtis Evans, *Masters of the 'Humdrum' Mystery: Cecil John Charles Street, Freeman Wills Crofts, Alfred Walter Stewart and the British Detective Novel, 1920–1961* (Jefferson, NC: McFarland, 2012). On the academic career of Alfred Walter Stewart, see his entry in *Oxford Dictionary of National Biography* (London and New York: Oxford University Press, 2004), vol. 52, 627–628.
2. The Gould-Stewart correspondence is discussed in considerable detail in *Masters of the 'Humdrum' Mystery*. For more on the life of the fascinating Rupert Thomas Gould, see Jonathan Betts, *Time Restored: The Harrison Timekeepers and R. T. Gould, the*

Man Who Knew (Almost) Everything (London and New York: Oxford University Press, 2006) and *Longitude,* the 2000 British film adaptation of Dava Sobel's book *Longitude:The True Story of a Lone Genius Who Solved the Greatest Scientific Problem of His Time* (London: Harper Collins, 1995), which details Gould's restoration of the marine chronometers built by in the eighteenth century by the clockmaker John Harrison.

3. Potential purchasers of *Murder in the Maze* should keep in mind that $2 in 1927 is worth over $26 today.

4. In a 1920 article in *The Strand Magazine,* Arthur Conan Doyle endorsed as real prank photographs of purported fairies taken by two English girls in the garden of a house in the village of Cottingley. In the aftermath of the Great War Doyle had become a fervent believer in Spiritualism and other paranormal phenomena. Especially embarrassing to Doyle's admirers today, he also published *The Coming of the Faeries* (1922), wherein he argued that these mystical creatures genuinely existed. 'When the spirits came in, the common sense oozed out,' Stewart once wrote bluntly to his friend Rupert Gould of the creator of Sherlock Holmes. Like Gould, however, Stewart had an intense interest in the subject of the Loch Ness Monster, believing that he, his wife and daughter had sighted a large marine creature of some sort in Loch Ness in 1935. A year earlier Gould had authored *The Loch Ness Monster and Others,* and it was this book that led Stewart, after he made his 'Nessie' sighting, to initiate correspondence with Gould.

5. A tontine is a financial arrangement wherein shareowners in a common fund receive annuities that increase in value with the death of each participant, with the entire amount of the fund going to the last survivor. The impetus that the tontine provided to the deadly creative imaginations of Golden Age mystery writers should be sufficiently obvious.

6. At Ardlamont, a large country estate in Argyll, Cecil Hambrough died from a gunshot wound while hunting. Cecil's tutor, Alfred John Monson, and another man, both of whom were out hunting with Cecil, claimed that Cecil had accidentally shot himself, but Monson was arrested and tried for Cecil's murder. The verdict delivered was 'not proven', but Monson was then – and is today – considered almost certain to have been guilty of the murder. On the Ardlamont case, see William Roughead, *Classic Crimes* (1951; repr., New York: New York Review Books Classics, 2000), 378–464.

7. For the genesis of the title, see Macaulay's 'The Battle of the Lake

Regillus', from his narrative poem collection *Lays of Ancient Rome*. In this poem Macaulay alludes to the ancient cult of Diana Nemorensis, which elevated its priests through trial by combat. Study of the practices of the Diana Nemorensis cult influenced Sir James George Frazer's cultural interpretation of religion in his most renowned work, *The Golden Bough: A Study in Magic and Religion*. As with *Tom Tiddler's Island* and *The Ha-Ha Case* the title *In Whose Dim Shadow* proved too esoteric for Connington's American publishers, Little, Brown and Co., who altered it to the more prosaic *The Tau Cross Mystery*.

8. Stewart analysed the Achet-Lepine case in detail in 'The Mystery of Chantelle', one of the best essays in his 1947 collection *Alias J. J. Connington*.

Chapter I

A REQUEST FROM THE CORONER

MARK BRAND—professionally known as The Counsellor —had gone through the correspondence selected and docketed for him by his staff, in preparation for his next broadcast from Radio Ardennes. From the mass, he had picked out the more useful letters and put them into a wire basket to the right of his desk. A larger pile of rejected material lay in the corresponding wire tray on his left. The Counsellor put his hands behind his head, tilted back his desk chair and stared at the cornice of his office.

He was bored; and, what was in his case a worse symptom, he was admitting this boredom to himself. This week's supply of correspondents had been a poor lot, presenting nothing that stimulated his imagination. *Lonely Betty*, living in a hostel for girls, wanted to get to know some nice men. *Perplexed's* young wife couldn't get on with her mother-in-law or her sisters-in-law, and what was to be done about it? *Billy* was leaving school and liked poetry, chemistry, music, engineering and French, but his father insisted on Billy going into his greengrocer's shop. (Billy had been sent a copy of Leaflet A. 25 dealing with the choice of a career.) *Heart-sick* had found that her boy-friend was taking an interest in other girls.

And so on. Not a single novel problem in the whole lot, The Counsellor acknowledged sourly. Each of them

1

of the utmost importance to the enquirer, of course; but as the bases of a broadcast, as dull as ditch water. He tilted his chair still further back and scanned the ceiling as if some fresh and interesting suggestion might be detected there.

The sound of the door opening softly brought him back with a jerk to a more normal attitude, and he turned his head to look at the intruder, a pretty chestnut-haired girl who paused on the threshold and examined him with a smile which was half quizzical, half sympathetic.

"You look frightfully bored, Mark," she commented as she came forward towards the desk.

Sandra Rainham was a distant relation of The Counsellor, and she treated him with more familiarity and less respect than an ordinary secretary would have ventured.

"I *am* bored," admitted The Counsellor crossly. "Devilish so, in fact. Has nothing come in except this? There's not a Chinaman's chance of being interesting on subjects like these."

"They did seem a pretty dud lot when I went through them before sending them in," Sandra admitted. "You've dealt with every one of them—or something like it—twice at least, already. You'd better give them a miss; turn them over to the Correspondence Department; and talk about something entirely fresh. Try a chat on Unsolved Mysteries and offer a prize for solutions. Offer that at the start, and every crime-hound will prick up his or her ears."

"Something in that, perhaps," The Counsellor conceded grudgingly. "Jack the Ripper, the Peasenhall affair, the Merstham Tunnel business, and the rest of the tunnel cases—things of that sort, you mean?"

"Yes, something like that. And you can end up with this."

She slid a paper across the desk towards The Counsellor as she spoke.

"That's just come in by Special Messenger, Express Delivery post. You'll have to get it into your broadcast, somehow, Mark. Read it, and then I'll tell you something more."

The Counsellor picked up the sheet and read the printed heading aloud:

"From John V. Frobisher. Coroner. Westerfield Hall, Fernhurst-Hordle. . . . Fernhurst-Hordle? I seem to remember that name."

"You've heard me mention it, probably. Go on, Mark; I'll explain when you've read it."

The Counsellor nodded absently and continued to read:

15th April, 1939.

"DEAR SIR,—Being cognisant of the valuable services which you rendered to the authorities in connection with the assassination of Mr. James Treverton of Grendon St. Giles last September, I venture to solicit your assistance in the following circumstances.

"At 2.30 a.m. this morning, in the vicinity of Tetherdown Cross Roads, within my jurisdiction, a motor car was discovered in flames. The driver appears to have been entrapped in the burning vehicle; and as he was unable to extricate himself, he perished in the catastrophe. The identification plates of the car had been removed. The vehicle, however, has been recognised as a six-cylinder, 16-h.p. Hernshaw-Davies car of a type which came upon the market in the autumn of 1937. Its body had been dark green, which was one of the standard tints for these cars at that date.

"Enquiries are being pursued by the local constabulary, as is their duty. But I am determined to leave no stone unturned in the matter; and as I am aware that you have an extensive audience who listen to your broadcasts (though they may neglect to give attention to the police messages from the B.B.C.) I request you to co-operate with me by giving the fullest possible publicity to the matter at the earliest possible moment, asking any of your listeners who may have seen this car to communicate immediately with me upon the subject.

"The identity of the deceased driver is as yet unascertained and any information relevant to this point would be of the utmost value to me in the inquest which I shall have to hold.

"Communications should be made to me by letter or by telegram at the address given above or by telephone to the number printed at the head of this note-paper.

"I have the honour to be, sir,

"Your obedient servant,

"JOHN V. FROBISHER."

"H'm!" ejaculated The Counsellor, laying the letter down on his desk and glancing up at Sandra Rainham. "Sounds a pompous bloke. Polysyllables are his long suit. Still, he must be a sound fellow after all. At any rate, he knows enough to come to the right man for this job."

"I'm sorry to disturb a pleasant illusion, Mark," Miss Rainham explained, "but I really doubt if he ever heard of you before this dreadful business. There was an enclosure addressed to me inside the envelope. You'd better read it."

4

She tendered a second sheet of paper.

"Same address," commented The Counsellor, glancing at the heading. "Signed 'Vera Glenarm,' " he added, turning to the signature. "Who's Vera Glenarm? I seem to remember the name. . . . Oh, yes, that's the girl who was such a pal of yours when you were taking your training at that secretarial college, isn't it?"

Miss Rainham confirmed this with a nod, and The Counsellor turned back to the letter in his hand.

"MY DEAR SANDRA,—I know you won't mind doing me a favour. Please read Uncle John's letter which goes along with this; and then do your best to persuade Mr. Brand to help.

"Uncle John has never got on well with the local police, somehow. They don't take him seriously enough, or something. Anyhow, whether it's merely his imagination or not, he thinks they're cold-shouldering him over this dreadful car affair. To cheer him up, I unfortunately suggested that he might enlist Mr. Brand's help in collecting information. So now my credit's at stake. And you know how difficult Uncle John can be when he doesn't get what he wants. He snapped at the idea like a lobster or a crocodile or whatever it is that does snap at things. If he can get on to something the police have missed, it'll put him in a good temper for a week. And that would be a blessing. So *please* do your best, dear.

"If Mr. Brand refuses, Uncle John will put it all on my back; and, really, he's difficult enough already without that, on account of this case. The things he says about the Chief Constable simply will not bear writing about. Like this: ——! **£%%? @½)("!!!!
                              "Yours,
                                    "VERA GLENARM."

5

The Counsellor laid the letter on his desk.

"Uncle John V. Frobisher doesn't sound specially amiable," he commented. "You've met him, I suppose? What's he like?"

"Not really so bad," Sandra explained, "but he always reminded me of a terrier with an uncertain temper. He eats out of your hand one day, and the next day something's happened and he'll snap at you before you know where you are. Frightfully touchy about slights, and generally detecting a lot that don't exist outside his own imagination."

"Sounds like the character in the poetry-book: 'When she was good, she was very, very good. But when she was bad, she was horrid.' How does this Vera girl come to be mixed up with him, if he's like that? Hasn't she a home of her own?"

"Her father and mother died when she was in her teens, and they left her enough to live on comfortably; but she wanted some sort of training to fall back on, just in case she got stranded in any way. That's what took her to the secretarial college, where I met her. After her mother died, her uncle took charge of her and she's lived with him most of the time since. She doesn't mind his little ways, really. The grousing in her letter's only a bit of fun. If she wanted to, she could leave him. She'd get a secretarial post easily enough. She's intelligent," she added impishly.

"Oh! Is she?" said The Counsellor, falling into the trap. "You mean freckled, snub-nosed, rather untidy, with black specs. That's what 'intelligent' usually means. At least, when you're talking about a girl."

"I said 'intelligent,' and I mean 'intelligent,' implying that she shows a high degree of understanding," retorted Sandra with a slight grimace. "You're all wrong in your fancy portrait, Mark. She's about a year older than I am—say twenty-six. She's about my height, slim, fair-haired, pretty, dresses well, wears fours in shoes, six-and-a-half in gloves, plays games, and reads as well. Her sight's quite normal. Just the sort of girl you might marry, Mark, if you were extra lucky."

"Leave me out of it," said The Counsellor hastily.

"Well, of course, she might not like your taste in tweeds, I admit. That's a new suit you're wearing, isn't it? I can't imagine where you pick up these patterns. Do you get them specially woven or what? If they get much louder I'll have to take to anti-glare glasses myself, I give you fair warning. At least, while you're about."

" 'Enough of this fooling. To business,' " quoted The Counsellor severely. "Take this down, will you?"

He dictated a few sentences, summarising the information given in the Coroner's letter.

"By the way," he added, "have we any grateful clients in Fernhurst-Hordle?"

Miss Rainham glanced at him with a shade of apprehension.

"Why do you want to know that?" she demanded. "All you're going to do is to put this stuff into the broadcast, as Mr. Frobisher wants. The thing's going no further."

"It *is* going further," declared The Counsellor firmly. "The Coroner has asked for my assistance. He'll get it, without stint. It's a matter of public interest."

"He asked you to put it into your broadcast. That was all," she pointed out in a faintly chilling tone. "He didn't invite you to put your finger into it beyond that."

"We never do things by halves in this office," retorted The Counsellor magnificently. "All our resources are at the disposal of the authorities."

"Meaning that you're going to poke your nose into

the affair, whether they like it or not?" translated Miss Rainham. "They *will* be pleased. Or will they? I'm not sure."

"Matter of public spirit," affirmed The Counsellor unctuously. "Besides, it's the sort of thing that interests me."

"I see," said Miss Rainham resignedly. "You fluked some sort of success when you took up the Treverton affair, and it's gone to your head. My advice to you, Mark, is to rest on your laurels and not risk a fiasco over this business."

"I asked a question," The Counsellor pointed out with an insufferable air of patience.

"Whether we'd any grateful clients? I put Records on to that as soon as I'd read Vera's letter, just as a matter of routine. I'm glad to say that we can trace none. Does that damp you?"

"Not a bit," responded The Counsellor cheerfully. "All the more credit to be got when one works without local assistance."

"I know what Wolf will say when he hears about it," said Miss Rainham ominously.

Wolfram Standish was The Counsellor's general manager.

"So do I," said The Counsellor blandly, "so we won't bother to call him into consultation at present. Wolf has no imagination, poor fellow. It's that strain of Scots blood in him. Or else his Saxon ancestry. Or both. All against my taking up the Treverton business, Wolf was; and precious silly he looked in the end over that. Enough about Wolf. Tell me something about this Coroner cove. It's always well to know about people before one meets them."

The Counsellor's lower lip was thrust forward in a way only too familiar to Miss Rainham. She recognised the symptom and shrugged her shoulders, as if abandoning a lost cause.

"He's about my height, spare, rather leathery-faced with bushy dark eyebrows, and he's got a high-pitched voice, a fault-finding kind of voice, if you know what I mean. He wears dark grey tweeds usually. You might copy his taste there with advantage, Mark. He's not difficult to deal with if you just agree with everything he says. That seems to cover his main peculiarities, I think."

"Except in special circumstances, a coroner must have been a solicitor, a barrister, or a doctor, I believe," said The Counsellor. "How does this Frobisher conform to that?"

Sandra reflected for a moment or two before she was able to answer this.

"I believe that he was called to the Bar when he was a young man," she said, at last. "At least, I seem to remember hearing Vera say something about it. I never heard of his practising, though; and some cousin of his died and left him Westerfield Hall—it's just a big house in some grounds—and enough to make him independent for life. I don't think he ever had to work for a living."

"Not a strug-for-lifeur, as the French say. That might account for his opinionatedness. Never found his level."

"Quite likely," agreed Miss Rainham rather acidly. "You never had to strug-for-life yourself, Mark; so it works out in two cases."

"Quiet determination is one thing; pig-headed obstinacy is another. I never can get you to see the difference," complained The Counsellor. "But enough of metaphysics. Let's return to the urgent affairs of Coroner Frobisher. Here's a blazing car with no number plates on it. Now just ask a question. How did the deceased manage to drive that car any distance without somebody spotting the lack of the numbers?"

"Because it was in the small hours of the morning, of course. There's hardly anyone about, then."

"But the police don't knock off for the night," The Counsellor pointed out. "And they've less to amuse them then than in the daytime. *Ergo*, they're more likely to look at any passing car and spot that it's got no number plates. The inference is . . ."

"That it was driven only a short distance minus number plates, of course. So it must be a local car."

"Thought you'd say that," said The Counsellor cheerfully. "All wrong, of course. For all I know, the deceased may have driven the car a hundred miles with the number plates on; then removed them and pitched them over a hedge; and then driven on a mile or so to where the car was found ablaze."

"It doesn't sound very sane," objected Sandra.

"No? But it sounds like suicide to me."

"Why should a suicide take such pains to conceal the identity of the car?" asked Sandra, rather contemptuously. "If it had been murder, one could see the point of that."

"Something in that," admitted The Counsellor. "Let's follow it up a bit. A. takes B. out in A.'s car. A. murders B. and leaves the body in the car. If the car's identified, then A. has to explain how his car came to be mixed up in the business. Hence he attempts to make it unrecognisable by taking off the number plates. That seems to fit. Now try it the other way round. B. is taken out by A. in A.'s car. B. murders A., and puts a match to the petrol. In that case, you've got A.'s body in A.'s car, which would look like suicide. Then why remove the number plates? That doesn't seem to fit, not to any extent. Suicide's more likely."

"You make it sound so," Sandra admitted doubt-fully.

"But now, just ask a question," continued The Counsellor. "What's become of other things that would help to identify the car? The licence disc on the windscreen, for instance."

"Burnt, of course," said Sandra contemptuously.

"And the engine number? And the chassis number? Burnt, of course, I suppose?"

Sandra considered for a moment or two before answering.

"Just remember that the car was found ablaze between two and three o'clock this morning, Mark. And Mr. Frobisher must have sent off his letter to you shortly after breakfast-time, since it reached here in the forenoon. On that basis, you can take your pick of three solutions. First, that car may have been nearly red-hot with the blaze; in which case the police couldn't hunt for engine and chassis numbers until it cooled down a bit. They may not have discovered them by the time that letter was sent off. Second, I've shown you Vera's letter; and you can guess from that that the constabulary aren't likely to put themselves out to help Mr. Frobisher more than strict duty demands. I doubt if they'd fall over their own feet in their hurry to pass on the news, even if they'd got it. And, third, the engine and chassis numbers may have been obliterated, just as the number plates were removed. Now then, start counting round, *Eeny-meeny-miney-mo!* Which of the three is It?"

"Wait and see," advised The Counsellor, refraining from giving an opinion. "I'll tell you one thing, Sandra. This affair interests me more and more as I think over it. Scope for my peculiar talents in it, evidently. Even Wolf could see that if it were carefully explained to

11

him. My plans are complete to the last detail. I shall broadcast it, asking for information. I shall then take that information down to Fernhurst-Hordle in a public-spirited way. Then I shall endeavour to play off old Frobisher against the police, thus giving scope to my peculiar diplomatic capacity. *Tertius gaudens*, in fact. A providential opportunity, no less."

"You're quite exceptional, Mark. We all admit it. I've never met the match of your conceit anywhere. But I hope you won't make a fool of yourself, that's all. Shall I give you a note to Vera? She might be able to keep you from the more obvious blunders amongst these strangers. She's intelligent, you see."

"Right!" said The Counsellor. "I'll be glad to meet an intelligent girl. And now, if you'll take dictation, we'll do our best to lighten the troubles of Lonely Betty, Perplexed, Little Billy, Heart-sick and the rest of them. Ready?"

Chapter II

BLUE GLASS

THE COUNSELLOR'S confidence in the success of his broadcast appeal for information declined slightly when Monday passed without bringing any results; but on Tuesday morning his anxiety was relieved by the arrival of several letters. With these in his pocket, he set off for Fernhurst-Hordle to interview the Coroner.

He was shown into a room, half lounge, half study, and was kept waiting for a few minutes before his host appeared. Mr. John V. Frobisher turned out to be almost exactly as Sandra Rainham had described him: a rather fussy, distinctly touchy personage with an exaggerated idea of his own acuteness and importance. He came into the room with mincing steps, pointing his toes like an old-time dancing-master; and before speaking, he subjected The Counsellor to a silent scrutiny which lasted several seconds.

"You are Mr. Brand?" he enquired, glancing at the visiting card in his hand as if doubtful of its genuineness. "Mr. *Mark* Brand, I believe."

The Counsellor confirmed this with a nod, whereupon Frobisher glanced again at the visiting card as if to refresh his memory and then laid it aside on his desk.

"Now, Mr. Brand," he went on, staring at The Counsellor under his bushy eyebrows, "I admit candidly that I am not acquainted with your activities. In fact,

I never heard of you until my niece, Miss Glenarm, mentioned your rather peculiar cognomen. She advocated my making use of you. She pressed her view strongly, so that I was at last persuaded to avail myself of your services."

The Counsellor reflected that this account hardly tallied with the one given in Vera Glenarm's letter, but he refrained from comment.

"Now," continued Frobisher in his high-pitched, rather querulous voice, "I am quite aware that by utilising your services I have departed from routine methods. I have, in fact, gone outside the beaten track. But the circumstances justify that, I think. I think they do. The fact is, Mr. Brand, I am continually hampered in my duties as Coroner by a certain obstructive spirit in the local police. Naturally, I name no names. But I am undoubtedly hampered by a lack of frankness. I have often great difficulty in extracting information which should immediately be placed at my disposal. They say, of course, that the publishing of certain evidence might be inexpedient. Take this motor-car case as an example. It is, on the face of it, a simple suicide. All the facts point to *felo de se*. But now some fussy fellow, some half-educated Jack-in-the-box—Jack-in-office, I mean—has got it into his head that it might be homicide. Homicide! And the result of this delusion is that he wishes to suppress certain evidence which should come before the jury at the inquest if they are to be in a position to bring in a proper verdict. That, in my opinion, is tampering with the course of justice and putting the jury—and even myself—into a most unfair position. In fact, Mr. Brand, I am being hampered—I use the word deliberately—by people who should be a help instead of a hindrance."

"Of course. Of course," said The Counsellor sympathetically.

And having thus inserted himself into the conversation, he hastened to broaden the wedge.

"This is how it is, Mr. Frobisher. I've received several letters in response to my broadcast on Sunday. . . ."

"Permit me," interrupted the Coroner, not too suavely. "I wish to make my point clear. Here are the facts. When you hear them, I am certain you will take my view—namely, that suicide is the only possible explanation. First, two empty petrol containers were discovered, which had been thrown over the hedge bordering the road at that point. From the vehemence of the conflagration, it is evident that this unfortunate fellow—whoever he is—deliberately emptied four gallons of petrol into the car before taking his life. Second, that petrol must have been ignited from within the car, since there are no signs of a petrol trail having been led to the car, by means of which fire could have been set to the liquid from a distance. I have satisfied myself on that point by my own observations and even the police do not deny the fact."

"Might have chucked a match through the car window, perhaps," The Counsellor suggested, but he was not allowed to go further.

"Allow me to state the facts first, as they dispose of your explanation," declared the Coroner, steamrolling over the interruption. "The catastrophe was discovered by two young men and a girl, who were returning from a dance. They are respectable persons whose word can be credited completely. According to them, they saw the car standing just off the road, on a broad grass edging; and when they first came into view of it, its lights were out and there was no sign of any flame. The road at that point is straight, so they had a perfectly clear view; and their sight had been sharpened by a walk of a mile or more through the night. They are quite convinced that there was no one near the car from the time it came in sight. They pursued their way, and when they had come within a dozen yards of the vehicle, it suddenly burst into flame, becoming a mere furnace almost immediately. It became, in fact, a beacon throwing illumination over the whole neighbourhood; and any person who was near enough to have thrown a match into the car through the window to ignite the petrol would inevitably have been discovered to them by the flare. They saw no one. And they looked carefully around them by the light of the burning car for this reason. It had not then crossed their minds that a human creature was imprisoned in the vehicle. They leaped to the conclusion that this was a case of someone wilfully destroying his car in order to perpetrate a fraud upon his insurance company. Hence they expected to see someone running away and looked for him. But they saw no one decamping; and when I interviewed them individually, each of them was perfectly definite on the point that no one had set fire to the car and then escaped unseen. They were quite close, they explained to me, and no one could have got away without one or more of them detecting him. They were absolutely convinced on that point."

"Yes, go on," said The Counsellor as the lecturer paused for breath.

Now that they had really come to the business in hand, The Counsellor was no longer bored, but was listening with all his ears.

"These facts, I think, dispose completely of the idea that a second person was present when the car caught fire," continued the Coroner. "But there is further evidence, and of a striking character. When the remains of the car had cooled down sufficiently to make an examination possible, it was found that the body of the deceased man was in the driving seat, where one would naturally expect to find the owner of the car. The two rear doors and the door next the driving seat had been locked by the usual method of adjusting the inside handles. The front near-side door, which locks from outside with a key, was not so secured, as was to be expected if only one man were present. It seems evident to me that the deceased wished so far as possible to hinder any involuntary or instinctive effort to escape which he might make at the last moment."

"One question," interrupted The Counsellor firmly. "Was the sliding roof open or shut?"

"Open. Open," replied the Coroner. "Obviously to give full access to the air and so stimulate the flames."

"Yes, go on," repeated The Counsellor, with the inward decision to consider these last pieces of evidence in conjunction at a later moment. A merely handle-locked door, he reflected, doesn't hinder people inside the car from getting out easily enough, but it does prevent people outside the car from getting into it.

"Now I come to what seems to me the crucial piece of evidence in this matter," the Coroner went on with a barely suppressed air of triumph. "Amongst the remains of the car were found some fragments of blue glass with a ribbed surface. From the position in which these were discovered, it was apparent that the glass object had been dropped at the feet of the deceased. Can you suggest what that glass object was in its original form?"

"Easily enough," said The Counsellor immediately, to the obvious annoyance of the Coroner. "A poison bottle. Druggists use ribbed blue glass bottles to hold poisonous drugs, so that people can't make mistakes and swallow the stuff by accident."

"Very acute. Very acute indeed, Mr. Brand," admitted Frobisher hastily and in a tone which showed his vexation at being robbed of what he had hoped would be a sensational disclosure. "A poison bottle, as you suggest. That is, in fact, what the object was. And the reason for its presence will not have escaped you either," he went on hurriedly to forestall any interruption. "Evidently the deceased had this poison with him, a quick-acting drug, no doubt; and as soon as he set fire to the petrol, he must have swallowed the poison to ensure a quick death for himself. Then the phial fell from his hand on to the floor of the car at his feet. There is not the slightest difficulty in reconstructing the whole process. And yet these pigheaded persons are not convinced that it is a case of *felo de se*! Imagine that, Mr. Brand. Incredible, one would think. But there is no accounting for the vagaries of some so-called intellects. If there is anything clear in this affair it is that we have to do with a very determined case of suicide."

The Counsellor contented himself with nodding sagely in response to this. Then, after a moment's thought, he put a question.

"Now that the heat's gone out of the car, they've examined it carefully, I suppose?"

"The police have examined it to the best of their ability," the Coroner admitted grudgingly. "And I have inspected it carefully myself."

"What about the licence disc on the wind-screen?" asked The Counsellor. "Was that burned? If not, it will have given you the identity of the car."

"The metal ring of the casing was discovered," the Coroner explained sardonically. "I am not entirely devoid of brains, like some people with whom I have to work, Mr. Brand. But, unfortunately, the paper disc with the particulars of the car was missing and had probably been consumed by the flames."

"But the numbers stamped on the engine and on the metal of the chassis wouldn't be obliterated by fire," pointed out The Counsellor. "What about them? They'd give a clue."

An expression of mingled annoyance and confusion appeared on the Coroner's face.

"I'm afraid I did not carry my investigations to that extent," he said crossly. "I had time only for a cursory inspection and was forced to delegate a more minute examination to the police. I have been very busy with other things, at the moment. A friend of mine died suddenly last week, poor George Earlswood, and as I am one of the trustees appointed under his will, I have naturally had a good deal on my hands, with funeral arrangements and other matters."

The Counsellor discounted this rather feeble explanation.

"The old bird never thought of the engine number at all," he decided mentally. "He's one of these people who are *never* wrong. No wonder the police can't stick him."

The Coroner seemed anxious to pass from the subject of chassis and engine numbers and he accomplished the evasion by producing a fresh piece of evidence.

"It occurs to me," he said hastily, "that I may be able to utilise your services further, in the endeavour to identify the deceased man. On the bones of the ring-finger, the police discovered the remains of a seal-ring. The gold circlet was almost unaffected by the heat to which it had been subjected; but the stone forming the actual seal had apparently been cracked and splintered, so that only two fragments were left adhering to the setting."

"Any engraving on the fragments? Bits of a crest or initials?" demanded The Counsellor, who was wearying of Frobisher's verbose style of narration.

"The stone itself was carnelian," Frobisher informed him. "The shape of it was a rectangular oblong, like a postage stamp, but much smaller, naturally. The residual fragments of stone were in the top left-hand corner and in the middle of the base. On the first of these were some engraved lines, almost unrecognisable in themselves; but the clue to them was given by the lower fragment, on which it was easy to distinguish a bird's claw resting upon some irregular object which formed a plinth or base in the design. The lines in the other fragment, with this guide, revealed themselves as part of the curved beak of the bird. There was no sign of any inscription having existed."

"A crest of sorts," summarised The Counsellor, pulling out a notebook. "Just give me that description again, please. I want to jot it down."

The Coroner complied without deviating from his original story.

"What sort of clothes had the dead man been wearing?" demanded The Counsellor. "They'd be burned, no doubt. Still, some bits must have been left. Seat of his trousers, probably. The flames wouldn't reach that."

"You are quite correct," said the Coroner in the tone of a master commending a promising pupil. "Some fragments of cloth did survive almost intact; and from an examination of them I inferred that the deceased had been wearing evening clothes. A set of plain gold studs and a pair of gold sleeve-links were also discovered among the débris, but they were of a common pattern and suggested nothing individual in the wearer's taste."

"Was wearing an evening suit with plain gold studs and links," mumbled The Counsellor as he made a note in his book. "Anything else? Anything remaining from the contents of his pockets? Wrist-watch? Eyeglasses? Latch-key? . . ."

"I was just coming to these matters," said Frobisher irritably. "There were some silver and copper coins discovered among the débris. Probably he had been carrying them in his trouser pockets. There was no wrist-watch or any remains of one; nor was any eye-glass frame found."

"Body badly burned?" enquired The Counsellor alliteratively.

"It was quite unrecognisable," Frobisher assured him. "Quite. The police surgeon estimated that the deceased had been a man about five feet seven inches in height, judging from the length of some of the limbs; but I should allow a fair margin of error in that."

The Counsellor reflected for a second or two. Obviously the police had something up their sleeve in the way of evidence, for all that Frobisher had given him pointed straight to suicide. The Coroner had not given him this extra evidence, but The Counsellor guessed that it could easily be wheedled out of him by playing upon his vanity.

"I agree with you," he said. "All you've given me suggests plain suicide. It would take something pretty definite to alter my opinion. But you say the police don't agree with us. They must have something striking to go on, surely."

Frobisher fell into the trap at once.

"Striking!" he echoed with withering contempt. "Childish is a better word for it. They found a tooth amongst the débris, that was all. And they found the corresponding tooth missing from the jaw of the deceased. They put the tooth into the gap, and it fitted. That's their evidence! And on this basis they evolved, by means of what I suppose they are pleased to call their intelligence (save the mark!), some wild theory that a struggle had taken place between the deceased and a second man, during which that tooth had been knocked out of its socket by a blow. Sheer dementia, sir! Nothing less. Consider one other possibility and the whole thing vanishes into thin air. Any man in the midst of flames will writhe with pain; and in writhing he might quite well knock his jaw against the wheel of the car and so dislodge a tooth. There's the whole of this tooth business put into proper perspective immediately. But would they listen to common sense? Not a bit of it. They've got this bee in their bonnet about a second man being present, although there's no proof whatever of anything of the kind."

"The evidence you gave me certainly doesn't point that way," agreed The Counsellor at once. "Still, everybody has his own views. *Quot homines, tot sententiæ,* as my old friend Terence remarked. And Terence said quite a lot of good things in his time, you know."

Frobisher had evidently no desire to discuss Terence or his ideas.

"Some opinions are sound; some are not," he said oracularly, and then made his views plainer by adding: "And the opinions of that troublesome Jackanapes, Inspector Hartwell, are certainly not sound. A more pig-headed, misguided . . ." he suddenly realised that he was saying too much and changed the subject: "But I think you have some information to give me. Pray do so."

The Counsellor was now satisfied that he had

extracted all the information he was likely to get from the Coroner. He felt in his breast-pocket and produced a sheaf of papers which he proceeded to smooth out on his knee.

"I'd better give you the lot," he suggested. "Some of this stuff is obviously off the mark. The Hernshaw-Davies is a fairly common make of car and green is one of their standard colours. So these reports probably include two or three different cars. Still, they'll always help, if we can sift them out."

He lifted the top sheet from his packet and handed it to Frobisher, who found that it was a sort of time-schedule:

Time	Place		Witnesses
*9.00 p.m.	5 Savernake Park	. .	Maidservant
9.10 p.m.	Arthur Street .	. .	Schoolboy
*9.25 p.m.	Caplatzi's Dance Rooms	.	Door-keeper
9.30 p.m.	George Street .	. .	Motorist
11.00 p.m.	Regal Cinema	. .	Commissionaire
*11.15 p.m.	Caplatzi's Dance Rooms	.	Door-keeper
11.20 p.m.	Anderly Road .	. .	Tramway-driver
*11.30 p.m.	Ranger's Copse	. .	Married couple
*12.20 a.m.	16 Avon Drive	. .	Taxi-driver
*2.15 a.m.	Tetherdown Cross Roads	.	Lorry-driver

"Now, this is how it is," explained The Counsellor. "The one item which seems definitely connected with your affair is the last one on the list, since it was seen by a lorry-driver who passed it just about Tetherdown Cross Roads. It's most unlikely that there was a second Hernshaw-Davies car just at that place at that time. This lorry-driver, anyhow, saw no signs of one. So, on that basis, the blazing car must have stood, there or thereabouts, for ten minutes or a quarter of an hour before your witnesses saw it go up in flames."

"That seems probably so," Frobisher conceded rather grudgingly.

"Now turn to the head of the list," continued The Counsellor. "Just before nine o'clock, the maid-servant at 3 Savernake Park went out to post a letter at the pillar-box near by. As she was going to the pillar-box, a dark-green car drew up at the gate of No. 5 and a man in evening dress got out and went up to the front door. Just as she passed the car again on her way back, a girl came out of the gate with the man and got into the car, which then drove away. This maid seems to have her wits about her. When she heard me offering a reward for information, she went to look at a Hernshaw-Davies in a shop-window display and recognised it as the same make as the car she'd noticed. So that's that."

"A reward?" interrupted Frobisher suspiciously. "Who's going to pay that, Mr. Brand?"

"I am, naturally. I always offer a flat rate of one quid for information supplied. Why not? Thou shalt not muzzle the labourer who is worthy of his hire. The Bible says that, or something like it. But that's by the way. We proceed. I've bought a map of your town, and it's plain enough that if a car was at Savernake Park at nine o'clock it wasn't in Arthur Street at 9.10 p.m. unless it was doing about 50 m.p.h. all the way. Leave out the Arthur Street car at present. Caplatzi's Dance Rooms are out in the suburbs or a shade beyond. A kind of road-house, or something. Just about twenty minutes easy driving from Savernake Park, according to the map. The Caplatzi doorkeeper remembers a Hernshaw-Davies arriving with a man and a girl aboard at about 9.25 p.m. In evening dress, naturally, as they went in to dance. That looks like the pair from Savernake Park.

"The car seen in George Street at 9.30 p.m. can't have been this car. You couldn't make George Street from Caplatzi's in five minutes, nohow. Then there's the car seen by the commissionaire at the Regal Cinema at 11 p.m. It was in the park there, and had been so for two hours before its owners came out of the cinema and went off in it. So it's not the Savernake Park car either.

"At 11.15 p.m. the man and the girl came out of Caplatzi's and the commissionaire saw them go off in their car. That car can't have been in Anderly Road five minutes later. Besides, the witness in Anderly Road was a tramway-driver just off duty and looking out for a lift home. He got it in a Hernshaw-Davies driven by a man with a male passenger aboard, and they dropped him about ten minutes later close to his home, miles away from Caplatzi's. That was about half-past eleven.

"Now at 11.30 p.m. the Savernake Park car turns up again at a place called Ranger's Copse. I gather it hasn't got too good a reputation. Cars get parked under the trees, with lights out, and some of the doings might not bear the light of day too well."

"It's a plague-spot," interrupted Frobisher. "If the police did their work properly, instead of obstructing public officials in their duty, they would find full scope for their so-called efficiency. Ranger's Copse should be under constant supervision. I have heard a good deal about it from various quarters."

"Well, here's the Stop Press News about it," broke in The Counsellor, picking up a letter from his sheaf of documents. "This comes from a Mr. Ilton, apparently a greengrocer in a moderate way, since he has three shop addresses at the head of his paper. I'll read it to you:

"DEAR SIR,—In reply to your inquiry per broadcast on Sunday, I can give you the following information. The wife and I had gone for a spin in our car on Friday night and we came back by the road which skirts Ranger's Copse. That's a small wood near here with no fencing between it and the highway and it's a place where young fellows are apt to take girls in their cars after they've picked them up in town. I've often seen a dozen cars parked there with lights out.

"We were coming along that bit of the road slowly at half-past eleven o'clock. We were going slow, because the crew that park their cars there are sometimes a bit above themselves and one never knows when they mayn't open a door on the wrong side carelessly or do something else that's silly.

"There were perhaps ten cars parked, most of them off the road and under the trees on the edge of the wood. Just as we came up to one of them and drew out to pass it, the off-side rear door burst open and a girl stumbled out on the road. Lucky my brakes are good; and I pulled up just before I knocked her over.

"As soon as she saw my car, she made a dash for it and seeing the wife beside me, she spoke to her and begged us to give her a lift. She was in one of these dance frocks and my wife said afterwards that it looked a good one and not cheap. She was a red-haired girl, a bit slim, about average height for a girl, and the wife reminds me to say that her frock was green and she had a string of beads round her neck. She was all excited, gasping and panting, and from what she said we gathered that the man who brought her there hadn't been behaving well to her.

"The wife told her to hop into the back seat. Just as she did that, the man stepped out of his car (which I forgot to say before was a Hernshaw-Davies Sixteen) and I had a good look at him in the light of my lamps. He was ordinary, clean-shaven, round about thirty, I'd say at a guess, dark, with a light coat, and as he turned to get into the driver's seat, I saw his white shirt front and made out he was in evening togs. He didn't come near us, but just slammed the doors of his car and began to move off at once. I couldn't see all of his number plate, but I remember there were two Y's on it and the last figure nearest the tail light was 6, in a four-figure number.

"We offered to take the girl right home to her door, but she said it would be all right if we dropped her in Edendale Road, which happened to be almost on our way home. So we did that for her, and left her on the pavement.

"Hoping that this may be of service to you,

"I am,

"Your obedient servant,

"SAMUEL J. ILTON."

"I've looked up the map," The Counsellor explained, "and I found that Edendale Road is only a stone's-throw from Savernake Park, where a man picked up a girl at her house at 9 o'clock, you remember."

"I know the geography of my own town," said Frobisher testily.

"So nice," said The Counsellor flippantly. "Useful in helping you to find your way home, no doubt. But to business. I forgot to mention that the doorkeeper at Caplatzi's remembered that YZ67 was part of the number of the car that the man and girl used. Put all that together, and the actual number might be YYZ676. You can get it tracked down by the proper licensing authority if you tell them it's a 16-h.p. Hernshaw-Davies. And now here's a further chapter in its history. About twenty past twelve, a taxi came along Avon Drive behind a 16 h.p. Hernshaw-Davies car. The driver was on his way back to put up his car for the night and he was in a hurry. Just as he was going to pass the Hernshaw-Davies, it swung to the right, without bothering to give a signal; and he had to be nippy to avoid a smash. The Hernshaw-Davies went into the garden of No. 16. As there'd been no smash and as he was dog-tired, the taxi-man did not wait to have a slanging match with the Hernshaw-Davies driver. He looked at the number but didn't write it down. He remembers YYZ6 . . . but that's all. Seems to identify the car as the one that was at Ranger's Copse, though. And the time of transit seems about right, too."

Frobisher seemed a shade more interested in this item than he had hitherto been. He got up, took a local directory from a shelf, and began to skim through it.

"Avon Drive. . . . 16, you said? Here it is: Sydney Barrington. . . . I wonder. . . ."

He picked up the telephone directory from his desk and consulted it in its turn.

"Yes. . . . Of course. . . . Barrington and Hawkstone, Solicitors . . . I thought so. . . . I don't know Mr. Barrington except professionally, so I couldn't be sure about his private address when you mentioned it. But now I have a faint recollection that he does live in Avon Drive, though I cannot exactly remember how I came to know that. My dealings with him have been merely in the matter of a trusteeship I hold. He is not my own solicitor. . . . One moment. . . ."

He pulled open a drawer in his desk, rummaged for a few seconds, and finally produced a letter.

"Yes. . . . Quite correct," he announced, reading out the heading of the paper, " 'Barrington and Hawkstone . . . Sydney Barrington, Vincent Hawkstone.' . . . Their office is in Anne Street."

The Counsellor made a rapid jotting on one of his papers.

"That seems to be all the information I have for you," he said as he rose to his feet. "Here's a *précis* of the evidence in these witnesses' letters, along with their addresses in each case. I thought you'd want that."

Frobisher took the sheet, but showed no particular gratitude for the trouble The Counsellor had taken.

"Thanks. This will help to put a spoke in the wheel of these officious people at police headquarters. It makes the case crystal-clear, I think."

"Do you?" said The Counsellor respectfully. "Not quite so clear about it myself. But then I haven't had your experience."

"Naturally. Naturally," agreed Frobisher, unable to refrain from blurting out his ideas, just as The Counsellor had foreseen. "To you, of course, it would not be obvious. Clearly, however, this is the sequence of events. The deceased, it is evident, took this girl to Caplatzi's Dance Rooms . . ."

"Mind my glancing at your directory?" interrupted The Counsellor as he reached over and picked up the volume. "Just a moment. . . . Savernake Park. . . . Here we are. . . . No. 5. . . . Percy Campion. . . . Girl might be either his wife or his daughter. Yes, sorry. . . .".

"As I was saying," Frobisher continued in a tone which showed his feelings had been ruffled by the interruption, "clearly the deceased took this girl—whose

29

name may be Campion or may not be Campion, since it is by no means proved that she is any relation to the householder—he took this girl, I say, to Caplatzi's Dance Rooms, stayed there for some two hours, and then conveyed her in his car to Ranger's Copse. At Ranger's Copse one must suppose that he committed, or attempted to commit, an assault upon her which she did her best to repulse, either successfully or not. In any event, she ran away from him. His next step, taken immediately, was to visit a solicitor at the solicitor's private residence some time after midnight. That is not a usual hour for consultations. It is fair to assume, then, that he called on his legal adviser to make a clean breast of his recent doings and to learn how he stood with regard to his misdeed. Barrington's opinion may have been unfavourable. It may even have suggested that the deceased stood a chance of social disgrace. It may even have hinted plainly at a criminal trial and a heavy sentence. In the small hours of the morning, most men are not so well-balanced as in the daytime. Troubles are apt to seem blacker then. The deceased may have been shocked by the prospect before him; and, with this on his mind, he may have taken his car out to Tetherdown Cross Roads, and then, unable to face what he saw coming upon him, he may have put a match to his petrol and an end to his life."

The Counsellor seemed wholly unimpressed by this rhetorical statement of the case.

"A match?" he said doubtfully. "To judge from the remains found in the car—or the lack of some—he was a non-smoker. What would he be carrying matches for? Happy thought! Perhaps he borrowed this match from a passer-by."

"Some non-smokers carry matches," declared the Coroner.

"I was thinking of something else," answered The Counsellor vaguely. "Who's in charge of this case, by the way?"

"I am," said the Coroner in a tone which blended surprise and asperity.

"I know. I know," answered The Counsellor. "On the police side, I mean."

"There's an Inspector, Hartwell by name, who looks after the district in which Tetherdown Cross Roads is situated. No doubt he considers himself in charge, as you put it."

"Thanks. Now I think I've given you all my information, I'd like to see Miss Glenarm, if she happens to be in. I've got a message for her from my secretary, Miss Rainham. They're friends, I'm told."

"Ah, yes," said Frobisher. "I know Miss Rainham. She's stayed with us at times. A very charming young lady."

"She'll be glad to hear your opinion," said The Counsellor drily. "Well, I'd like to meet Miss Glenarm now, if she's available."

Chapter III

ANOTHER VIEW OF THE CASE

"Sandra showed me your letter to her," The Counsellor explained with an unconcealed grin, after he had established relations with Vera Glenarm. "I've done as you wished. Now I want a favour from you in return."

"What's that?"

"Oh, just a few bits of information. Now that you've dragged me into this business, I've got interested. I want to know more about some people."

Vera glanced at him with amusement in her face.

"Just what Sandra foretold," she said. "I've had a letter from her, warning me to look out for you."

"And she advised you to damp me down?" hazarded The Counsellor. "Pay no attention. It's just one of her fads, damping my enthusiasm. You're more broad-minded. I can see that at a glance. Besides, I did you a favour and I'm not above reminding you of that."

"I like candid people."

"Then you like me? That's so nice. We start on a firm footing. But to business. Your uncle mentioned an Inspector Hartwell. Know anything about him?"

"Nothing whatever," said Vera. "I've never even seen him."

"Then that doesn't count towards the score. Let's try again. Ever come across one Barrington, Sydney by Christian name, and solicitor by trade?"

"I've met him," Vera admitted. "You want a picture of him? Well, then, he's about thirty-five, and he looks like the model for the strong, silent man you read about. Taciturn, you know, with an air that makes you think he'd say something worth listening to, if he opened his mouth. As a matter of fact, I don't remember him talking about anything except the weather, and he didn't say anything I could put in my diary as a notable utterance. A friend of mine knows him better than I do; and she seems to like him pretty well."

"Married?"

"My friend is, yes. Oh, you mean Mr. Barrington. No, he's a bachelor. His brother lives with him."

"What's the brother like?" persisted The Counsellor.

"You're writing a *Who's Who* of the town, are you?" retorted Vera with a smile. "Dull work, I'd imagine. We're not a very interesting lot, I admit frankly. Well, Mr. Richard Barrington is, I believe, a dentist. He's the younger of the two and quite unlike his brother. Volatile, shall we say?"

From a study of Miss Glenarm's expression, The Counsellor inferred that "volatile" might be translated into "rackety" without doing any injustice to Richard Barrington. He recalled another name.

"Your uncle mentioned a Mr. Earlswood."

Vera's face clouded a little and she obviously stiffened her attitude.

"That was rather sad," she said soberly. "Poor Mr. Earlswood died very suddenly just about a week ago— blood-poisoning, or something like that. My uncle is one of the trustees for the estate and, now I come to think of it, it's Mr. Barrington's firm that's handling the legal side of the matter."

"The other partner in the firm is a Mr. Hawkstone, isn't he?" queried The Counsellor, who could see from

33

Vera's manner that she had no wish to discuss Earlswood and his affairs.

"You seem to have picked up quite a lot," Vera
retorted. "You're exactly what I imagined you'd be
like, from Sandra's description of you. 'Eaten up with
inquisitiveness' was her account of you. But this time
you're going to be baffled, Mr. Brand. Mr. Hawkstone
happens to be married to a friend of mine, so I don't
intend to dissect his character for your amusement.
Sandra's met him. Apply to her for her impressions.
I shan't give you mine. *Sans rancune*, you understand?"

"*Sans rancune* so far as I'm concerned," agreed The
Counsellor without discomfiture at this snub. "It's a fact
that I'm interested in people and their doings. Sandra
calls it inquisitiveness. I call it a deep concern for
humanity. Sounds better that way, I think. In my line,
one simply has to be interested in the most unlikely
people; and the habit grows on one. Like to tell me your
own life-story? I'm all ears."

Vera glanced at her wrist-watch.

"I'd love to," she said sardonically. "The whole tale
illustrated with snapshots from the family album.
Unfortunately, duty tears me away. I've an appointment with a dog, about a walk. That'll be all for the
present, Mr. Brand. Give my love to Sandra when you
get back to Town."

The Counsellor took his dismissal philosophically,
since he had secured more information than he expected.
He walked down the steps of the front entrance and
gave his chauffeur a low-voiced direction.

"Go into the town and find the Police Headquarters."

At the police station, The Counsellor explained that
he had come on a matter connected with the blazing car
case and wished to see Inspector Hartwell. He was kept

waiting for a time, but at last a tall, heavily-built, square-jawed man appeared.

"My name's Hartwell. You asked to see me."

Evidently a dealer in incontrovertible statements, The Counsellor reflected. He noticed that the Inspector had a trick of moving his lower jaw without parting his lips, which was possibly a symptom of impatience. This was the kind of man who wanted people to come to the point at once, so The Counsellor wasted no time.

"I've come to see you about that Tetherdown Cross Roads affair. Got some evidence which may be new to you."

"I'm listening," said Hartwell, who seemed a man of few words.

The Counsellor produced a second copy of the time-schedule which he had given to the Coroner and passed it to the Inspector. Hartwell studied it attentively.

"These asterisks show different appearances of the same car?"

"Probably," said The Counsellor cautiously.

He remembered that the Coroner had not troubled about the asterisks.

"Where's your evidence?" demanded the Inspector.

The Counsellor produced his sheaf of documents.

"These are replies to your broadcast on Sunday?" continued the Inspector. "I heard about that. I rang up your office an hour or two ago about it, but you'd gone. They said you were coming down here, so I expected a call from you."

"Why didn't you ring up yesterday?" demanded The Counsellor.

"I didn't expect you'd have your answers until to-day."

"Quite correct," admitted The Counsellor with an increased respect for the Inspector's acumen. Obviously

Hartwell was not a fussy fellow like Frobisher. He could bide his time before making his move, and yet move at the earliest useful moment.

"Let's hear the details," Hartwell continued.

The Counsellor gave him much the same summary as he had given to the Coroner, and the Inspector listened throughout without a single interruption. When The Counsellor had finished, Hartwell reflected for a moment or two before speaking.

"Now, about this maidservant," he began. "She's employed next door to No. 5, Savernake Park. How comes it that she didn't recognise the girl in evening dress when she met her at the car?"

"Quite all right," explained The Counsellor. "She'd just come to her place that day. Hadn't had time to find her bearings or get to know the neighbours. She says so in her letter."

"Pass that," said Hartwell. "Now I put my cards on the table with people, Mr. Brand. This is new evidence to us. Thanks. Going on to the Caplatzi Rooms, we'll make further enquiries from that door-keeper. He ought to have given us his information."

"Humanity's human," declared The Counsellor. "He got a quid from me for his news. Probably he didn't expect to get more than thanks from you."

"Pass that," said the Inspector. "What about this married couple who picked up the girl?"

"A man who's got three greengrocer's shops to manage is bound to be pretty busy," The Counsellor pointed out. "He'd be on the go all day and pretty tired at the end of it. Some people hardly look at the newspapers. But on Sunday he has a day off and listens to the wireless. That's probably how he slipped through your net and fell into mine."

"Like enough," admitted Hartwell. "He's new to us,

anyhow. Thanks. It's the taxi-driver I can't make out at all. They're usually keen to stand in with the police. That's natural. Why didn't he make a report?"

"Because, as you'll find in his letter, he was on the sick list immediately after getting home that night, and more interested in his inside than in the outer world. He was a bit better by Sunday, and listened to the wireless. He'd lost a couple of days' earnings. A quid meant something to him. So he wrote to me to get it."

"You don't stint expenses, evidently," commented Hartwell. "Not that I complain. It's money well spent —from our point of view."

"I could spend a bit more without grudging it," said The Counsellor, meaningly. "But not blindfold. I want to see where I'm going."

Hartwell pondered this remark for a time without answering. Then, apparently, he came to a resolution.

"You want to know as much as we can tell you?" he enquired.

"I can't help you much unless I do," interrupted The Counsellor. "My broadcasts need the human touch, the personal touch, if they're to fetch home the goods. If you merely want a police message read during my hour at Radio Ardennes, apply to my Advertising Department and they'll quote you the cheapest rates. If you want *me*, then you'll have to give me the background I need."

"It can be done. To a certain extent, anyhow. But any expense falls on you, if you offer rewards. That's plain, I think."

"Perfectly," agreed The Counsellor, without ado.

"Then here are the things we want to know about. First of all, we found the remains of a poison-bottle in the wreck. It was a two-ounce ribbed hexagonal phial of blue glass. You might broadcast an enquiry about the sale of any poison-bottle of that make in the last few weeks."

The Counsellor shook his head slowly but decisively.

"Nothing doing. How many bottles of that sort have been sold up and down the country in the last few weeks? Hundreds, I expect. I'm rich, Inspector, but not so damn' rich as all that. Besides, I don't believe much in this quick-acting poison notion which I hear mentioned in some quarters."

The Inspector had evidently not made his proposal seriously. He laughed when he heard it rejected.

"I can guess the author," he rejoined. "No need for names. So you don't agree with him? Neither does the expert we put on to the *post-mortem*. He found the post-nasal space practically free from any carbon particles such as would be inhaled by a man sitting amongst smoke. Therefore the man was dead when the fire started. And there wasn't anything in the way of a common poison to be found in the remains of the stomach. My view is that the blue phial was put there just as a blind."

The Counsellor rubbed his chin thoughtfully.

"A blind? Like enough. But I think it had another use as well, perhaps. No use asking me what I think about it yet. Not enough data to go on, and I don't want to look a fool if I'm wrong. By the way, you found no metal match-box or cigarette-lighter amongst the débris?"

Hartwell shook his head conclusively.

"Nothing of the sort. He may have carried wooden vestas in a pasteboard box, of course. That would go up in the blaze and leave no trace."

"Would it?" queried The Counsellor. "Have you ever tried burning a box of Swan vestas? Not so easy as you think. Friend of mine had a fire in his house, once, a regular furnace in one room. When he examined the remains of a desk afterwards—it was practically burned away out of all shape—he found two boxes of Swan vestas badly scorched but quite recognisable. The heads had exploded, but the stems weren't so much damaged as you'd think. And matchheads are mineral matter. They don't burn away to gas. If you really were thorough in going through the remains of that car . . ."

"We were," said Hartwell confidently.

"Then the man had no box of matches on him, that's all I say."

"I'll try putting a box of matches into a hot fire," said the Inspector. "I'm always willing to learn. Thanks. For, you see, Mr. Brand, you're helping to confirm my view of this affair."

The Counsellor did not think it necessary to ask for an elucidation of this. It was plain enough that the Inspector had murder, and not suicide, in his mind.

"What's your second enquiry?" he asked, dismissing the bottle and matches problems as finished.

"We found no watch amongst the remains," explained the Inspector. "Most men carry a watch. So either a watch was removed from the body or else the deceased had sent it to be repaired and hadn't a spare one to wear in the meanwhile. We're making enquiries at the local watchmakers; but that takes time and uses men who might be better employed. If you put the point in a broadcast, you might be lucky. Especially if you appealed to shops in the small towns round about here, which we haven't been able to touch yet."

"I get you," said The Counsellor. "There's nothing yet which directly connects that body in the car with the fellow who picked up the girl in Savernake Park. Even if the girl gives you the name of her friend, that doesn't prove beyond dispute that it's his car and his remains that turned up at Tetherdown Cross Roads. But if you can prove that the fellow's watch was under repair, it's an extra link in the chain, eh?"

"That's it," admitted the Inspector. "You see, Mr. Brand, we've had no enquiries for a missing man, although this fellow has been dead for some days. We have to try to get every scrap of evidence to prove identity. Now here's another thing you might help us with. Just a moment."

He left the room and returned a few minutes later with a small cardboard box.

"We found the remains of a signet-ring on the body's finger," he explained, opening the box and disclosing the object inside. "If we could find anyone who could recognise that ring, we'd be a step forward. You might help here. But it's been badly damaged, and there's not much left to base a description on. Have a look at it."

The Counsellor scrutinised the ring with the help of an aplanatic hand-lens which the Inspector fished out of his pocket.

"Looks as if the design had been some bird with a curved beak standing with its claws on some object or other," he said at last, returning the lens to its owner. "I can put out an enquiry about it, but that's the best I can do in the way of a description. We can but try. Perhaps I can get at it another way, though. Too early to say, yet. That reminds me of a question. You've looked for the engine number and the chassis number of the car? The fire can't have destroyed them."

"No, but a file did," retorted Hartwell with a smile. "They'd both been erased. And thoroughly, too. It must have taken a longish time to do that, the way it was done."

"That's interesting," said The Counsellor thoughtfully.

This evidence, which he had expected, obviously exploded the Coroner's explanation of the affair. Frobisher's hypothesis had been based on the idea of a sudden panic produced by the dead man's visit to his solicitor. Was it likely that a man thrown off his balance to the extent of suicide would have enough wits left to file away the engine and chassis numbers from his car before actually taking his own life? Not likely, The Counsellor decided. Besides, what point was there in doing it, if the case was one of suicide? None that Brand could see. Further, there was the poison-phial. That was plain proof that the thing had been planned before the dead man had gone to Barrington at all. You can't knock up a druggist at midnight and get him to sell you a dose of poison so easily as all that. Not without raising his suspicions, at any rate. And no druggist had spoken up, so far, evidently. Suicide it might be, but not according to the Coroner's reconstruction of the case.

"That's very interesting," repeated The Counsellor, coming out of his brown study. "And rum, too. What do you make of it?"

"It may have been a stolen car he had," Hartwell suggested, with no marked conviction in his tone. "He may have bought it from a car-snatcher. And the car-snatcher would probably file off the numbers to make sure that it couldn't be identified."

"True, O King," said The Counsellor flippantly. "I guess you believe that tale just as much as I do. You don't want me to broadcast an enquiry for some suffering owner who had his Hernshaw-Davies snaffled somewhere in the Kingdom within the last eighteen months."

"You can if you like," said Hartwell. "Nothing to do with me."

"Then I don't think I shall, so long as I've other things to talk about. By the way, I suppose the inquest has been adjourned till you get your evidence together?"

"It has. If you're thinking of attending when it comes on again, I'll see that you get in."

"Shan't be called as a witness, shall I?"

"That's the Coroner's affair," said the Inspector with a slight acidity in his voice. Then, with a change in tone, he went on with more cordiality than he had hitherto shown: "You've given us some useful pointers, Mr. Brand. Thanks. We'll question these two women in Savernake Park, first of all. And if you can pick up anything about the poison-bottle, the watch, or the signet-ring, we'll be glad to hear of it. I've got your address on your card. . . ."

"And you may count on any help I can give you," said The Counsellor, interpreting the Inspector's pause. "I've a vague idea about that ring. It hangs on the deceased's sense of humour, to some extent. Now, you're a busy man. So am I, sometimes. I'll not waste your time."

With that The Counsellor took his leave without giving the Inspector a chance to question him further. A glance at his watch, as he reached his car, showed him that it would be after office hours before he got back to London. He gave his chauffeur the address of Sandra Rainham's flat.

Chapter IV

THE SEAL

WHEN The Counsellor reached the flat, he was lucky enough to find Sandra at home.

"Have you given it up?" she asked hopefully, when he had been shown into her sitting-room.

The Counsellor shook his head decidedly, to her obvious disappointment.

"No. Too interesting. Your friend Vera's a nice girl. Her uncle didn't catch my fancy, though. Pompous old beggar. But I met an efficient-looking police inspector. Been quite busy, in fact, playing *Accident, Suicide or Murder?* A new round game. All the rage down there. The rules are much the same as for *Animal, Vegetable or Mineral?*"

"Have you had any dinner?" Sandra enquired, ignoring all this.

"Dinner?" echoed The Counsellor, doubtfully. "Now I come to think of it, I don't believe I have. But don't let that worry you. I'll get some when I reach home. No need to kill the fatted calf on my account. But my man must be hungry. You might send down some sandwiches and a couple of bottles of beer to him. Or else, as the night's chilly, you might invite him in to sup with your maid, if she happens to be supping."

"I'll see about that," said Sandra, and she left the room to give instructions.

When she returned, The Counsellor was in an

43

arm-chair with his hands stretched out towards the fire.

"Anybody coming in to-night?" he asked, over his shoulder.

"Three people for bridge, later on."

"Well, I'm only a bird of passage," explained The Counsellor. "I'll be gone before they arrive. Just dropped in to ask a question or two. Your friend Vera referred me to you. By the way, she sent her love and kisses."

Sandra glanced with intention at the clock on the mantelpiece.

"I can take a hint," declared The Counsellor. "To business, then. Can you tell me anything about a Mr. Earlswood? Your friend Vera didn't exactly gush with information on the subject."

"I hope you haven't been putting your flat feet into it, Mark," said Sandra seriously. "Mr. Earlswood's dead; he died quite recently. Vera mentioned it in a letter. Something went wrong with his antrum, whatever that is, and he died of blood-poisoning or something. It was very sudden."

"Great friend of Vera's?" queried The Counsellor, rather uneasily.

"Well, it wasn't exactly tragic," Sandra admitted. "Still, it was rather sad. I don't think Vera was in love with him, or anything like that. Still, they were very close friends always, and they might have got engaged if things had been normal. I know she liked him. But he had some trouble . . . something that made him think he shouldn't get married. . . .Catalexy? No, that's not it."

"Catalepsy?" suggested The Counsellor.

"Catalepsy. That's the word. Something about trances, isn't it? He used to lose power over his muscles or something like that. I never noticed anything myself, except that he always seemed rather nervous and high-strung. It was Vera told me about it."

"That's hard lines," said The Counsellor with a gravity unusual to him.

"Very hard," Sandra agreed. "The Earlswoods were an old family in that part of the country. Something equivalent to Lords of the Manor at one time, though they didn't call themselves that. And he was the last of them; so when he didn't feel he should marry, the old name was bound to die out. I think he felt that, too. It was sad."

"Vera rather shied away from the subject when I mentioned him, now I think of it," mused The Counsellor. "And, despite your forebodings, I did *not* pursue it. Knew I could get what I wanted from you instead, so it didn't matter. She shied away even more markedly when I asked her about a man Hawkstone. He's a lawyer, I believe. Ever met him?"

"I didn't like him much," Sandra said, bluntly. "I happened to be left alone with him once for a few minutes; and he gave me a vivid impression of being— h'm!—rather too impetuous for my taste. I had to shake him off pretty sharply."

"I understand," said The Counsellor. "Like the bit in Dryden:

> "*Lovely Thais sits beside thee,*
> *Take the goods the gods provide thee.* . . .

You were the goods, eh?"

"If you must quote, I wish you'd do it accurately," said Sandra in only half-feigned vexation. "It's 'good' in the original. The movies are corrupting you, Mark."

"Same thing in practice," protested The Counsellor.

" 'Once aboard the lugger' or once alone in the drawing-room. I get you, Steve. Draw a veil and continue the character sketch."

"Well, he's one of those men who can't keep their paws off a girl if they get her alone; the sort of creature who thinks he's irresistible and has a hide like a rhino when it comes to snubs. I don't care for the type; and I didn't seek his society after that experience. No doubt he attracts some women, but not me. I've an idea he played the same game with Vera, and she was no better pleased than I was."

"Makes his wife jealous?" asked The Counsellor.

"She didn't show it; and I doubt if she was, really, though he gave her plenty of grounds for it. Why he can't content himself with her, I can't imagine. She's quite out of the common: tall, tawny-haired, with eyes like emeralds. Most people have greeny-grey eyes or greenish-blue ones, but hers are a real green and they 'go' amazingly with her hair. She carries her clothes well, too, and she walks with a sort of lazy, feline movement, rather like a sleepy tigress, if you see what I mean, Mark."

"One of the larger carnivores, eh? I don't know she'd be quite pleased with that last bit. You don't often rave like this, Sandra," he added, with a grin. "She must have impressed you. And, as you aren't a man, it can't be merely sex-appeal."

"Of course it isn't. She's quite uncommonly good-looking, that's all. As to sex-appeal, she certainly didn't put herself out to exercise it, any time I saw her. She was friendly with men, no more than that."

"Not jealous of her husband, you say?"

"Not a scrap, so far as I saw. In fact, she seemed to accept his peccadilloes—when she heard of them—as something quite to be expected. I suppose she's lost interest in him, just as he's lost interest in her to some extent. They've no children to complicate their affairs."

"What age are they—the Hawkstones, I mean."

"She'd be under thirty, I think; and he must be between thirty and thirty-five, probably."

"Married long?"

"Seven or eight years, I think. Vera told me that he'd been rather a catch financially—in a small way. But I don't think it was that that induced her to marry him. She's not that kind. Probably he was the first man to propose to her—he's rather a dasher, as you may have guessed—and she was pretty young then and likely to be carried away easily enough."

"What sort of hands has he?" asked The Counsellor inconsequently.

"What on earth do you want to know that for?" Sandra enquired in surprise. "As a matter of fact, I didn't like his hands. Too fat and stubby-fingered."

"Sounds the sort of man who would wear rings," opined The Counsellor with a depreciatory sniff.

"Don't try your 'would-be-clever' tricks on me," said Sandra contemptuously. "You've been talking to Vera about him and heard he wore a ring; and now you come and pretend to have guessed it."

"You're wrong. Honest Injun," protested The Counsellor. "Your friend Vera said nothing about him. I told you she referred me to you for information. But as a reward for my smartness, you can tell me about his rings. Make it thrilling."

"Nothing to be thrilled about, so far as I can see. He wears a plain gold ring with a stone signet—chalcedony, the stone might be. Nothing very rare, I know."

" 'Chalcedony dispels illusions and all vain imaginations,' " quoted The Counsellor. "So Albertus Magnus says, anyhow. Looks to me as if that ring had got on to the wrong finger. Mrs. Hawkstone ought to be wearing it. Then one could account for her disillusioned state of mind which you described so elegantly. Amethyst would have done better for him. Promotes chastity, they say."

"Is this another sample of your second-sightedness?" Sandra enquired to the surprise of The Counsellor. "Or did Vera tell you about the other ring—the one Mrs. Hawkstone has?"

"No, she didn't," declared The Counsellor with obvious candour. "What about it?"

"Well, she had a duplicate of his ring. I think he gave it to her when they got engaged. She didn't wear it, but she used it as a seal. . . ." She broke off for a moment, thinking, and then added: "I believe I've got an impression of it, if you're so keen about it. She sent me a knitting pattern once, with some wool samples; and I think she sealed the envelope because the contents were bulky. . . . Wait a moment and I'll see if I can find it."

She went across to her writing-desk and searched among its pigeon-holes for a few moments. Then she came back with a large envelope in her hand.

"Here it is. There's the seal, if you want to look at it."

One glance was enough for The Counsellor. The seal represented a hawk perched on a stone; and he recognised the beak and the claw which Hartwell had shown him on the shattered signet taken from the blazing car.

"I thought so," he said, concealing his interest from Sandra. "A hawk and a stone. Pun on the name Hawkstone, evidently. Mind if I take this, Sandra? It's no use to you."

Without waiting for her permission, he tore off the seal and handed the rest of the envelope back to her.

"What does this Hawkstone man do for a living?" he enquired casually, to divert Sandra's attention from the seal.

"Oh, he's a half-asleep partner in a firm of lawyers. He bought a share in it just after he got married, Vera told me, once, when we were talking about him. Barrington's his partner's name. I've met the partner: a big, heavy, silent sort of man. I liked him better than Mr. Hawkstone, I must say."

"Barrington has a brother, hasn't he?"

"You don't seem to have wasted your time down at Fernhurst to-day," Sandra admitted, though there was no trace of compliment in her tone. "As a gossip-hunter, Mark, you must be in the first flight. Yes, there is a brother, a bit of a ne'er-do-well from what I heard about him. The lawyer brother has had to get him out of a good many scrapes. One of them, I heard, was a pretty big one, rather nasty and very expensive to hush up. His brother was said to have paid through the nose to keep their name clear. But you know how people talk. Personally, I'd prefer him to Mr. Hawkstone, though. He doesn't take so much for granted, for one thing," she added drily.

"Hawkstone didn't smoke much, did he?" enquired The Counsellor with apparent irrelevance.

"Second sight? Or Vera again? You're quite right, though. He was a non-smoker. So was his wife, if that interests you."

"I'm fascinated," said The Counsellor. "And, by the way, from what you say, I gather that Barrington came about the Hawkstone house. You met him there? So they were friends as well as partners?"

"Yes," Sandra confirmed, though with a shade of doubt in her tone. "The impression I got was that Barrington took more interest in Mrs. Hawkstone than in her husband, though. He'd known her before Hawk-stone appeared on the scene and married her, Vera told me. In fact, it was the marriage that brought the two men into contact and so led to the partnership deal."

"You seem to have done pretty well in the gossip line yourself," The Counsellor pointed out.

"I've been down to stay with Vera often enough," said Sandra defensively; "and naturally one gets to hear things in one visit after another. I didn't go nosing things out, the way you seem to have been doing."

The Counsellor glanced at the clock on the mantel-piece.

"Time's a-bouncing. Your bridgettes will be here in a few minutes, so I'd better tear myself away."

He rose from his chair and took his leave, without giving Sandra any chance of putting questions in her turn. When he reached home, he went straight to the telephone and rang up Hartwell.

"I can give you the name of the fellow found dead in that blazing car," he announced when the Inspector came to the phone. "Have you made anything out of your enquiries at Savernake Park?"

"A sergeant's making them now. He hasn't got back yet to report," explained Hartwell. "You say you've identified the man?"

"Yes. I told you my guess depended on his sense of humour. What I meant was that it hung on whether he was amused by a pun, or not. The beak on the one fragment of the seal looked to me like a hawk's bill; and the claw on the other bit of it was gripping a stone. Hence Hawk, Stone. Meaning that Hawkstone was the name of the owner. And Hawkstone was a partner of Barrington, which might account for that late visit to Avon Drive."

"Are you sure about this?" demanded Hartwell

suspiciously. "It sounds a bit far-fetched, especially as most of the design of the seal's still missing."

"Don't fret. I can show you an impression of the Hawkstone seal in wax, if that'll help to convince you. I've got it in my pocket now."

"That sounds like evidence," admitted the Inspector. "You'll have to produce it if it's needed. Don't lose it, please."

"I'll put it into my safe now, if that'll let you sleep easier to-night," said The Counsellor lightly. "It won't get lost. Good . . ."

"Here! Hold on a tick!" said the Inspector, before The Counsellor could finish the word. "If that body is Hawkstone's, why has no one reported Hawkstone as missing? It's days since that car went west. Why hasn't anyone enquired after him?"

"Why?" echoed The Counsellor. "Because some people don't want him to be known as missing and some other people think they know where he is, but don't want his whereabouts advertised. That's how I read it, anyhow." Then, without giving the Inspector any chance of putting a question to clear up this cryptic statement, he concluded, "I've had no dinner yet. Starving is the word. Tell you some more another time. Good-bye!"

Chapter V

THE INQUEST

THE proceedings at the opening of the inquest had been purely formal; and when the second session was held, The Counsellor was not summoned as a witness. Mindful of his promise, however, Inspector Hartwell notified his unofficial helper and reserved a seat for him in the little hall. As The Counsellor was about to enter, Frobisher bustled past him, returning The Counsellor's salutation with a curt and rather unfriendly nod. When The Counsellor took his seat, he found the place almost uncomfortably crowded, and a number of Pressmen had been accommodated at a table. Evidently the blazing car case attracted the public's attention, as The Counsellor had anticipated.

The first witness called was a frank-looking young man, Angus Tattershall, a railway porter. He, along with his sister and a friend, had attended a dance, a subscription dance, on the night of April 13th/14th. They had left the dance premises at 2 a.m. or shortly after that and walked home. Their road took them past Tetherdown Cross Roads. Just before reaching the Cross Roads, Tattershall had kicked something lying in the road, and on picking it up he found it was a bicycle tyre inflator. Thinking it might damage the tyre of any car which passed, he had pitched it on to the grass edging of the road. He had not examined it closely; it was a darkish night; and he did not profess to be able to identify it. Shown an inflator by Inspector Hartwell, he stated that it was about the size and make of the one he had handled in the dark, but he could not identify it definitely.

After throwing aside the inflator, he and his companions had gone on their way for perhaps a quarter of a mile past the Cross Roads. There they had noticed a car standing on the grass edging of the road, with lights out. They saw no one near it. As they came up to it, flames burst out and lit up the whole neighbourhood. He had seen no lights of any description near the car as he came up; no sign of anyone striking a match and throwing it into the car. After having walked in the dark for a while, his eyes would have spotted anything of the kind at once, he believed. The flames seemed to originate inside the car.

By the time he and his companions had run up the road to the car, it was "all a-blaze, with the flames shooting up through the sunshine roof like a blowpipe." It was too hot to go near it. He thought he could see a man in the driving seat; and at that he had pulled his sister past the car so that she shouldn't get a shock. There was nothing to be done in the way of help, so they had run on to the village, a mile beyond the crossroads, and waked the police constable who lived there. His friend had gone back with the constable to the car, while he himself took his sister home as she was "a bit hysterical-like" at the thought of the dead man in the car. He had then gone back and joined the constable at the car, but they had been unable to do anything owing to the heat.

His companion was the next witness and confirmed this evidence without adding anything fresh.

The constable deposed to being awakened and going to the car which was still blazing furiously when he reached it. He had sent for assistance and Inspector Hartwell had arrived some time later. It was out of the question to do anything for the man in the car. The heat was so intense that it was impossible even to approach the vehicle. When the car cooled down, he had assisted in removing the remains of the deceased to the mortuary, and he had also helped in the search made among the débris of the car.

Inspector Hartwell gave his evidence next. As he began, he threw a faintly derisory glance at the Coroner. Then he appeared to address himself to the jury, except when interrupted by Frobisher. After describing formally his appearance on the scene of the disaster and the delay necessitated by waiting until the metal-work of the car had cooled down, he proceeded to deal with the discoveries he had made among the débris. He exhibited the fragments of blue glass, the coins, the gold studs and sleeve links, the signet ring, the metal buckle from the back of a waistcoat and a number of buttons.

"These six are braces-buttons from the trousers," he explained. "This lot here are from the trouser-fly. These ones, you see, have been cloth-covered originally and make up the set on a dinner waistcoat. This larger cloth-covered one belonged to a dinner jacket. This piece of cloth is part of the trousers, from their seat. When we came upon it, it smelt strongly of petrol which has probably evaporated by now."

"You mean to say that some petrol actually failed to evaporate although the interior of the car was a perfect furnace?" demanded the Coroner sceptically.

"I'm explaining what we found," said Hartwell bluntly.

The Counsellor had no difficulty in believing this; he recalled that a similar phenomenon had been described in a previous blazing car case, at the Rouse trial. But clearly petrol must have been splashed abroad very lavishly if it had saturated the seat of a man's trousers, he reflected.

"There was a patch of some white mineral material on the remains of the car seat where the deceased had been sitting," the Inspector continued, since the Coroner made no further comment. "It was collected and submitted to an analytical expert, who will deal with it in his own evidence. Then we found a tooth among the débris."

He exhibited the tooth to the jury.

"On examining the remains of the deceased man," he went on, "I found he had a complete set of teeth in the upper and lower jaws, except that one pre-molar in the upper jaw was not in place. The tooth found among the car débris was somewhat damaged by the fire, but it fitted exactly into the gap in the deceased's teeth, so there is no doubt whatever that this detached tooth was his. My opinion is that it was knocked out of its socket by a blow."

"A blow?" asked the Coroner, with an assumption of surprise. "What kind of blow?"

Hartwell shrugged his shoulders almost imperceptibly as he answered:

"A good hard knock, I should say."

Obviously this was not what the Coroner had expected.

"A blow from what?" he demanded, in an irritated tone.

"Some blunt object, such as a human fist, perhaps," retorted Hartwell with a straight face, though The Counsellor thought he detected a twinkle in the Inspector's eye.

"Could the displacement of this tooth have been caused by an impact between the deceased's jaw and the steering-wheel during the writhings consequent upon the pain of burning?" Frobisher propounded weightily.

"From an actual trial, with myself in the driving seat of an intact Hernshaw-Davies car, I think it's unlikely, sir."

"Very well, very well," said Frobisher testily. "The jury will no doubt take note of your interesting experiment and place whatever weight they choose upon your results."

Hartwell paid no attention to this, but proceeded with his evidence:

"As in most modern makes, the petrol-tank of the Hernshaw-Davies car is at the rear. It seemed unlikely that even if the tank caught fire at once, flames could have reached the front of the car as quickly as previous witnesses described. It seemed more likely that petrol had been splashed about inside the car from some source other than the tank, before the fire occurred. I therefore ordered a search to be made in the neighbourhood of the car. Two empty petrol tins were found behind the hedge bordering the road. They are among the exhibits. There is nothing characteristic about them."

"You suggest, then, that the deceased had these two tins in his car, that he poured the contents about the interior of the vehicle, that he then threw the tins over the hedge, and, after returning to the driving seat, set fire to the scattered petrol?"

"No, sir. I'm giving the facts, merely. I shouldn't care to back this hypothesis, at least until I see some evidence to support it," said Hartwell measuredly. Then, without giving the Coroner time to interrupt, he continued, "Examination of the car showed that the front and rear number plates were missing. They had been unscrewed, not wrenched off. Further inspection established that the engine number and the chassis number had been filed away. Thus at that time there was nothing to indicate the identity of the burned car. The licence disc had been burned away from the wind-screen, though we found the metal ring container among the débris. Most of the clothing of the deceased had been burned away also; but from one or two fragments which survived, it appears that he had been wearing evening clothes. This is supported by our finding gold sleeve-links and a set of gold studs, such as men wear in dress shirts, among the débris. The body of the deceased was so badly burned as to be quite unrecognisable."

"You had, in fact, discovered nothing which could identify either the deceased or the burned car?" interrupted the Coroner in a depreciatory tone.

"Not at that time, sir," the Inspector admitted politely. "The inflator mentioned by a previous witness was recovered from the grass edging on to which he had thrown it."

"What made you attach any importance to it?" enquired the Coroner suavely.

"To check the accuracy of the previous witness's statements, sir," retorted Hartwell with equal blandness. "At a later stage, I ordered a rigorous search to be made in the neighbourhood of the burnt-out car. As a result of this, two car number plates were found in a clump of thorn bushes which stands in a field alongside the road near where the inflator was picked up. The numbers on the plates were YYZ.6756. A white-painted gate leads into the field at this point. On examination, a dark streak of paint was detected on this gate: a straight, vertical streak. The ground there was rather wet and there were clear traces of the print of a cycle tyre with a definite pattern in the mud at one point between the road and the gate."

"From which you infer?" enquired the Coroner.

"That somebody had leaned a cycle against the gate while he went into the field and that the gate had shifted slightly, dislodging the cycle, which had slipped down and left a long scratch on the paint of the gate as a result. Probably the inflator had become dislodged from its clips at the same time, if it was fixed to the top bar of the cycle or to the rear tube of the diamond frame, and the owner, in picking up his machine in the dark, did not notice his loss."

"Quite so, quite so," said the Coroner. "But I must point out to the jury that no connection has been established between this bicycle and the deceased. This clump of thorn bushes is evidently a convenient hiding-place, close to where the burned car was standing. It was natural that it should be chosen as a place of concealment by anyone wishing to dispose of the number plates from the car. The deceased, who evidently took pains to obliterate everything which could betray his identity, might quite well have thrown the number plates among the thorns, feeling sure that no one would look there for them. The traces of a bicycle may have no relation whatever to the rest of the facts."

"I was giving the jury the facts, sir," explained the Inspector with more than usual meekness, but with a glance at the foreman of the jury which evidently spoke volumes.

"Quite so, quite so," said the Coroner. "And have you any other facts to place before the jury?"

"From information received," continued Hartwell, "we had before this been able to identify the deceased. The number plates of the car enabled us to check the other evidence in our possession. He was Vincent Hawkstone, residing at 2 Kingsmere Avenue, and he was the junior partner in the firm of Barrington and

Hawkstone. The number plates are those of the Hernshaw-Davies 16 h.p. car owned by him, which is missing from his garage. The seal-ring found on the remains corresponds with one which he was accustomed to wear. We found no wrist-watch on the body; and we have ascertained that a few days before the disaster he had left his wrist-watch with a watchmaker for repairs.

"From information received," continued the Inspector, "we have traced the movements of the deceased on the night of April 14th/15th. He left home in his car—the burnt Hernshaw-Davies Sixteen—at 8.40 p.m. At 9 p.m., he called at the house of Mr. Percy Campion, 5 Savernake Park, where he picked up Mrs. Campion and took her to Caplatzi's Dance Rooms. He stayed there with her from 9.26 p.m. to 11.15 p.m., when he drove her to Ranger's Copse. They parted there; and he drove back to town, reaching the house of his partner, Mr. Sydney Barrington, 16 Avon Drive, at 12.20 a.m. He stayed there for a time, and left the house about ten minutes to one in the morning. At 2.15 a.m., his car was seen near Tetherdown Cross Roads, in the vicinity of which the disaster occurred at 2.30 a.m."

"No one was seen in the car with him at 2.15 a.m.?" demanded the Coroner, sharply.

"The witness was a lorry driver. He'll be giving his own evidence later," said the Inspector stiffly.

The next witness was the medical man who had made the autopsy. He gave a gruesome description of the remains. Death was apparently due to burning. He had found no trace of poison in the deceased's stomach. There were no signs of violence discoverable, except the displaced tooth; but considering the state of the body, this did not exclude the possibility that violence had been used. The remains of the hyoid bone showed that it had not been fractured, as it might have been had the deceased been strangled. The displaced tooth was slightly decayed and was part of the natural set of teeth of the deceased.

The doctor was followed by an analytical chemist. He had examined the fragments of blue glass found in the débris of the car. After being subjected to such a high temperature, little could be detected on the glass unless the poison had been an inorganic one. Analysis had revealed the presence of traces of sulphur and phosphorus on the glass. The glass itself was of a common composition. Some white powder found in the remains of the car and near the body gave tests for calcium and chlorine.

Witness had assisted the pathologist to examine the deceased's internal organs. No mineral poison was present. Nor was any alkaloidal poison detectable. The conditions were not favourable to the detection of organic poisons.

Next came the maid who had seen Hawkstone and Mrs. Campion in Savernake Park. From the concise and colourless manner in which she gave her evidence, The Counsellor inferred that she had been well coached by Hartwell beforehand.

Mark Brand had listened to these witnesses with attention, but with no acute eagerness. The evidence was all so strictly impersonal. It lacked human interest. But now they were coming to the real kernel of the case. Lorna Campion's name was called, and as she came forward to take the oath, The Counsellor straightened himself up in his chair and examined her attentively. Here, at last, was one of the persons who had been near the centre of the drama and who had something fresh to tell.

There was nothing of the tragedy heroine about her. Under her Titian-red hair, her rather peaky little face was not unattractive, though without the slightest sign of character in its lines. She had dressed quietly for this occasion, but had evidently not been able to resist the temptation to put on sundry articles of jewellery, the size of the stones convincing The Counsellor that they were paste. She gave her evidence in a pleasant voice marred by a faint trace of a common accent and broken from time to time by a nervous titter at awkward moments. Her manner alternated between nervousness and a self-confidence which came near effrontery.

"You were acquainted with the deceased?" demanded the Coroner sternly, when she had admitted the facts as to her identity.

"I knew him, yes, certainly."

"How do you know that the deceased was this acquaintance of yours?"

"Inspector Hartwell, over there, showed me a ring he'd found on the body's finger. It was all in bits, but I recognised what was left of it. There was a bit of a bird on it. That's how I knew."

"Under what name did you know the deceased?"

"Well, he called himself Merlin and I thought that was his name. He showed me the stone in his ring with the bird on it and said it was a merlin. Some kind of bird of prey, he said it was. I never heard of a merlin, but it sounded all right."

"You had no idea that this was a false name and that his real name was Hawkstone?"

"Oh, no. I just believed what he said. It didn't really matter, did it?" Mrs. Campion answered, with a nervous titter.

"How did you make his acquaintance?"

"I picked him up in a tea-shop," the witness explained candidly. "I never knew his address, nor even his phone number."

"When did you meet him first?"

"That would be about four months ago, I think."

"And you met him frequently thereafter?"

"Well, I met him now and again, once or twice a week if Mr. Campion was out of town. He's a commercial gentleman and often away from home on his rounds. Mr. Merlin used to take me to dinner sometimes and sometimes to a dance hall in the evenings."

"Did Mr. Campion know the deceased?"

"Oh, no! Leastways, they never met, to my knowledge."

"Did your husband know of these assignations with the deceased?"

"Pardon?"

"Were you carrying on this affair without your husband's knowledge?" demanded the Coroner, obviously annoyed at having to paraphrase his question.

Lorna Campion seemed to lose her self-assurance. She glanced round the room as though seeking inspiration.

"Well, that's as it may be," she replied at last, with a repetition of her peculiar titter.

"Please answer my question."

"Well, he'll know now, thanks to you and the rest of them. I don't think he knew before. He might have guessed, but I don't think so. He's terribly jealous of me, my husband, and likely he'd have said something about it, if he'd got to know."

She looked at the Coroner, as though expecting him to pay her the compliment of saying he could quite understand that; but Frobisher did not rise to the bait, obviously to her disappointment.

"Where is your husband at present?"

"He's gone to America. The firm sent him out there to see if there was an opening for their goods. He sailed from Liverpool on the 16th, but he left here on the morning of the 14th—that was the Friday—because he hoped to do some business in Liverpool before sailing."

"You made an appointment with the deceased at 9 p.m. on the 14th. How did you make that appointment? In writing?"

"Sometimes we arranged at one meeting when we'd see each other again, and sometimes he wrote to me, and sometimes he used to put an ad. in the newspaper. Sometimes I'd advertise. But this time you're talking about, he wrote me a letter saying he'd pick me up in his car. I'd told him that my husband was going off for some weeks. The Inspector, there, asked me if I'd kept that letter; but when I looked for it I couldn't find it. It came on Tuesday. I know that, because Mr. Campion was at home that day and we had pork fillets for dinner. That's what makes me remember the exact day."

"What was the tenor of this letter which you received from the deceased on Tuesday?"

"Pardon?"

"What did he say in that letter?"

"You do put things in a funny way," complained Mrs. Campion with a certain irritation in her tone. "What did he say in the letter? He just asked me to meet him on Friday night and go to Caplatzi's. He was going to call for me with his car about nine o'clock."

"You went to Caplatzi's Dance Rooms with him?"

"Yes, I did. No harm in that, is there?"

"And after that what did you do?"

Mrs. Campion showed some signs of confusion when this question was put.

"We went on in his car to Ranger's Copse. We stopped the car there for a while. He got a bit rough, and I began to feel a wee bit frightened. He was stronger than I was, you see, and he was getting above himself, altogether. You never know what a man in that sort of temper might do, alone in that car of his. So I tore myself away from him and jumped out of the car. Lucky for me, another car drove up then and I got a lift home in it."

"Where in the car were you and he sitting when this happened? In the front seats?"

"No, we'd shifted over. We were in the back seats, so that passing people wouldn't see us so well, you know."

"Were there any petrol tins in the car, on the floor or on the seats?"

"Oh, no," said Mrs. Campion, with a slight titter. "I couldn't have helped seeing them, if there had been, could I?"

"You didn't see the deceased again that night, after you entered the other car?"

"No, I didn't."

Frobisher evidently racked his brains to evolve some further questions to put to the witness; but apparently he failed, and she was allowed to stand down.

The next witness called was Sydney Barrington. As he took the oath, The Counsellor examined him with interest to see if he corresponded to the descriptions of him given by Sandra and Vera Glenarm. They had not been far out in their verbal portraits. Barrington was a slow-moving, heavily-built man, with deep lines running from his nostrils to his mouth-corners, full lips tightly closed, and a general air of reserved competence.

Frobisher evidently regarded him as a brother in the Law who deserved careful handling; for when he began to put his questions, his tone was more courteous than that which he had used with earlier witnesses.

"The deceased's body was identified by you, I believe?"

A rather grim smile twitched the corners of the lawyer's mouth.

"Identified is rather a strong expression in this case," he qualified in a pleasant bass voice. "I saw the body; but the only recognisable thing about it was a seal-ring which I identified as his. The general proportions of the body corresponded with those of Mr. Hawkstone. Naturally, seeing him every day, I was familiar with his build."

"A cautious devil," The Counsellor reflected. "Not likely to go beyond his book in any evidence he gives."

"Mr. Hawkstone was your partner?" continued the Coroner.

"He'd been in partnership with me for a number of years," the witness agreed.

Frobisher nodded sagely, though this was no news to anyone present.

"I wish to put one or two questions to you," he went on. "I am putting them for the purpose of clearing away sundry rumours which I understand have been drifting about this town and which are better disposed of."

Evidently this had been pre-arranged, The Counsellor decided. Some people had been gossiping and the coming questions were being put in order that Barrington might dispose of malicious rumours. The solicitor deliberately clasped his hands on the table before him, gave the Coroner a brief nod of acknowledgment, and waited for the questions.

"Your firm was an old-established one at the time when you took the deceased into partnership, I believe?"

"It was," agreed Barrington. "It was founded by my father, and I succeeded to it after his death. It was after that that I admitted the deceased into partnership."

"He furnished some financial consideration in return for the partnership?"

"He did. He paid me £15,000 under our agreement.

In return for that, he secured a fixed proportion of the firm's income; and in the event of his death, his widow was entitled to either a return of the £15,000 or to a slightly reduced share in the income of the firm."

"I see," said Frobisher weightily. "This means, in plain language, that financially you had no interest in his death."

"Hardly that," corrected the lawyer, with a rather wry smile. "It means that I may have to find £15,000 at very short notice, if Mrs. Hawkstone asks for the capital. And I shall have to engage someone to do the part of the firm's work which Mr. Hawkstone did."

"Quite so. Quite so," said Frobisher, testily. "What I wished to elicit is that you are not standing to gain, say, £15,000 by this death. That is what I want to have clear."

"I shall certainly not gain £15,000," Barrington declared.

"Thank you," said Frobisher, turning to the jury. "That has, I think, cleared up this matter entirely and proved the baselessness of these rumours which I am told have been in circulation. I have no doubt that the members of the jury have already rated them at their true value; but it seemed advisable to remove any doubt on the point. I now turn to another matter. You inspected the body which had been taken from the blazing car. Did you examine the teeth?"

"I did. The body had a full set of teeth, with the exception of one tooth which had been knocked out, apparently. The deceased also had a full set of teeth. So far as I saw, the teeth of the body were very similar to those of Mr. Hawkstone. I cannot profess to be an expert in the matter; I am giving merely my impression as a witness who was familiar with the general appearance of Mr. Hawkstone's mouth."

"Thank you," repeated Frobisher. "Now will you tell us when you last saw Mr. Hawkstone alive?"

"He arrived at my house, unexpectedly, between 12.15 a.m. and 12.30 a.m. That was the night between Friday and Saturday. I wasn't pleased to see him at that hour. I wasn't feeling very well—a sick turn, probably I'd eaten something that disagreed with me. My maids had gone to bed long before. I let him in myself."

"Did anything strike you about him then?"

"He looked as if he'd had quite enough to drink, and he was excitable. He asked for a whisky and soda and insisted on having it. I gave it to him. I didn't drink myself, as I was out of sorts."

"Did he explain what brought him there at that hour of the morning?"

"Yes, he did. It seemed he'd got into trouble with some woman. He didn't mention her name and I didn't ask it. I gathered that she wasn't the only one. They had been away for week-ends together; the woman's husband had grown suspicious; he was furiously jealous, it seems; and then the two of them had landed themselves in the usual trouble. It would all come out. In fact, I got the impression that Hawkstone was in a pitiable state of consternation over what the result might be. He wasn't a very courageous man, either morally or physically. I pointed out to him that any scandal would have an adverse effect on our firm and warned him that I didn't propose to have our name mixed up in his discreditable affairs. If there was a scandal, I'd take steps to break up our partnership; and then, although I didn't remind him of it, he'd have lost the money he'd put into the firm, according to our agreement. That didn't seem to be his worst trouble. He was more than half-intoxicated and he'd got to the state of repeating the same sentence over and over again: 'What'll *he* do? What'll *he* do?' I'm afraid I wasn't very patient with him, especially as I was feeling sickish and wanted to get to bed. Finally, I told him to go home and sleep over it. His head would be straighter in the morning. I saw him into his car and he drove away, rather more competently than I'd expected. That was about ten minutes to one in the morning."

"When you saw him into his car, you did not notice any petrol tins in it?"

"No, none. If there had been any there, I think I'd have noticed them in the light of the lamp over my front door."

The Coroner fumbled among his papers, glanced over one of them, and then turned back to the witness. The Counsellor inferred that another of these "pre-arranged" questions was coming next.

"After you had shown the deceased off your premises, what did you do?"

"I went up to my room and went to bed. Then I was taken ill. My brother shares the house with me; but he was away that week-end at a little fishing cottage we keep, ten miles down in the country. I had to rouse my maids and get them to telephone for Dr. Arkwright, who lives a few doors down the road. He came round very quickly and did what he could for me. I was not then in much of a state to bother about the time; but I've enquired from Dr. Arkwright and my maids, and it appears that the doctor arrived about 2.15 in the morning and went away again about half an hour later."

"Thank you," said Frobisher. Then he added, severely: "I hope this will serve to put an end to other stupid rumours which have come to my ears and which may, possibly, have reached the members of the jury also."

"Phew!" said The Counsellor to himself. "So the local gossips had their little theories, too, had they? Everybody's doing it. Well, that seems to settle *their* hash. Can't get behind the united evidence of two maids and a G.P. nohow."

"Now I come to another point," the Coroner went on. "Mr. Hawkstone wore no jewellery except the seal-ring of which we have heard. Was it usual for him to carry any metallic objects in his pockets: a cigar-cutter, a cigarette-case, a metal match-box, or a bunch of keys, for example?"

"He was a non-smoker," Barrington explained. "He did carry a key-ring and a latch-key which was on the ring with the rest of his keys. But he was careless at times; and, as it happened, he left his key-ring in the office, after opening our strong-room, the afternoon before his death. I showed this key-ring to Inspector Hartwell; and with his consent I detached from it the keys of our office locks before returning the remainder to Mrs. Hawkstone. As to other metallic objects which might have been in his possession at the time of his decease, I cannot recollect any which he would be carrying on his person if he were in evening dress— except the coins, of course."

"Thank you," said the Coroner, who had apparently decided not to put any further questions to Barrington.

The next two witnesses—the taxi-driver who had seen Hawkstone's car at Barrington's gate and the door-keeper of Caplatzi's Dance Rooms—added nothing to The Counsellor's knowledge when they gave their evidence. Nor did the Iltons, who had given Mrs. Campion a lift home from Ranger's Copse. The lorry-driver who had seen the Hernshaw-Davies car near

Tetherdown Cross Roads declared that he noticed only one man in it, though he admitted that he had paid no special attention to the point at the time and could not swear that only the driver was in the car.

The next witness was Mrs. Hawkstone: a tall, graceful woman with striking features and arresting eyes. She was evidently nervous in the face of the audience, but she kept her feelings well in check and seemed anxious only to get through her ordeal as soon as possible. Apparently to give her time to recover herself, Frobisher first asked her formally to identify the ring. When she spoke, The Counsellor found that her voice was in keeping with the rest of her personality: low, but clear, with the faintest trace of a drawl which harmonised with her unhurried movements.

"Now, I must ask you one or two other questions, Mrs. Hawkstone," said Frobisher in a courteous tone which seemed to suggest that he had fallen under her charm. "When did you last see your husband alive?"

"At dinner on the evening of Friday, the 14th."

"Did he seem then in his normal state of mind? I mean, did he seem quite collected and free from anxiety?"

"He seemed to be in rather better spirits than usual," Mrs. Hawkstone answered. "He had told me he was going off for the week-end, and I imagined that the prospect had brightened him up."

"He had actually communicated his project to you?"

"Oh, yes. He said that he was going with a friend to some links he hadn't played on before. He was going to the office on Saturday morning and then straight to the station, so he warned me not to expect him home for luncheon. He had packed his week-end suit-case that morning—Friday morning, I mean—and took it away along with his clubs, meaning to leave them in the left luggage office at the station, so that he could pick them up on the Saturday. He couldn't take our car on Saturday, since he wasn't coming back; and by taking the suit-case down with him on Friday, it saved carrying it in his hand next morning."

"He went away frequently at week-ends?"

"From time to time," Mrs. Hawkstone answered in a tone which suggested that she had no desire to be more precise.

"He did not mention the name of this friend with whom he was spending the week-end?"

"Oh, no. He had a number of friends whom he did not bring to the house. I knew them only as names and had no particular interest in them."

"You saw him at dinner," continued the Coroner. "What happened after that?"

"I went into our drawing-room and switched on the wireless. He looked in for a moment or two, and then went out. That was the last I saw of him."

"He didn't return later in the evening?"

"No—not to my knowledge, at least. I went upstairs to my room at the usual time."

"When he did not appear at breakfast next morning, were you not alarmed?"

"Oh, no. My husband was often rather erratic in his movements. I mean, he changed his plans often on the spur of the moment. I had got quite accustomed to that. When he did not appear at breakfast, I concluded that he had altered his mind and had gone off on Friday night instead of Saturday morning."

"Without telling you of his change in plan?"

"Without telling me, of course. It was quite usual for him to do things like that."

Mrs. Hawkstone seemed faintly surprised that Frobisher should find anything strange in the matter.

"You saw in the newspapers some account of this blazing car having been found?"

"Well, I read it, or rather I glanced over it. But it didn't seem to have anything to do with me. The car had not been identified, you will remember. One doesn't think of such things in connection with oneself, somehow. It certainly never crossed my mind that the car described in the newspapers was our Hernshaw-Davies."

"You went out to your garage to get your car. When you found it missing, did that not raise a suspicion in your mind?"

"Not the slightest," Mrs. Hawkstone replied frankly. "I did not need the car on Saturday, nor on Sunday morning, so I did not go to the garage until Sunday afternoon. When I found the car gone, I supposed that my husband had changed his mind about going by train —just as he had changed his mind about going on Friday instead of Saturday—and that he had forgotten to mention to me that he was taking the car. There was no reason to think anything else. By that time I had almost forgotten about the blazing car. I don't read accounts of things like that in the newspapers except by accident. They don't appeal to me."

"When did you first feel uneasy in your mind?"

"Not until Tuesday night, when my husband did not come back. But, even then, I shouldn't say I felt uneasy. At times, he had often stayed away longer than the week-end, and I simply took it that this was another long stay. I merely wondered a little; but I assumed that he would come back when it suited him."

"That accounts, then, for your not lodging any information with the police about your husband's disappearance?"

"It never crossed my mind to appeal to the police,"

said Mrs. Hawkstone in a faintly surprised tone. "Why should it? I wasn't anxious about my husband. He was doing nothing that he hadn't done before. I was expecting him back at any moment."

"When he went away for week-ends did he not send you a wire to let you know that he had arrived at his destination?"

"Never!" said Mrs. Hawkstone, quite obviously surprised at the suggestion. "I wasn't anxious about him. He was quite well able to look after himself, surely. Why should he trouble to send a wire?"

Frobisher seemed to look on the matter from a different point of view. Evidently such a lack of sentiment surprised him. He glanced at the jury as though to discover their opinions. Then he went on to his next enquiry.

"Then how did you actually learn the truth about your husband's death?"

"Inspector Hartwell called. I think it was late on the Tuesday evening. He brought my husband's seal-ring and asked if I knew it. Then he told me about the car."

"Thank you," said Frobisher. "Now, another point, Mrs. Hawkstone. Was it customary for spare petrol tins to be kept in your garage?"

"No," said Mrs. Hawkstone decidedly. "Our garage is part of our house and we had no permit to keep a store of petrol beyond what we had in the tank. My husband was very strict on that point, perhaps because he knew the legal position. I'm quite sure that we never had any spare petrol on our premises."

"Thank you, Mrs. Hawkstone. That is all I have to ask you at present," said the Coroner.

And as she moved away from the witnesses' seat, he closed the proceedings and adjourned his inquest until more evidence should become available.

Chapter VI

DELAYED ACTION

AT the end of the proceedings, The Counsellor rapidly made his way outside and posted himself conveniently for intercepting Hartwell when he emerged in his turn. While awaiting the Inspector, he passed the time by examining the various witnesses as they came out into the open air.

The young men who had been the first to give their evidence seemed rather pleased by their experience, and made apparently jocular remarks about it to two or three friends who had come to see them perform. Next came the Coroner, looking very official, with a book under his arm. He glanced neither to right nor left, recognised no one, but walked straight to his car and drove away. Mrs. Campion appeared next, accompanied by some other woman whom she had apparently brought with her to act as a moral support. She showed a certain perkiness, glancing here and there at the groups of people standing in the street and giving a nod or a smile to anyone she recognised. She kept up a steady nervous chattering to her companion all the while.

"Not much of the grand passion there, so far as I can see," mused The Counsellor. "If Hawkstone got himself snuffed out on her account, he made a poor bargain of it. Common little thing. A certain physical attractiveness, but no brains whatever. Don't suppose he was looking for brains, though."

Sydney Barrington's massive shoulders appeared at the door and he walked deliberately down the steps, pausing at the foot of them and glancing back as though he were waiting for someone. The Counsellor ran his glance over the group of cars beside the pavement; and in the driving-seat of a two-seater he recognised Vera Glenarm. She nodded to him, but quite plainly did not expect him to go over to speak to her, though he was only a pace or two away. She, also, seemed to be waiting for someone. The Counsellor did not remember seeing her during the proceedings. Apparently she had stayed outside in her car.

When at last Mrs. Hawkstone came out, Barrington joined her and for a few moments they stood talking together, almost at The Counsellor's elbow. Without wishing to do so, he none the less caught fragments of the conversation, which seemed to have nothing to do with the inquest.

"Well, think it over, Sheila," Barrington said once. "No hurry."

More talk followed, in a rather lower tone, rather to the relief of The Counsellor, who had no wish to eavesdrop, even involuntarily. Then Sydney Barrington raised his voice in what seemed to be a final remark:

"It's not for me to advise. But in your shoes, Sheila, I think I'd take the income rather than the capital. Think it over carefully before you make up your mind."

The Counsellor could not help guessing that they had been discussing the financial affairs of the firm as they were affected by Hawkstone's death. It seemed rather cold-blooded, coming immediately on the heels of the inquest. Yet Barrington's tone was not unsympathetic. Quite otherwise, in fact. He seemed like an old friend pressing caution upon someone for whom he had a marked regard and who, he feared, might take

a wrong decision in haste, merely for the sake of getting some irksome problem settled and done with.
Mrs. Hawkstone nodded, at last, as though giving way
to the lawyer's suggestion.

She evidently had the gift of unself-consciousness
under the gaze of curious eyes, for, although she was
obviously a focus of interest for the bystanders, she
seemed quite unaware of it. She took leave of her companion with a graceful gesture; walked along the line
of cars to Vera's two-seater; and got in. Vera drove off
at once as soon as Mrs. Hawkstone had taken her place.

"Of course!" The Counsellor said to himself after a
moment's reflection. "I'd forgotten she has no car of
her own, now. Decent of Vera Glenarm to remember
that and to come and fetch her."

As he turned away from watching the disappearing
car, Hartwell emerged from the building, and The
Counsellor stepped forward to intercept him.

"I've got something fresh," he explained as the
Inspector was going to pass on with a nod of recognition. "Might interest you. But if you're in a hurry, it
can keep."

Hartwell gave a surreptitious glance at his watch.

"Are you likely to take long?" he demanded. "I'm
on my way to lunch. If I don't get it now, I mayn't
be able to fit it in."

"Depends how far it is to a newspaper office," said
The Counsellor, who knew the advantage of rousing
curiosity. "I want to talk it over with you first. Suppose you have luncheon with me, if there's any place
you fancy. My car's here."

The Inspector pretended to consider for a moment
or two. Before he had time to reply, Barrington moved
deliberately over to join the Inspector, whom he
greeted with a pleasant smile.

"Congratulations on your evidence, Hartwell," he said with an almost imperceptible twinkle of humour in his eyes. "But I'm rather afraid that you didn't please the Coroner with some of it. He doesn't like to see his theories weakened. And, by the way, I suppose from something he said to me that your phrase 'from information received' covered the activities of that wireless person who calls himself The Counsellor."

"This is the gentleman you're speaking about," said Hartwell hastily, with a gesture of introduction towards The Counsellor.

Barrington cast a glance over The Counsellor's conspicuous tweeds; but there was no offence in it and he greeted their owner as though he were really interested in him.

"I had a suspicion that it was you," he admitted frankly. "I heard from Frobisher that he'd asked for your help; and naturally I was interested and listened to your talk from Radio Ardennes that Sunday to see what you would say. To be candid, the troubles of Lonely Betty, Blighted Billy, Heart-sick and the rest of them left me cold. It's not my kind of pathos, though perhaps that's my fault. A solicitor gets more than enough of other people's troubles in the course of his business, you know."

"Perhaps you don't treat 'em in the right spirit," retorted The Counsellor with a smile. "I've a solicitor friend whose favourite remark is: 'I can't help your troubles; but I *can* add to them.' I suppose he's thinking of his bill when he says that. Not quite the way to undam the stream of confidence, though."

"Perhaps not. But I sympathise with your friend. There are some kinds of confidence which one could well do without. I've been dragged into this miserable affair owing to one of them, as you know. Are you proposing to interest yourself further in it or have you had enough?"

"Listen to me next week," retorted The Counsellor. "Then you'll know all that can be made public."

"I'd rather forget all about it, if I could," said Barrington gravely. "It's a nasty affair."

"Especially for Mrs. Hawkstone," agreed The Counsellor with equal gravity.

"Especially for Mrs. Hawkstone," the solicitor confirmed soberly. "She has the worst end of it, undoubtedly. However, I see you want to be off," he added to the Inspector. "You'll remember our appointment to-morrow?"

"I'll be there," Hartwell assured him.

"Then that's all right," said Barrington, turning away. "I just wanted to make sure it hadn't slipped your mind."

He nodded to The Counsellor in a friendly way, walked over to his car, and drove off. The Counsellor's chauffeur came up at a gesture from his master, and was given his orders as the Inspector got into the car.

"By the way," said The Counsellor, taking his seat in turn, "just a question. Every little helps. That keyring of Hawkstone's. You saw it, I suppose, before Barrington handed it back to Mrs. Hawkstone. Had it an insurance tag on it? You know what I mean? A metal tag telling a finder that he'll get five bob for it at the Chief Police Office if he dumps it there. Bet you five bob myself that there was such a tag on the ring."

"Well, there was," Hartwell confirmed, "so it's no use my taking your bet. But what made you think there was?"

"It just occurred to me," declared The Counsellor, lightly. "Now, here's our restaurant. No chance of a private room, I suppose. Waiters have ears, like the rest of us. Let's keep off the subject of the inquest while we're feeding. Talk about nothing but high life and high-lived company, with other fashionable topics, such as pictures, taste, Shakespeare and the musical glasses. Goldsmith wrote that—the cove Garrick said wrote like an angel and talked like poor Poll. *Vicar of Wakefield*, you know."

"It's a wonderful thing to be well-read, sir," said Hartwell sardonically. "No doubt you had *The Vicar of Wakefield* in your lessons at school—same as me."

"Pinked!" admitted The Counsellor, unabashed. "You know my methods, Watson, evidently. But, out you get. And now, mum's the word! Be as mute as a mackerel. After banqueting, we'll take a spin in my car for a quarter of an hour; and then, if the fancy takes us, we can talk of graves, of worms, of epitaphs. Shakespeare. But no doubt you had him at school—same as me. Come along!"

The Counsellor was a good host, with a shrewd choice in liquids, and the Inspector enjoyed his lunch. When they returned to the car, he was much readier to talk than he had been before.

"Speaking of the fear of death," he said, recurring to a subject they had touched on incidentally in their conversation, "it's a natural enough feeling. But did you ever come across anyone suffering from the fear of life?"

"I once averted a suicide," said The Counsellor. "Come to think of it, he must have been afraid of life. Else why commit suicide?"

"Something in that," admitted the Inspector, evidently not ill-pleased to cap The Counsellor's reminiscence. "But I know a queerer twist to it. I once knew a man who was terrified of being buried alive. You'd

be afraid of life in these circumstances, wouldn't you?
Waking up six feet under the sod and stifling your life
out. He made most careful provisions about it. In fact,
I came into a little bit under his will in that connection.
You heard me making an appointment before lunch?
That had something to do with it."

The Counsellor gave a slight shudder as if the subject
struck him cold.

"I've had enough of graves, worms and epitaphs for
the present, I think," he declared. "What I really
wanted to talk to you about was the Hawkstone affair.
I gathered from this morning's proceedings that the
Coroner is still sticking to his suicide theory. Seems
like rubbish to me. If this was a tec novel and I was
reading it, I'd get suspicious at once. What's the motive
for flying straight in the face of plain facts? I'd say.
Has this Coroner person any interest in the removal
of the deceased? Is he using his official position to screen
himself from the results of a crime? But, in real life,
I can't see it so. I take it that he just wants to disagree
with his competitors in the Elucidation Stakes."

"He's got no interest in Hawkstone's death," said
the Inspector. "He hardly knew the man."

"Exactly. Rule him out, then. What about the
Campion imbroglio, for a change. Did you swallow her
evidence?"

"It sounded all right," said the Inspector, without
much conviction in his tone. "And it *was* right, so far
as we've checked it up. Her husband *has* gone to
America, just as she said."

"A very convenient departure," commented The
Counsellor. "But leave that aside. We'll come back to
it by-and-by. Listening to the evidence, I saw a lot of
snags sticking up out of the smooth current. First of
all, where did those two petrol tins come from—the

ones that had been emptied into the car and then chucked over the hedge? Have you found out?"

The inspector shook his head.

"One petrol tin's like another," he said.

"True. But just ask a question. These tins weren't in the car while Hawkstone and the Campion dame were having their dust-up at Ranger's Copse. That's her evidence. They weren't visible when Barrington looked into the car just as it drove away from his house. That's his evidence. Then how did Hawkstone come to have them aboard after that?"

"They may have been in the boot of the car all the time," the Inspector pointed out, with a certain tone of "caught you that time" in his voice.

"I'll let you stop the next ten cars we meet, and give you a quid for every petrol tin you find in their boots," said The Counsellor contemptuously. "Nobody carries spare petrol nowadays, with all these pumps by the roadside. No, if he had these tins aboard from start to finish, then it was suicide after all and he'd planned it all beforehand. And that doesn't make sense. If he picked them up after leaving Barrington's house, it's certain he didn't get them in his own garage, because he kept no tins there. That's his wife's evidence. They must have come from somewhere. Where did they come from? Obviously the murderer had them handy, wherever he got them. And that leads on to another point. Hawkstone left Barrington's house at 12.50 a.m. He didn't get himself incinerated until 2.15 a.m. or later. What was he doing in between? It wouldn't have taken him more than twenty minutes to get from the one place to the other; and yet he spent about an hour and a half on the road. I haven't been able to trace him during that spell. Had you any better luck?"

The Inspector shook his head.

"No. I've made enquiries, the fullest enquiries, but nothing's come of them."

"Then there's another point," The Counsellor went on. "When were the engine number and the chassis number filed off his car? That's a job that takes time. Might have been done between his leaving Barrington and arriving at the Cross Roads. But there was no point in his doing it, if he meant suicide. And if another man did it, he must have got Hawkstone away from his car while he was busy with the filing job. Even half-drunk, no man would let another man start on his car with a file. That wants clearing up, and badly. Those missing number plates, too. Why take them away at all, if they were to be dumped so near at hand? And, by the way, did you take my tip about matches?"

"We've combed that débris over and over again, looking for any signs of match-heads," said the Inspector rather crossly. "Your tip wasted a lot of our time and led to absolutely nothing. I'd take a fair-sized bet that we'd have found even a single match-head if it had been there."

"Then obviously it wasn't," said The Counsellor, who seemed rather relieved than otherwise by this evidence. "That seems to put the lid on the suicide hypothesis, anyhow, unless Hawkstone kindled his blaze with sparks from a wayside flint. Now another thing. Did you ask Mrs. Campion if she knew the number of Hawkstone's car?"

"She'd never bothered about that," said Hartwell. "Why should she? She wasn't interested in Hawkstone barring the fact that he could give her what she reckoned as a good time."

The Counsellor seemed to reflect for a few seconds before speaking again.

"Tell you what strikes me most," he said at last.

"There's a sort of delayed-action scheme in this affair. Like the fuse of a Mills bomb. Nothing shows for a time, and then things begin to happen. On the face of it, lots of precautions were taken to conceal Hawkstone's identity. No number plates on car. No engine number. No chassis number. No licence disc left intact. Corpse quite unrecognisable. No personal jewellery or wrist-watch. A clean sweep, in fact, bar one thing: the signet ring. And even the signet ring was a bit knocked about to make recognition difficult."

"Then where's your delayed action?" demanded the Inspector. "The murderer took every step he could to make identification impossible."

"Say *immediate* identification, and I'm with you," said The Counsellor. "He wanted to keep you off the track for some days. That's plain as print. But he wanted it to be known eventually that it was Hawkstone's body. That's equally plain. He left the number plates of the car near at hand in a place that was bound to be searched in due course. He left the seal ring, after damaging it enough to make it useless as a clue by itself. It's as plain as daylight that what he really wanted was to gain a day or two before Hawkstone was identified. Why? Because during that day or two, any possible witnesses's memories would get a bit blunted and they might not put two and two together and see that their evidence had any importance. That's what I mean by delayed action. What he was after was merely to make your investigations hang fire for a while, even if you got at the truth in the end. Now that's got one very significant fact attached to it, if you think for a moment."

"I'll spare myself thinking," said the Inspector. "You tell me, and it'll save brain tissue."

"Well, then. Suppose you disappear this afternoon.

How long would it be before one or two people begin to say: 'Where's that tall handsome Inspector we used to see about the place?' About twelve hours would do it. Why did nobody get excited about Hawkstone's disappearance? Because his circle knew he was erratic and likely to dash off at any time on some of those dubious excursions of his. And that suggests that the murderer knew about these excursions, too. He could count on having a week-end in hand before Hawkstone's circle began to sit up and notice that their late friend was no longer in their midst. See that? In normal life, who'd be the first to spot the disappearance of a husband? His wife, of course. But you heard Mrs. Hawkstone's evidence. . . . By the way, have you any notion how she's been left—financially, I mean—by this affair?"

"She won't be much worse off, if at all," said the Inspector. "You heard the evidence. She can either demand £15,000 cash from Mr. Barrington or else take a slightly reduced share of the firm's profits, whichever she chooses. And now she won't have Hawkstone there, spending money on those week-ends of his."

"What sort of reputation has that firm got?" enquired The Counsellor. "A good, old-fashioned affair?"

"So I'm told," said Hartwell. "I don't employ them myself," he added with a smile. "Rather too grand for folk like me. They do the work of most of the big families round about here, I believe."

"The Earlswoods and that lot?"

"Yes, that lot," said the Inspector. "But the only dealings I've had with them have been strictly professional on my side: a matter of the theft of some lead piping from an empty house they had in their charge, temporarily. That was a week or two back, and I had to see Mr. Barrington about it. He took the sensible view of the affair. I'll say that for him. He's not the sort to cry over spilt milk, I gathered; and he doesn't expect the police to be everywhere at once. I'd like to lay that thief by the heels if I could; but so far we haven't got him."

The Counsellor seemed amused by a thought which had crossed his mind.

"It's always the simplest things that worry one most," he declared weightily. "I'll lay you an even quid, Mr. Hartwell, that it'll take you longer than twenty-four hours to give me . . . let's see . . . Well, say the address of Hawkstone's outfitter and the name of the firm that did his washing. And another even quid that you can't tell me in the same time . . . well, let's say whether or not he wore a hat usually when he went out at night in his car. Care to snap at it?"

"Snap!" said the Inspector. "I'll phone you the news well under the time limit. That will be two quid you owe me, Mr. Brand."

"I pay by results," retorted The Counsellor, drily. "Produce them and I'll pull out my note-case."

Chapter VII

THE ADVERTISEMENTS

THE COUNSELLOR seemed to have no further interest in Mrs. Hawkstone's finances.

"Now, I've got something fresh for you," he said, taking a sheet of paper from his pocket. "I run a Problem Department as part of my business. Anyone can send in puzzles and ask for solutions. I keep a tame Solutionist for that work. Fellow who lives on acrostics and dreams o' nights about gardens with nine trees arranged in eight rows of three. Yesterday he came into my office. Everybody on my staff knows I'm interested in this Hawkstone affair. Now it seems somebody sent in some cipher advertisements to be deciphered. The address given was in Fernhurst-Hordle here; and when my Solutionist saw that and had worried them out—it didn't take him long—he brought them straight to me, thinking them of interest. The address given by the sender was Swinbrook, c/o Shipman, 12 Wilkin Lane. No such address, is there? I thought not. There's more in this than a mere enquiry. Now here are copies of the ads."

He unfolded the sheet and handed it to the Inspector, who stared at it uncomprehendingly, for it showed only a series of pasted-on newspaper cuttings with the names of journals appended:

Fernhurst Courier, March 30th:
    SNAP. Xzm blf hvv nv glnliild? ERM.

Fernhurst Herald, March 31st:
  SNIP. Ml gfvhwzb kviszkh mvch ozgvi olimz.

Fernhurst Herald, April 1st.
  SNIP. Sv droo yv zdzb gfvhwzb mrtsg xlnv sviv
    uli hfkkvi xxxxx olimz.

Fernhurst Courier, April 2nd.
  SNAP. Droo yv drgs blf 8.30. ERM.

Fernhurst Herald, April 5th.
  SNIP. Szh sv wvxrwvw gl tl Mligs uli dvvp-vmw.
    ERM.

Fernhurst Herald, April 6th.
  SNAP. Xzm hkvmw dvvp-vmw zugvi mvcg drgs
    blf. Xzoo uli nv 5.30 Uirwzb. Ivgfim Hfmwzb
    mrtsg. XXXXX. OLIMZ.

"Might be Russian or Chinese for all I can tell. I
don't speak either of them," Hartwell commented, after
a second careful perusal. "The *Herald* and the *Courier*
are our two local papers. That's all I make out of it."

"Here's what my Solutionist makes of it," said The
Counsellor, producing a second sheet of paper and
passing it to the inspector.

Courier, March 30th.
  SNAP. Can you see me to-morrow? VIN.

Herald, March 31st.
  SNIP. No tuesday perhaps news later. lorna.

Herald, April 1st.
  SNIP. He will be away tuesday night come here
    for supper xxxxx lorna.

Courier, April 2nd.
  SNAP. Will be with you 8.30. VIN.

Herald, April 5th.
    SNIP. Has he decided to go North for week-end?
    VIN.

Herald, April 6th.
    SNAP. Can spend week-end after next with you.
    Call for me 5.30 Friday. Return Sunday night.
    XXXXX. LORNA.

"It makes more sense when you write it that way," Hartwell admitted. "Vin's short for Vincent, obviously. That's Hawkstone, plain enough. Lorna's this Mrs. Campion, plain enough. He calls her Snip and she calls him Snap. H'm! The 'he' in it means her husband, I suppose. Well, one thing's clear to me, Mr. Brand. That little hussy went on her oath before the jury and committed the blandest bit of perjury I've seen done for a while. She swore it was all a nice boy-and-girl business between her and Hawkstone. Nothing nasty about it. And here, in plain print—or in cipher, anyway —she's telling him she'll spend the week-end with him when the tom-cat's away. Well, well, you never can trust anyone on oath when it comes down to these hormones they talk about so much nowadays."

"There's more in it than that," The Counsellor declared, holding out his hand for the papers, which the Inspector mechanically passed back to him. "You've missed one or two points, Inspector."

But instead of elucidating the matter further, he put the documents back into his pocket and glanced at Hartwell with something approaching a grin.

"And what's the next move?" he demanded.

"I'll have to see that young woman and put a question or two. She won't like it," answered the Inspector.

"You haven't got it quite right," The Counsellor corrected, his grin becoming unmistakable. "It reads: *We'll* have to see that young woman, etc."

"I'm not so sure I could agree to that, sir," said the Inspector in a more formal tone. "That would be a bit too irregular."

"You think so? All right! Good hunting! Don't let me keep you off the trail. Nose down, and go to it!"

"But I need those documents," protested the Inspector, seeing the meaning of The Counsellor's tactics.

"Sorry, and all that. I want them myself. My need is greater than his, as Sir Philip Sidney did *not* say. I've given you the tip and served the ends of justice. Now you can run down to the newspaper offices, hunt up the ads., decipher them, and go ahead. As you don't want my company, I'll wish you farewell, *au revoir, auf Wiedersehen, buon viaggio*, and the rest. Expect you'll puzzle out that cipher in no time. My Solutionist tells me a child could solve it. Now where would you like me to drop you? Not being needed here, I'm going back to Town now to attend to my own business."

The Inspector knew that he had no gift for cipher-solving; and he had no Solutionist to call upon for help. It might be long enough before he could worry out the meaning of the advertisements; and without the exact text, his questioning of Mrs. Campion would lose half its point. He recognised the fix into which he had got; and, being a sensible man, he decided to put formalities aside and to concede The Counsellor's demands so as to secure the use of the documents at once.

"You've got me in a cleft stick," he admitted, not ill-naturedly. "Have it your own way."

"Spoke like a real gent," declared The Counsellor vulgarly. "And I'll give you a tip in return for that.

Don't you get crusty if I shove my oar into this duet you're planning. Trios are more interesting. I've got an idea or two in reserve, as I hinted before. The first thing to do is to find out what newspaper our friend Campion favours at breakfast time. But don't start on that at once. Bring it in naturally. But bring it in."

He picked up the speaking-tube and ordered his chauffeur to drive to 5 Savernake Park. When they arrived there, The Counsellor got out and glanced up and down the road.

"A bit simple in the architecture," he commented to the Inspector. "The four-rooms-and-kitchen style of box, with a one-car garage included. By the way, what about those petrol tins? Could they have come from here? She swore in her evidence that Hawkstone didn't visit her that night after the trouble at Ranger's Copse. Still . . ."

"I'll ask about that point, sir," the Inspector assured him.

The house-door was opened at their ring by Lorna Campion herself, still in the same costume that she had worn at the inquest. She looked much less self-confident than she had done before the Coroner, and The Counsellor had little difficulty in inferring that she had been "having a good cry," as no doubt she would have described the process herself.

"Oh, it's you again, is it?" she said ungraciously, at the sight of Hartwell. "Haven't you made enough trouble already? I thought I'd finished with the lot of you, after having to go up and be questioned about my private affairs by that Coroner this morning. Can't you leave people in peace?"

She threw an inquisitve and rather suspicious glance at The Counsellor as she spoke. But if she expected an introduction, Hartwell disappointed her.

"I've just come to ask a question or two," he explained civilly. "We'd better go inside, I think. You don't want the neighbours . . ."

Evidently Lorna Campion agreed with him in not wishing to be examined on her own doorstep. She led the way into a little sitting-room rather glaringly furnished in ill-chosen colours. As she preceded them, The Counsellor took the opportunity of passing to the Inspector the cipher and the translation.

"Now, first of all," the Inspector began, "I want to know what you called Mr. Hawkstone—or Mr. Merlin, if you like. Did you call him Mister, or had you got on to a Christian-name footing?"

Evidently this seemed to Lorna Campion merely a silly question.

"We knew each other *quite* well, in a way," she answered. "We soon dropped the Mister and Missus. He called me Lorna, and he told me his name was Vincent, so I used to call him Vin. What's that got to do with you?"

"You used to communicate with him sometimes by advertisements in the newspapers. Why did you use advertisements, since you could use the post?"

"Why? Because he never told me his address, so I couldn't get hold of him by letter. He could write to me if he wanted, for he knew where I stayed. But I had to advertise if I had a message for him. That's plain enough, isn't it?"

"Quite," agreed the Inspector, placidly, as he unfolded The Counsellor's documents. "Now here's an advertisement beginning SNAP. Did you use that in your advertisements?"

Lorna Campion considered for a moment or two before replying. She was evidently taken aback by finding the Inspector had hit on that particular advertisement.

"Yes, I did," she admitted. "I don't see how you found that out. You couldn't read the message after it, anyhow," she ended, with a triumphant smile.

"Think so?" said Hartwell, indifferently. "It's in some sort of cipher, so I suppose you thought no one could read it. But that kind of cipher's mere child's play to an expert."

The Counsellor smiled covertly at the way in which the Inspector left Lorna Campion to assume that the police had done the deciphering. Hartwell gave his statement time to sink in and then added:

"By the way, how did you hit on that particular cipher?"

"It was Vin showed me how to work it."

"Ah, indeed? Well, this message reads: 'SNAP. *Can you see me to-morrow?* VIN.' You remember that?"

"Can't say I do," retorted Mrs. Campion. "He may have put it in, or he may not. Honestly, I don't remember it particularly. There's not much in it to take hold of, is there?" she added with a shrewd glance at her questioner.

Hartwell frowned in obvious displeasure.

"It's no good fencing with me, Mrs. Campion. We know a bit too much for that to pay you. Here's your reply in the paper next day: 'SNIP. *No. Tuesday, perhaps. News later.* LORNA.' Now do you remember that?"

"Can't say," she retorted with a certain pertness.

"Very well, then. Here's the next one in the paper of April 1st. 'SNIP. *He will be away Tuesday night. Come here for supper.* XXXXX. LORNA.' Did you, or did you not, insert that?"

"Have I got to say?"

The Inspector contented himself with shrugging his shoulders. The Counsellor was amused to see how he evaded a direct answer. Lorna Campion evidently took the shrug as an affirmative reply; and she decided that she would do herself little good by persisting in her pretence of ignorance.

"Well, then, yes. I think I did. Something like it, anyhow. I can't remember just how I put it, but it was something like what you read out. What does it matter to you if I did ask him to supper when Percy was away from home? That's no business of yours, is it?"

"I suppose the crosses or X's were meant for kisses?" queried the Inspector, stolidly.

"What if they were? There's no harm in a kiss or two, is there? So long as it doesn't go any further, anyhow. Yes, I did have him to supper. And we did have a bit of fun afterwards. But nothing wrong in it, from start to finish. I wouldn't let him."

"H'm!" said the Inspector, making no concealment of his scepticism. "Quite sure about that?"

Lorna Campion's face flushed at the direct question.

"I'm dead certain about it, if you want to know," she retorted angrily. "That's slander, that is. And I've got a witness here"—she glanced at The Counsellor—"and I'll have the law on you, I will, as sure as you're here, if you dare to say that kind of thing about me to anyone. Percy would go half mad if he heard you hinting at that kind of thing about me. Furious, he'd be. You'd better be careful. I warn you! How dare you suggest such a thing? Of course I never let him touch me—not *that* way."

The Inspector felt that he now had the game in his hands. He held the paper before her, marking the place with a blunt forefinger to emphasise his words:

"And yet five days later you put this in: 'SNAP. *Can spend week-end after next with you. Call for me* 5.30 *Friday. Return Sunday night. XXXXX.* LORNA.' It's not usual for people like you and Hawkstone to spend a week-end just holding hands. You could do that without paying an hotel bill."

Lorna Campion's reaction to this insinuation satisfied the Inspector that he had scored a bull's-eye. She threw up her hands in an involuntary gesture, her pointed little face grew drawn, and her eyes seemed to expand with fear as she took in the meaning of Hartwell's words. She looked like some little animal which has just realised that it is caught in a trap and sees no way of escape. The Counsellor had set a trap of his own, and he was inwardly amused to see the Inspector fall into it. That, he reflected, would make Hartwell more amenable in future.

"I never put that in," Lorna Campion gasped, when she had regained some control over her voice. "I never wrote anything of the sort. I never *dreamed* of going off with him for a week-end, let alone offering to do it. I didn't, say what you like. I don't understand this. You're inventing it, just to ruin my character. I'll have the law on you, if I can, for daring to suggest it. I will, see if I don't. Oh! What'll Percy do if he hears about that? I never wrote anything of the sort. I never did. Never!"

"There's the cutting in cipher. You can work it out for yourself," said the Inspector impatiently. "What's the good of denying it when it's there in print, exactly the same as the other messages? You'll never get anywhere with that line of talk."

"I never put it in," Mrs. Campion repeated sullenly.

The Counsellor suddenly intervened, silently, in the scene. With a sharp frown, he telegraphed to the Inspector to be wary. Hartwell saw the contraction of the Counsellor's brows and was puzzled.

"Well, how do you account for it, then?" he asked,

rather lamely. "Same cipher. Same newspaper. Same code-word at the start. I don't see how you can get round it, Mrs. Campion, and I advise you to think again carefully before you speak."

Lorna Campion seemed half-dazed for a moment or two. Then she broke into a feeble titter, and The Counsellor feared that she would collapse into hysterics. However, after gulping spasmodically once or twice, she seemed to pull herself together a little.

"I never put it in," she protested with a kind of shaky doggedness. "Believe it or not, it's the honest truth I'm telling you; and if you like to bring a Bible and put me on my oath, I'd swear the same. I don't understand it, any more than you do."

She thought for a moment or two and then her face lighted up as though she had found some way of escape:

"Besides, if I'd been so ready to go off for week-ends with him, why did I quarrel with him at Ranger's Copse just because he wanted me to spend a week-end with him and I wouldn't? You're not going to deny that I did quarrel with him then, are you? For there's two witnesses to that, as you well know."

"I don't know what you and he quarrelled about, and these two witnesses—if you mean the Iltons—don't know, either," said the Inspector, acidly. "All they know is that there was a quarrel of some sort between you and Hawkstone. They certainly don't know what you squabbled about. That doesn't help."

"Well, it's true," Lorna Campion persisted obstinately, though with a note of depression in her voice as she recognised that her argument had failed to convince. "And I'd never think of putting an advertisement like that in the paper."

The Inspector decided that nothing would be gained by pursuing the matter further at the moment.

"Let it go at that, then, for the present," he said, with no attempt to conceal his disbelief. "But just remember this. If there's a criminal case comes out of this affair, you'll be called up again as a witness. And you'd better make a clean breast of it if you're questioned about these advertisements when you're in the box. You'll be on oath then."

"I tell you I didn't do it," declared Lorna Campion in a tone of almost physical anguish. "I don't understand it, any more than you seem to do. Things seem to have got all upside down, and I can't make head or tail of it, I tell you. It's no good your questioning me about it, for I simply can't answer questions about something I know nothing about. Can I?" she ended, turning to The Counsellor as if appealing to his judgment against the Inspector's.

"Just let's see, first, if that advertisement really appeared in the paper," suggested The Counsellor soothingly, with a quick side-glance at the Inspector to warn him not to interfere for the moment. "Have you a copy of the *Fernhurst Herald* in the house? I'd like to compare the types."

Lorna Campion seemed to think that she had found a sympathetic defender in The Counsellor. She gave him a grateful glance as she answered.

"I haven't got a copy of the *Herald*," she explained with obvious regret. "I'm sorry. It's the *Courier* we take in."

"But you used to advertise in the *Herald* when you communicated with Mr. Hawkstone?" asked The Counsellor, to give her more time to recover her nerve.

"Yes, I did. And he used to put his reply advertisement in the *Courier*, because it was the paper we took, so I saw it every day and didn't need to go buying a second paper to see if there was any message from him."

"How long has this sort of thing been going on—advertising, I mean," asked The Counsellor quietly.

"A couple of months or more," Lorna Campion admitted with apparent frankness. "Only, we didn't do it often, you see. Usually when we met, we'd fix up a time for our next meeting. It was when we forgot, or couldn't be sure my husband would be away, that we advertised."

"I understand. And you'd no difficulty with this cipher business—no bother in reading the cipher or making it up?"

"Oh, no. It was dead easy, you see. All you do is to write the alphabet, A, B, C, D, . . . down to M, in a line and then begin working back, putting N under M, O under L, and so on until you come to Z under the A. Then if you want to put any letter into cipher, you take the one above it—or below it. A for Z or Z for A, if you see what I mean."

"I see perfectly," said The Counsellor, with a swift side-glance at the expression on the Inspector's face. "Very simple, indeed. Now just another question, Mrs. Campion. You've a garage here. Have you any petrol stored in it?"

"Pardon?" queried Lorna Campion, who evidently had not been quick enough to follow this sudden switch to a fresh topic.

"I merely asked if you have any spare petrol tins in your garage."

"No, we haven't. We used to keep quite a lot, a dozen tins or so, because my husband wanted it ready to fill up the tank if he had to make a long journey at short notice, as he often had to do in the way of business. Then somebody went off and told the police about it. It must have been somebody with a spite against us. There's a lot of cats about this neighbour-hood, as I could tell you. My husband, he's quick-tempered; and I think he got across the police over it. Anyway, he was fined for keeping too much petrol in a garage that's part of the house; and he was furious about that and said he wouldn't give them a chance again; and he wouldn't go crawling to them for any permit. So, since then, we've never had any spare petrol on the premises at all. Sometimes it's very awkward."

"Some people have a spite against you?" ruminated The Counsellor, aloud. "Nasty, that. Women, I suppose?"

"Well, gentlemen, too," Mrs. Campion admitted. "My husband's a bit inclined to quarrel with some people. There was some trouble over the tennis club. It's very awkward when he quarrels with the husband of some lady that's a friend of mine."

"Obviously," agreed The Counsellor in a sympathetic tone. "Now, another question. Did you ever tell anyone about this cipher advertisement business?"

"Pardon?"

"I mean, did you mention it—perhaps as a kind of joke—to any of your friends?"

Lorna Campion was evidently struck by this enquiry. She put her little pointed chin into her hands and thought hard for a few moments, her contracted brows testifying to the intensity of her memory-searching.

"No," she said, at length. "Not that I can remember, anyhow. I may have done, but I don't think so."

"Do you read much?" demanded The Counsellor, unexpectedly.

"Pardon?"

"I mean, in the evenings, to pass the time?"

"No, not much," Lorna Campion confessed readily. "Generally I go to the pictures if I get bored. My husband reads a bit, when he has time."

This answer hardly surprised The Counsellor. His roving glance had already catalogued the single untidy shelf which constituted the Campion library: a dozen tattered paper-backed editions of detective stories, Dudeney's *Canterbury Puzzles*, one or two battered numbers of the *Strand Magazine*, a crossword puzzle book, and a very old and dishevelled copy of *One Thousand Pink Uns from the Pink Un*.

"Interested in crossword puzzles?" demanded The Counsellor abruptly.

"Pardon?" repeated Mrs. Campion, obviously at sea.

"Do you like crossword puzzles?" The Counsellor paraphrased, speaking with careful deliberation.

"Me? Not a bit. But my husband's good at them," Mrs. Campion answered with a touch of pride. "He once won a prize. It was only five and threepence, because so many other people got it out as well. But he got it right. That started him off, and now if a puzzle comes his way, he sits down to it and worries at it for hours, if he has the time to spare. When he gets a *Strand Magazine*, the first thing he settles down to read is the puzzle page. It's a queer taste. Needs brains, you know. I never had the head for things of that sort," she ended frankly.

The Counsellor had a momentary vision of the home life of the Campions: the husband, tired after a day's travelling, sitting by the fire dozing over crossword puzzles, the wife out at some picture house, trying to scrape acquaintance with any man who would give her an amusing hour or two. Evidently the first flush of passion had passed, so far as those two were concerned. But that did not mean that jealousy had vanished also, he reflected.

Hartwell, gathering that The Counsellor had no further questions to ask, intervened to put some more of his own.

"When you heard about this blazing car affair, you never connected it with Hawkstone in any way?"

"Why should I? One reads about these things in the papers, of course, but one never thinks they might happen to anyone that one knows. I certainly didn't."

The Inspector put the sheet with the cuttings before her.

"Which of these do you admit having inserted? Be careful, now."

Lorna Campion seemed to lose some of her regained self-possession at the reappearance of the advertisements. She read through the series with knitted brows as though carefully considering her ground before making her reply.

"That one there in the *Herald* of March 31st and the next one. I do remember writing them out. And there's nothing wrong with either of them. Even *you* can't say there is."

"Then you remember his messages in the *Courier* on March 30th and April 2nd, since they belong to the same set?"

"Ye-e-s, I suppose I do," she admitted, reluctantly.

"And what about the last two, in the *Herald* of April 5th and April 6th? Do you still deny any knowledge of them?"

"Of course I deny it. I told you so before. I'd never set eyes on them till you showed me them."

"You denied some of the others as well, before you knew how much I had in my hand," declared Hartwell, not altogether accurately.

"I remember the first lot now," Lorna Campion admitted sulkily, keeping her eyes fixed on the carpet. "It must have slipped my memory or something, when you asked me before. I haven't a good memory, really. I forget a lot of things sometimes."

"You don't care to remember the one about the week-end?" demanded the Inspector sardonically. "I'm not going to ask again."

"No, I don't. I never wrote such a thing. You can bully me till you're tired, but I never wrote anything of the sort. I never did, and I'm not going to be frightened into saying I did. I appeal to this gentleman here. He's a witness."

"He is," said the Inspector meaningly. "Now there's another thing I've got to ask you. After that little affair at Ranger's Copse, you were brought back to Edendale Road by Mr. Ilton. What happened after the Iltons left you?"

"I walked round here and went straight to bed."

"Anyone who can prove that? Have you a maid who could corroborate your story?"

"Pardon?"

"Have you a maid who saw you come in that night?"

Mrs. Campion shook her head despondently.

"No. We don't keep a maid. I do the housework myself."

"Your husband didn't come home, by any chance? No? Then there's nothing to prove that you didn't go out again? In fact, there's only your own word for it that you *did* come in and go to bed."

"Well, I did. There!"

The inspector's only comment was a faint shrug.

"Hawkstone didn't pay you another visit later on, trying to make up your quarrel? He knew the coast was clear, didn't he? He knew your husband was away from home, didn't he? Now, don't try to put me off. It doesn't pay. We know too much, as you've seen already. Just the truth, please, and nothing else. It saves time."

Lorna Campion seemed to be again on the brink of hysterics.

"I never saw Mr. Hawkstone after I parted with him at Ranger's Copse. That's the truth. I did just as I said, came home here and went straight to bed because I was all upset after that row I'd had with him."

"Let it go at that," said the Inspector sceptically. "I've nothing more to ask you at present. I may have, later on; and I'd advise you to have your memory in good order when I do. Now, I'll just jot down an outline of the evidence you've given me; and after you've signed it, you'll be quit of us."

He sat down and wrote out a *précis*, which he made her read over before she signed it.

"That's all for the present," he said, rising and moving toward the door.

The Counsellor followed him. Mrs. Campion rose to her feet, but made no attempt to show them off the premises. Whatever inference she drew from the Inspector's final set of questions, they had evidently stupefied her.

"That's a silly little liar," said the Inspector crossly, when he had taken his seat beside The Counsellor in the car. "It's these would-be clever people who give half the trouble in a case by wasting time instead of admitting plain facts. If she'd told the truth at the start, I'd have believed her when she said she'd had no hanky-panky business with Hawkstone. Now, confound her, I don't know what to think about it. And it may be important, for all one can tell."

The Counsellor refused to be drawn on that subject. Instead, he suggested that the Inspector might like to be set down at one of the newspaper offices.

"You can look up their file. Just on the cards there may be earlier cipher messages than the ones I got. They might throw further light. Shall I tell my man to drive to the *Herald* office?"

"Thanks," said the Inspector gratefully. "And while we're on that subject, I want to ask a question."

"You're in practice," said The Counsellor, with a grin, after he had directed his chauffeur. "Go on."

"I've an impression that you've seen more in these ads. than I did," Hartwell admitted reluctantly. "What was it?"

"I did see a point or two," The Counsellor confessed. "You've got the documents. Fish 'em out and let's look at 'em. Glance at the signatures, first. ERM in capitals, each time. But in her ads. you find 'olimz' in small letters and not even a capital at the beginning of the name in the ads. of March 31st and April 1st; but when you get to the message of April 6th, you get OLIMZ all in capitals, just like the ERM of the man's. Further, there are no capitals at all and no punctuation marks—bar the ones put in by the printer, obviously—in either of her messages of March 31st and April 1st; whereas in the final message there are full stops, and capitals at the beginning of phrases and names of days. For instance, 'Uirwzb' means Friday, and the capital U corresponds to the capital F. Again, you find ERM using a capital in the message of April 5th. 'Mligs' is cipher for 'North' and he puts a capital to it. You'll find all these peculiarities faithfully reproduced in my Solutionist's deciphering."

"Wait a minute! Wait a minute!" interrupted the Inspector. "I want to get this straight. I think I see it. You mean that she's a rather brainless little idiot and that it would be enough trouble for her to put a message into cipher without bothering about capitals or stops in the finished product? Is that it?"

"That's what I guessed, after seeing her give her evidence at the inquest," The Counsellor admitted with an air of mild triumph. "She's no flyer in the brain competition. So she was glad enough to find the cipher equivalents of the letters in her messages, without bothering about refinements like capitals and punctuation."

"Obvious when you see it," agreed the Inspector, without troubling to congratulate The Counsellor on his acuteness. "And since the last two messages have the capitals and punctuation right, you say she didn't produce them?"

"Form your own opinion," The Counsellor advised. "What do the plain facts suggest to you?"

"That someone else put them in, perhaps," said the Inspector doubtfully. "It might have been Hawkstone, since he knew the cipher. In fact, he'd taught it to her, you remember."

"Oh, the cipher!" said The Counsellor contemptuously. "It's the simplest one of the lot. I used it myself when I was at school, for passing surreptitious notes along the class to a pal of mine. Anyone with a turn for that kind of thing would have it solved in a jiffy."

"Ah!" ejaculated the Inspector. "*Now* I see what you were getting at about crossword puzzles and the *Strand Magazine*. Campion could have solved these things. He had 'a turn for that kind of thing' evidently, from what she said."

"So have thousands of other people," said The Counsellor roughly. " 'The murderer had brown hair, so all we have to do is to arrest the nearest brown-haired man, and our job's done.' Are these your methods? About as much use as toothache to an epicure, I'd say. Here's something more interesting. Look at the papers that these ads. appeared in. When ERM wants to communicate with her, he puts his ad. into the *Courier*; and she gave us the correct reason for that. The Campions take in the *Courier*."

"So Campion had a chance of seeing ERM'S ads. without going out of his way," interjected the Inspector.

"Will you let me finish what I've got to say?" demanded The Counsellor testily. "ERM advertises in the *Courier*, which she sees daily. She replies in the *Herald*, which avoids the same subscribers seeing both sets of ads. Then will you tell me why on April 5th, ERM puts his ad. into the *Herald*, which she does *not* see daily? And that ad. is one of the two which she declares she knows nothing about. Which is what one might expect on the face of things."

"Something in that, perhaps," said the Inspector with marked reluctance. "But he might have told her he was going to use the *Herald*, so that she could buy a copy specially."

"Why diverge from the routine?" retorted The Counsellor.

"Why should Hawkstone go to the trouble of putting in an ad. which he didn't mean her to see, then?" countered the Inspector.

"Yes. Why should he?" said The Counsellor, with an almost imperceptible stress on the final word of his question. "Hullo! Is this Avon Drive we're in? I saw the name-plate as we turned the corner. Which is Barrington's house, do you know?"

"That's it," answered Hartwell, pointing to a roomy villa with a double-fronted garage adjacent to it, set in a garden of trim lawns.

"Seems big enough for two bachelors," commented The Counsellor, glancing at it as they passed. "Nice neighbourhood, too." Then, dismissing this subject, he went on: "Pity Mrs. Campion can't produce a witness to prove she did come straight home that night. A loose end, there. And, by the by, what about that crossword puzzle winner? Have you tested this tale about an American trip?"

"His firm say his berth was booked in that liner. We haven't gone to the expense of wirelessing to find out if he actually went on board. No point in wasting public money on that till we see some need of it. He's not in the picture, so far."

"No," conceded The Counsellor. "I like this zeal for economy in public funds. *O si sic omnia!* Now, another matter, ere we part. Cheer up! We'll meet again shortly, never fear. You've got an appointment with Barrington to-morrow. What time?"

"Ten-thirty," admitted the Inspector incautiously.

"Frobisher will be there, too, perhaps? Full of his suicide notions. You'll be able to give him a tip or two. Anyone else?"

"Most likely a surgeon, a Mr. Wyndcliffe. He attended Mr. Earlswood in his last illness. . . . But what are you asking this for?" demanded the Inspector suspiciously.

"Because I also shall be among those present," said The Counsellor magnificently.

"Oh, you will will you?" retorted the Inspector, obviously nettled at having been pumped successfully. "And where will you meet us, may I ask? I haven't said anything about that."

"Meet you?" queried The Counsellor blandly. "Why, in the Langthorne Cemetery, of course. Where else? At ten-thirty, you say? You'll find me pottering about, reading the epitaphs. 'This is the grave of Solomon Grundy, . . .' etc. You know what an enthusiast I am for worms, graves and epitaphs. Spend all my spare time on the hobby."

"You're too sharp for me there, I'll admit," confessed the Inspector frankly. "How did you know?"

"Ah, you *don't* know my methods. Pity to unveil

them. Too simple, really. You told me you'd come into a small legacy because someone was afraid of premature burial. The late Mr. Earlswood suffered from catalepsy. He died recently and is buried in Langthorne Cemetery. Barrington is one of his trustees. So is Frobisher. I guessed there'd be a third. You yourself were put into the will to make sure that the police don't get suspicious. You're all going to-morrow to see that Earlswood's well and truly dead. That's how it runs."

"Very smart," admitted the Inspector rather grudgingly. "But what do you make of it? We can't exhume a body without the direct authority of the Home Secretary."

"Then I suppose you aren't going to exhume it. Right? It's amazing how clever I am when I set about it. I shall now await your proceedings with interest. No doubt it's a case of opening ponderous and marble jaws. You can't beat old Shakespeare, Inspector. He turns up trumps every time."

"I had *Hamlet* myself at school," said the Inspector sourly.

"And never looked at him since? I know. I know. Still, there's a lot in *Hamlet*. Five acts and twenty scenes—no less. Not to speak of much in the way of suggestive thoughts. For instance, what are your views on the relations between Hamlet and Ophelia? But I seem to gather from your expression that the Swan of Avon isn't one of your favourites, so we'll drop him. And, most fortunately, here we are at the *Herald* office. This is where I drop you. See you to-morrow at about 10.30 a.m. I look forward to it. And—last bit of advice —see if you can discover who inserted these mysterious ads. It seems not unimportant."

107

Chapter VIII

HIC JACET

OUTSIDE of his bathroom, The Counsellor seldom sang except when he was in unusually high spirits; so when Sandra Rainham heard his voice uplifted in a creaky old chanty, she turned the handle of the door with the certainty that she would find him more than ordinarily delighted with himself.

" '*I am not a man-o'-war, nor a privateer,' said he.*
  '*Blow high, blow low! What care we?*
'*But I am a jolly pirate, and I'm sailing for my fee,*
  '*Down on the coast of the High Barbaree!*' "

The Counsellor trolled the verse to its end, then, taking his feet off his desk, he looked up at Sandra with a smile.

"A shade flat," she said critically as she came forward. "And so you've burst out in yet another line, have you, Mark? Piracy, no less. This versatility will be the death of you, sooner or later."

"That's purely metaphorical. The song, I mean," explained The Counsellor blandly. "The man-o'-war's represented by my friend Inspector Hartwell. The privateer's your pal Frobisher, the Coroner. Both of them have to play their game according to certain rules. I, on the other hand, having a free hand like the pirate, can play as I choose. See? My job, in fact, is summarised in the third line of another verse, which I will now proceed to sing:

" *'Lay aloft, lay aloft,' the jolly bo'sun cried.*
'Blow high, blow low, what care we?
'Look ahead, look astern, look a-windward, look a-lee,
'Down on the coast of the High Barbaree.'

So this morning I was down at Fernhurst-Hordle, looking all ways at once, with more success than you'd imagine."

"Don't sing any more," pleaded Sandra, who had an ear for music. "Tell me all about it, instead. It'll ease your mind just as much and be less painful to us."

The Counsellor put his hand into a drawer of his desk and extracted several quarter-plate photographs.

"The story's illustrated," he explained. "The pictures aren't all that one could wish, but you can't expect marvels when you get them developed and printed in less than no time and then dried with alcohol. As was done in this case. By me. Alone I did it. Now we're ready to start."

"Make it short, please," suggested Sandra, who saw signs that The Counsellor might spread himself in his narration if he were not given a plain hint.

"Short?" echoed The Counsellor. "There's only one length for a story and that's its right length. Which is what you're going to get. Sit down. Now this is how it is. I went down this morning to Fernhurst-Hordle (hereinafter referred to as Fernhurst, to save breath). I'd made an appointment with Inspector Hartwell at Langthorne Cemetery. Recognise that?" He produced the first of his prints. "That's one of Langthorne Church, just as a guarantee of good faith. You recognise it? That's so nice. Well, I arrived there about 10 a.m. and informed the caretaker, whom I met at the gate, that I wanted to take a photo of Mr. Earlswood's grave. That was merely a bit of humbug—throwing out a tub to amuse a whale, as Dean Swift advises. Most successful, as the whale burst into a bucolic smile and informed me that there wasn't no grave to photograph. Having expected this, on the strength of some inferences from Inspector Hartwell's remarks, I was not so much taken aback as I seemed. The caretaker kindly informed me that the Earlswoods were not buried in graves. They retire to a family vault in the crypt of the church, well underground, where their coffins repose on shelves."

"I could have told you all that if you'd asked me," said Sandra.

"I preferred to work it out myself," retorted The Counsellor, "and I got it right. But to continue. Having lent the caretaker a fill of tobacco and watched him palm some more out of my pouch without protest, I drew him out a bit while he smoked several of my matches in keeping his pipe alight. It seems that poor Earlswood was obsessed by the fear that he might be buried alive in one of these cataleptic trances of his. So he left instructions in his will on the point. Electric gadget in the coffin which rings a bell in the caretaker's house if anything moves in the coffin. Trustees visit the vault once a week for one calendar month to ensure that the wiring of the gadget is *in situ* and in working order. Then, when the month's up, the big stone slabs are put into place at the head of the crypt stairs, the soil's shovelled back on top of them, and grass is sown."

"What a dreadful idea," commented Sandra, shuddering. "But I suppose it's reasonable enough. It would be ghastly to be buried by mistake during a trance and then to wake up. . . ."

"Quite so. Quite so," said The Counsellor hurriedly. "But I didn't go there on that account. I wanted to have a chat with some of the people who'd be there:

Barrington, Frobisher, etc. And that seemed better than forcing myself on them at their various places of abode. So I just made conversation with the caretaker for a minute or two, asking if he was superstitious, and how he liked living in a cemetery and going his rounds after dark amongst the gravestones. He relieved my mind completely by saying that he didn't believe in ghosts and goblins and that he never bothered to go round the cemetery after dark. So, in all love, we parted, as Calverley puts it; and I went up to the church, where I took that snapshot. Nice old church-yard, with yews and elms and mouldering graves, and a rather fine lych-gate. The old burial-ground is full up. I gather they extended the premises not long ago, taking in a lot of fresh ground down by where the new entrance and the caretaker's cottage stand."

"Is this where I say, 'Go on! Go on!' breathlessly?" asked Sandra. "In any case, I wish you would go on, Mark. I've heaps of work to do this afternoon."

"All right!" said The Counsellor testily. "I go on. The next scene opened with a Masque of Executors, in the style of Cyril Tourneur, only they didn't dance, which was disappointing. Enter Hartwell, Frobisher, Barrington—accompanied by a brother who looks like a magnified King Charles's spaniel about the face and has a very slight lisp—and an unknown who turned out to be a Mr. Wyndcliffe. I had gathered myself together into a group at the top of the stairs leading down to the crypt and excused my presence by taking a snapshot. Here's the print. You can see the mounds of clay excavated by the grave-diggers and the big stone slabs all a-tilt, ready to be let down into position. Also the head of the stairs."

He passed the photograph to Sandra, who examined it carefully.

"When the Big Five came up to me, I explained I was taking these photos on behalf of a friend who had known Earlswood. That was you, of course, but I kept your name out of it. This served as both excuse and introduction and it led on to general chat, under my skilful guidance. Finally, when they started to clear their throats and look official, I withdrew tactfully to one side and took a snap of them in an unobtrusive way. This is it."

He handed over a third photograph.

"I've met this Mr. Wyndcliffe," Sandra volunteered, after scanning the picture. "He's a rather precise, cold-blooded man, with thin lips and long teeth. Freezingly polite, I found him."

"Admirable summary," The Counsellor commended. "He's the surgeon who did the antrum operation on Earlswood which turned out so unfortunately. Some relation I gathered, though a pretty distant one. He comes into most of the estate, I learned. Seemed to have his wits about him, judging from his conversation."

Sandra handed back the print and The Counsellor examined it in his turn.

"Barrington senior's giving his well-known imitation of Dark Lochnagar just at that moment," he commented. "He wasn't at his brightest this morning, I thought. Gloomy. Pessimistic. As if his morning rasher hadn't been all he expected it to be. But perhaps it was hardly the occasion for a song and dance. Anyhow, he drew out a large and ancient key. Likewise a Yale on the same ring. Armed with these, he descended the steps and unlocked the door of the crypt. As shown in the next picture."

He passed yet another print to Sandra.

"I rather missed the boat, there," The Counsellor

continued. "As I was rolling up the film, Frobisher went down the steps. Some slobs of clay had fallen from the edges of the excavation. Frobisher stepped on one of them—he's always the Little Johnny Head in Air—and he came a perfect purler, legs and arms all everywhere and hat doing a one-step on its own. I wish I'd got a snap of the performance. Funny without being vulgar in the least. A thing you could have shown to a child on a wet day, just to cheer it up."

"Try it, next wet day, on yourself, Mark," said Sandra crossly. "You're no better than a child if that's what makes you laugh. Poor Mr. Frobisher might have hurt himself badly."

"Pomposity goes before a fall," retorted The Counsellor. "And I've had enough of his pomposity, so I'm entitled to get what enjoyment I can out of the rest of it. He wasn't hurt much, except in the temper. I never knew coroners had such a vocabulary. Shocking! Shall I repeat his remarks? No? Well, to continue. The whole crew tripped downstairs in turn—no, not like Frobisher. They'd profited by his experience. I remained above-ground, as they didn't invite me to join them. But the crypt echoed a bit and I heard most of what they said while they were performing their wonders. Seemed to me a softish job. They took the wires off the binding-screws on the coffin-lid, had a look at them to see they were clean at the ends. Then they put them back and screwed them up; and each of them tried the screws to see they were fast home. Somebody examined something else—seals on the coffin-lid, apparently—and found that O.K. And then they all came out and Barrington fastened the crypt door and locked it. And that seemed all they had to do. I suppose they tested the bell, but the caretaker would tell them about that when they got back to the gate—whether it rang or not. Didn't hear it myself, of course, a quarter of a mile or more away."

"I'm not very interested," said Sandra chillingly. "You seem to have intruded where you obviously weren't wanted."

"Well, *I* was interested, which was the main thing," retorted The Counsellor. "Never saw a show like it before. Not likely to see one of its kind again. And I was by way of contributing my mite towards the safety of Earlswood, if he *has* been buried alive by mistake."

"How?"

"When they came above-ground again, I tackled them boldly and pointed out that before the caretaker could pick up his feet and run a quarter of a mile with a screw-driver to unscrew the coffin-lid, poor Earlswood might be dead of suffocation. 'And what about that?' said I. But I needn't have worried. It's all right. Earlswood had given every thought to the matter, as well he might. It seems there's a sliding panel in the coffin-lid, just over the face, which springs open as soon as the electric gadget works. There's plenty of air available at once. Very neat indeed. So there's no likelihood of Earlswood coming to any harm if he does wake up. I was much relieved to hear that, I can tell you. Seeing that mausoleum gave me a chill, I don't mind confessing. This brightness you complain about is merely the natural reaction after the grue. Buried alive! Ugh! Makes me creep all up the back, the very thought of it, after seeing that place."

"Then why talk about it?" said Sandra sensibly. "What happened after all that was over?"

"Oh, we got quite chummy, once duty was done. Under my skilful guidance, the conversation passed from Earlswood to the other recently deceased, Hawkstone. And they began to reminisce. *Nil nisi bonum* does not hold, in that circle, I may say. None of them seemed to regret him. Frobisher pontificated about his morals or lack of 'em, and incautiously let slip that he'd had a couple of letters from relations of girls whom Hawkstone had treated badly. He gave the Inspector a nasty look as he brought that out, and I could see what was in his mind. He's still on the suicide tack and thinks that these letters show that Hawkstone had landed himself in a regular hole—bigamy, perhaps—so that suicide was the easiest way out. Didn't say so in plain words, but you can do a lot with cocking your eyebrow. Your friend Wyndcliffe seemed to think the Coroner was going a bit too far there. He turned the talk by recalling when he'd met Hawkstone for the last time, playing bridge at Barrington's house. Some man Jelf was the fourth. Know him? No matter. Hawkstone's car struck work and Wyndcliffe had given him a lift home. Hawkstone seems to have had one over the eight and entertained Wyndcliffe with his views on women and his wife in particular, which rather disgusted Wyndcliffe, I gather, though he doesn't seem too strait-laced. And Wyndcliffe wanted to get rid of him and go and look at his patient. Earlswood was on his last legs, that evening, poor chap. He died the next day. And this drunken owl insisted on sitting on and on in Wyndcliffe's car, even when they'd reached his gate, pouring out his dingy reminiscences and reflections until Wyndcliffe felt like kicking him."

"I can believe it," said Sandra, briefly. "And then?"

"Well, I wondered if Barrington would lend any support to the Coroner's suicide notion. There was that interview at his house at one in the morning, you remember. Subject, some woman or other. I hoped Barrington might tell us a little more about that. But he was strictly professional. Not a word about it. He seems more strait-laced than I'd have supposed, though. I noticed that he showed signs of peevishness when Wyndcliffe mentioned Hawkstone discussing Mrs. Hawkstone in the car."

"Well, can you wonder?" demanded Sandra. "I told you Mr. Barrington liked Mrs. Hawkstone. Naturally he wouldn't care to hear she'd been discussed in that way."

"Any old romance in it?" enquired The Counsellor. "Did Hawkstone cut Barrington out when he married Mrs. H.?"

"I don't think so," said Sandra. "I never heard anything of the kind. But . . ."

"But you don't hear everything, of course? What interests me more is whether Mrs. Hawkstone had a penchant for Barrington."

"I never saw the least sign of it, if she has," said Sandra decisively. "They liked each other, I know, but that was all."

"Would you expect to see anything, anyhow?" said The Counsellor. "She was a married woman. Not likely she'd advertise her fondness for another man. In fact, I'd expect them to be careful not to show it, if it was there. So that goes for nothing. But to continue. The talk drifted back to Earlswood, and it came out that Barrington junior was the dentist who spotted the trouble in the antrum and called in Wyndcliffe to operate. The two of them gave us an enlightening discourse full of boss words like maxilla, foramen, premolar, pterygoid sinus, and cavernous thrombosis, and others fresh to me. It bored Frobisher; it left me standing; Barrington senior was not amused; and the Inspector listened to the words of learned length and thundering sound, just like one of the gazing rustics ranged around in *The Deserted Village*. Hoping to pick up an idea, even by its tail, you know. But in vain, I gauged."

"You would sympathise with him, being in much the same state," commented Sandra.

"I did," agreed The Counsellor. "These experts are above my head, I admit. But I mean to do better. I'll ask my medico all about it and then dazzle Hartwell, if no one else. But to proceed. As we wended our way towards the gate, I fell into step with the enlarged King Charles's spaniel person, Barrington junior. I feared a further lecture on pterygoid sinuses; so I hurriedly turned the chat on to hobbies. I'd better have left it at sinuses. He's a fisherman, and full of it. Seems he has a cottage in the country beside a large puddle—he called it a small lake—which swarms with all the sorts of fish which are sought after in the best circles. He has the fishing rights on it and a small boat. Very down on trespassers, he is, and prosecutes poachers with vim. And he fishes. . . . Also, he eats fish with relish, I learned. A perfect connoosser in that field, and loaded up with strange recipes. . . . Well, I spare you these. Finally, I was driven to ask if he did anything else for a living except catching and devouring fish. There I struck it worse than ever. He's a toothache collector, or something. Bitten with the notion of writing a large and learned work on teeth and what can go wrong with 'em. Fully illustrated, it's to be, with photos of every tooth he's drawn from the public. Or some of 'em, at any rate. A gruesome subject. I was glad when we reached the gate. All this harangue was giving me imaginary neuralgia. Then, unable to bear more, I switched the talk on to Hawkstone again, while the remainder of the gang went into the caretaker's cottage to enquire if the bell had rung and see that it was in trim. Barrington junior snapped at the fresh theme. He'd quite a lot to say on that subject. I gathered that he and Hawkstone pooled information about various dames and damsels of the lighter sort. In fact, my spaniel-faced acquaintance had been introduced to Mrs. Campion by Hawkstone and had taken her out on his own once or twice. It was pretty plain that he regarded Hawkstone as not a bad sort. In fact, I got the impression that Barrington junior is completely amoral in some respects."

"Skip all that," Sandra suggested, being rather bored by this part of The Counsellor's report.

"Right! Perhaps it's really not important," admitted The Counsellor. "Though it gave me an idea or two. To continue. When the crew of executors reappeared, I offered the Inspector a lift in my car. Once we got away from the rest, I enquired how business was with him. I'd asked him to find out, if he could, who had inserted these fake ads. in the *Fernhurst Herald* that I told you about. Seems he'd done much better than I expected. He went to the counter in the *Herald* office where they take in ads. for publication. Nice-looking girl on duty there. The Inspector, who isn't emotional usually, described her as a stunner. I was glad to hear that word again. I haven't met it since I was reading about Rossetti and the rest of the pre-Raphaelites who all married stunners, by their way of it. And thereby hangs a tale. This blessed damozel had been on duty when these two cipher ads. were handed in. Handed in, notice, across the counter. She noticed them at the time because they were in cipher. But she had good reason to remember them. Using them as an excuse, the advertiser got up a flirtation of sorts with her and invited her out for the evening. Dull work, standing behind a counter all day, I expect, so she agreed. The flirtation got a bit too speedy for her ideas, and she quarrelled with the swain after one evening at Caplatzi's. Asked to describe the Knave of Hearts, she said, rather unpoetically, that he looked like some kind of dog and talked with a faint lisp. Whereat, sensation! and the Inspector pricked up his ears. He's not so dull, is Hartwell. He remembered that a while ago the *Herald* had published pictures of some local fishing competition and my spaniel-faced pal Barrington junior had figured in it. So at once he rushed the damsel off to the office file, confronted her with the picture, and asked if she recognised anyone in it. She did, and was quite positive about it. So that was that."

"But . . ." interrupted Sandra in a puzzled tone, "what made him hand in an advertisement of that sort across the counter? Why didn't he send it in by post?"

"With a false address? That's what one wonders," admitted The Counsellor. "And especially why did he start to flirt with the girl, unless she was really such a stunner that she fascinated him and he couldn't help doing it? Still, such things are not beyond all conjecture, as Sir T. Browne sagely remarked about something else. In fact, I've conjectured. Not unsuccessfully, I think. But I won't spoil your pleasure by giving my solution."

"You needn't bother," said Sandra. "It's one of two things. Either he was careless or he didn't mind being recognised."

"I'd put it stronger than that," said The Counsellor musingly. "But we can tie another knot in the string, perhaps. Will you please fish out that letter from the enquirer who wanted these cipher ads. deciphered. It should be in our files, somewhere."

Sandra Rainham left the room and returned in a few minutes with the document, which she handed to The Counsellor.

"H'm!" he said discontentedly. "I've handled it; you've handled it; the Solutionist's pawed it over; and the filing-clerk's done her worst. Not much chance for a finger-print expert, by this time, I fear. But leave that aside now. I think I told you that the address at the head of it—c/o Shipman, 12 Wilkin Lane, Fernhurst—is a fake; and I suspect that the signature Swinbrook is in the same state. Now, just ask a question. Why does an innocent enquirer after a decipherment choose to conceal his identity, whilst the advertiser almost takes pains to blaze a trail up to his own front door? Rum way of going about things, isn't it?"

"You mean it was the same man in both cases? Richard Barrington?"

"Well, I don't know, yet. Could offer you fairly long odds, though, if you want to bet on the point. But to business. Take down this letter, please. Ready?"

"Richard Barrington, Esq.,
   16 Avon Drive,
     Fernhurst-Hordle.

"DEAR MR. BARRINGTON,—May I ask you to do me a favour? One of my clients has enquired what is the best fly to use for tench at this season. Frankly, I do not know whether tench are in season at the moment or whether one fishes for them with a fly at all. If you could give me your expert advice in the matter, it would be of great assistance in answering my client's question and I should be much obliged for your help.

               "Yours faithfully."

That ought to get a rise. No fisherman of his brand could resist the temptation to lay down the law. Enclose a stamped envelope. We don't want to be indebted to him in mere filthy lucre."

"*Do* you fish for tench with flies?" asked Sandra doubtfully. "I thought they lived at the bottom of pools."

"Well, if they won't rise to the fly, *he* will," said The Counsellor. "I put it that way just to rouse his worst passion for instruction. He simply couldn't bear to miss the chance of correcting me."

"I'll see it's posted," said Sandra. "Do you know, Mark, I'm a bit puzzled by this latest affair. If the handwritings turn out to be the same, what does it mean?"

"That they're identical, of course," retorted The Counsellor irritatingly.

"But why should he be playing this weird game? That's what I don't see. It doesn't make sense."

"Perhaps he wants to be accused of murdering Hawkstone and then be acquitted for want of evidence," suggested The Counsellor flippantly. "Ambitious to become a martyr, maybe. Or perhaps he's shielding somebody else."

"That's hardly in character," Sandra declared in a decided tone. "From all I've heard of him, he wouldn't go a yard out of his way to help anybody. You'll have to think again, Mark."

"Not even a woman?" queried The Counsellor.

"Least of all, a woman," retorted Sandra.

"Well, no doubt you know best," conceded The Counsellor placidly. "Don't let's quarrel over it. Perhaps the two handwritings will not turn out to be the same, after all. And that reminds me. Did you like Hawkstone's taste in shirts? I dropped in at his outfitter's to-day and bought some. They said they were the same as the ones he bought last. And I tried another of his tradespeople as well. The Inspector got me the addresses, very kindly, winning a bet by doing so. Gave him a lot of pleasure to win, too, because I'd rather pulled his leg about it."

"If you'd tried his tailor, it would have been something," said Sandra. "He used to wear quiet tweeds, I remember."

Chapter IX

O SPECULATION! HORRID FIEND . . .

The door of The Counsellor's office bore a large plate inscribed "NO APPOINTMENTS"; but this was intended merely to stave off the ordinary busybody. When it suited him, The Counsellor was quite ready to fix an appointment with someone who had aroused his interest. A few minutes after Sandra Rainham left the private room, one of the clerks brought in a visiting-card on which The Counsellor read "Mr. A. F. Davenant," with the additional information in the lower left-hand corner: "*Condor and Chiltern Insurance Company.*"

"Show him in," directed The Counsellor. "I gave him an appointment over the phone."

When he appeared, Mr. Davenant proved to be a youngish, sleek-haired, suave individual with a pair of sharp eyes under heavy brows. He acknowledged The Counsellor's greeting and took the chair on the opposite side of the desk from his host.

"Well?" enquired The Counsellor non-committally.

Davenant gave him a shrewd glance, as though trying to sum him up. Then, evidently satisfied with the results of his scrutiny, he came to the point without any preliminary beating about the bush.

"My Company, Mr. Brand, is interested in the reported death of a Mr. Hawkstone, of Fernhurst-Hordle. Rather heavily interested, in fact. To the extent of £25,000, to be exact."

"Indeed?" said The Counsellor, pricking up his ears at the mention of this figure.

Davenant evidently misconstrued his host's expression.

"Naturally, we do much bigger business than that, at times," he explained. "Still, it's a considerable sum. I learned that in some way you have interested yourself in the affair. We also are interested, as you can see. I thought that perhaps we might get together. . . ."

"Meaning that you came here to pump me, get all you could out of me, say, 'Thank you, kind sir,' and retire gracefully with the information? Sorry, I don't do business on these terms. Fifty-fifty."

"Fifty-fifty?" queried Davenant. "I don't quite understand."

"Not financially," said The Counsellor with a grin. "What I mean is that if I give you information, you must make it worth my while by giving me information that you have."

Davenant made no concealment of the fact that he was thinking this over before answering. He examined the tips of his fingers as if looking for flaws in his fault-less manicuring. The Counsellor pushed a cigarette-box across the desk and Davenant mechanically helped himself from it. Lighting the cigarette gave him time for still further thought; and when he put the spent match into an ash-tray, he had evidently come to a conclusion.

"It's hardly regular," he objected tentatively.

"My usual business terms," said The Counsellor with finality in his tone. "Nothing for nothing, and damned little for threepence. You need me, or you wouldn't be here. If you want information, you've got to pay in kind. It's one of these barter agreements so fashion-able nowadays in international affairs. Is it a deal? If not, we're both busy men and can spend our time better than by sitting here fencing."

"You seem to know your own mind," said Davenant with a pleasant smile. "Call it a deal, then, on your terms."

"Good. Then you put your information on the table first," said The Counsellor firmly. "It'll help me to see what I've got that might be useful to you."

Davenant made no attempt to hide his amusement at The Counsellor's methods.

"Very well, then," he agreed. "But you needn't imagine you're going to get any fearful revelations. It's a plain business matter. Here is the gist of it. A number of years ago, we were approached by a Mr. Sydney Barrington, who is a solicitor of some standing in Fernhurst-Hordle, as you probably know. He was taking in a partner, this Mr. Vincent Hawkstone whose name has been mentioned lately in connection with that blazing car case."

The Counsellor's brows twitched momentarily as he heard this cautious description of the affair at the Crossroads, but he held his tongue.

"Mr. Barrington wished to take out a policy, value £15,000, on the life of his prospective partner. It's quite a usual proceeding in cases of the kind."

"Can't go insuring the first-comer in that way," objected The Counsellor. "Got to show some insurable interest, haven't you?"

"That was quite easy in this case," explained Davenant. "On becoming a partner, Hawkstone contributed £15,000 to the firm's finances. If he died, that £15,000 had to be returned to his widow or else she got some share in the firm's income. The policy was intended to cover the case of her demanding the cash on the death of Hawkstone. Barrington was to draw the £15,000 on the policy and, if necessary, pay it over to the widow. That left him covered."

"I see," said The Counsellor in a musing tone. "Yes, go on."

"The whole affair was a matter of amicable agreement, and all above-board," Davenant continued. "Hawkstone consented to a medical examination and was found to be a perfectly sound life. Barrington, of course, contributed the premiums annually, and they have always been paid punctually as they fell due. There was a second policy—for £10,000 which is payable by us to Hawkstone's widow on proof of his death. That's a total liability of £25,000. Now, on the face of things, there is nothing wrong; and I'm not suggesting that there's anything crooked in the business. But . . . we don't like deaths of that kind, which are out of the common run."

"So I imagine," The Counsellor admitted.

"Now, I put it to you, Mr. Brand," Davenant continued cautiously. "Are you satisfied that the body found in the car was the body of Hawkstone? I'm told that you were largely instrumental in securing evidence on that point, so I've come to the fountain-head."

The Counsellor deliberated for several seconds before answering.

"One of your representatives attended the inquest, I suppose?" he enquired. "Right! Then you know the facts that came out. My own contributions came under the heading, 'Information received.' Undoubtedly the body had articles on it which belonged to Hawkstone. His signet-ring and some studs, etc. Beyond that I'm not prepared to go. But I can make a guess at what's troubling you. The Rouse case?"

"The Rouse case did occur to us," Davenant

admitted, grudgingly. "One has to take all possibilities into account."

"Rouse murdered a man, put the body into his own car instead of himself, set a match to the petrol, and cleared off, meaning to drop his identity in this way and start afresh under a new name when the corpse was mistaken for himself. That's it?"

"You remember the case, evidently," said Davenant, but he made no attempt to go further.

"You're very cautious," said The Counsellor with a faint touch of contempt in his tone. "Very well. Put it as a John Doe and Richard Roe affair, if you like. John Doe's life has been insured by his partner, Richard Roe, to the tune of £15,000. Also for £10,000 in favour of Mrs. Doe. If John Doe dies, Richard Roe collects his £15,000. But he has to pay £15,000 over to Mrs. Doe under the partnership agreement. So on the face of it, there isn't much in it for poor Richard. But suppose John Doe murders someone and passes off the body as his own, while he quietly vamooses? Richard Roe collects his £15,000 and pays it over to Mrs. Doe, who has also pulled in her £10,000. Where does poor John Doe come in, unless his wife is in the ramp and splits the £25,000 with him on the Q.T.? And that leaves Mrs. Doe in the unfortunate position of being only a grass widow, while in the public eye she's a real widow. Which might tend to cramp her style in various ways, if she chanced to have a respect for the conventions. Do you know enough about Mrs. Doe to say whether such a course fits her character or not?"

Davenant shook his head with a smile.

"I never heard of any such person as Mrs. Doe, until you mentioned her," he declared slyly.

"No?" retorted The Counsellor. "Surprising. But that does not exhaust the possibilities. Try again.

Richard Roe, John Doe, and spouse, are all mixed up
in the racket. They get into your pocket to the tune
of £25,000 and then split it among themselves, making
over £8,000 apiece, which isn't such bad pay for a few
minutes' dirty work. Like that hypothesis any better?"

"There's one factor common to all your hypotheses . . ." began Davenant.

"I know. A murderee. And that means somebody
missing from the board, somewhere, eh? In Rouse's
case, no one ever discovered who the murderee was,
though they tried hard enough. Some poor tramp or
other that Rouse had the luck to pick up on the road.
But luck like that doesn't come twice."

"It's hardly likely, is it?" said Davenant.

"No, it isn't. *Ergo*, someone's missing from his home.
And now, I think, we're coming to the real reason for
your visit. You want me to start up my machinery and
find out the identity of this missing man. That's it?"

"We don't even know that there's a missing man,"
Davenant pointed out critically. "All we want to know
is, definitely, whether that body in the car was Hawkstone's or not."

"Well, well. Don't let's differ about it," said The
Counsellor cheerfully. "Let's say that you wouldn't be
peeved if I made some effort to trace an *ersatz* Hawkstone. I could make a try. But it would cost a few
pounds in paying rewards for red herrings. Care to foot
that bill? I make no pretence of being a philanthropist
when my client's a big insurance company. It's got
more money than I have."

"If you discovered anything worth while, my
principals might not be ungenerous," said Davenant
guardedly.

"H'm! 'If' and 'might' leave a lot of loopholes. Even
a fat insurance company might crawl through one of

them and come out at the other side with all saved except honour," said The Counsellor with a sardonic grin. " 'What is that honour? Air. A trim reckoning,' as Falstaff shrewdly remarked. . . ."

A thought seemed to cross his mind swiftly, and his expression changed to one of amusement.

"Well, I'll look into it," he said, altering his tone. "Now I come to think of it, I may manage it on the cheap, so I won't be much out of pocket at the worst."

"I'm sure that my company would show its gratitude if you discovered anything of real value," Davenant hastened to assure him, evidently delighted that he had apparently gained his point.

"Five guineas?" hazarded The Counsellor with a laugh. "Well, perhaps I might make a profit out of it, even on these generous terms. We'll see. Thanks for your most suggestive conversation," he added, rising. "I've enjoyed it."

When Davenant had taken his leave, The Counsellor rang for Sandra Rainham.

"You've a bit of telephoning in front of you," he announced when she came in. " 'O Speculation! Horrid fiend. . . .' "

"I don't know that one," Sandra confessed.

"Ah? So you can't correct me? That's so nice. It's from Samuel Butler's *Narcissus*."

"You haven't been gambling in shares, have you, Mark?" asked Sandra with half-feigned anxiety. "Not ruined, or anything of that sort?"

"That's the sort of speculation Butler meant," explained The Counsellor, "but the kind I mean is the sort you do with your brains, if you have any. Meditation, you know, study, cerebration, pondering, lucubration, and all that kind of thing. Reckoning up how many beans make five, in fact. Strangely fascinating process,

if you get a good start. And our Mr. Davenant gave me
something to think about and ruminate on. Hence the
telephoning required."

"Before you start on that," said Sandra, "there's
somebody anxious to see you—Mrs. Percy Campion.
She's in the waiting-room, now. I didn't promise an
interview until I found out whether you wanted to see
her as much as she seems to want to see you. She's got a
rather nasty look on her face, or so I thought."

"Talk of the Devil!" ejaculated The Counsellor.
"Well, that'll save you one phone-call, Sandra, so be
thankful. I'll see her. But first of all, here's the rest of it.
You're to ring up the firm whose name I'll send out to
you in a minute or two. Ask them if their Mr. Campion
has gone to the U.S.A. If so, in what boat? When you
get the boat's name, ring up the shipping company
and find out if Campion actually went aboard. If they
can't tell you, get on to the boat itself by wireless or
wireless phone if you can, and ask the purser if Campion
is actually aboard. That will be enough for the present,
I think. You can show the dame in here."

"Like me to be present?" asked Sandra.

"As Propriety in a poke-bonnet? No. I think I can
face her alone, nasty look and all. I'll scream for help
if it comes to the worst."

"I shall keep my ears strained," said Sandra. "But,
to tell you the truth, Mark, I don't like your friend's
looks. She's a common little thing and I don't take to
her."

"That'll be quite all right," The Counsellor assured
her. "I don't take to her much either. But she might
not be so communicative if you were here. And that
would be a pity. Just see to that telephoning, as soon
as you've shown the good lady in here."

When Mrs. Campion was ushered into his room, The

Counsellor recognised the expression on her face which Sandra had described as 'a nasty look.' She seemed to be in a bad temper which she endeavoured to conceal under a surface appeal for sympathy.

"I've come up to Town for the day, Mr. Counsellor . . ."

"Brand's my name," interjected The Counsellor. "It's shorter than the other."

"Mr. Brand, then. I've been wanting to do some shopping, and I thought I'd kill two birds with one stone, you see. I remember you came along with that policeman when he questioned me after the inquest, that day; and I've found out that it was you that told the police all about my knowing Hawkstone, and dragged me into all the bothers I've had since. That wasn't a nice thing for you to do, Mr. Brand, and I'm not going to pretend that I'm overlooking it, for I just can't do that. You don't guess what a lot of disagreeables you started up when you did that."

"Sorry to hear that," said The Counsellor sympathetically. "But I was asked to help by the Coroner, and I could hardly refuse. There were sound reasons. No good going into them."

"Well, that's as it may be," retorted Mrs. Campion, not much placated by the plea. "Anyhow, you stirred up a regular hornet's nest by your doings, and it's me that gets stung."

The Counsellor made a propitiatory gesture which merely spurred her on.

"You don't know what sort of life I've led since you dragged my name out in public. Some of my neighbours won't look at me in the street, saucy beasts! They go past with their noses in the air, as if I was pitch or something that they couldn't even look at without getting soiled. They do. And I expect, if all was known, some of them are a good deal worse than me, for I've never done anything I was really ashamed of. But it's aggravating, all the same, to be treated that way, no matter who they are. I expect they go home and say: 'I saw that Mrs. Campion on the street to-day. You know. The one that was mixed up in that blazing car affair. I wonder what length she *really* went. There's no smoke without fire, you know.' That's the sort of thing they'll say. It's what they look like, anyhow."

"Very annoying," agreed The Counsellor.

"It's just exasperating, that's what it is. Exasperating!"

She brought her hand down with a slap on the desk, and The Counsellor reflected that the ring she was wearing would have been worth about £500 if the stones had been genuine.

"And the other sort are no better," she went on, having relieved her feelings by the physical act. "They come soft-sawdering round to call on me, generally when I'm washing up; and they sit and sympathise— Oh, so very sympathetic—and then they start trying to worm the whole story out of me and find out if it isn't a bit hotter than what I told in Court. But I know them. I know them! They don't get any change out of me, I can tell you, Mr. Brand. But still, it's all very unpleasant. You can see that for yourself. And I feel inclined to get a bit of my own back. Pay some people out in their own coin, you understand?"

"Must be very irritating," The Counsellor admitted.

"Irritating? I should think it is! So I've made up my mind that if some people poke their noses into my affairs, I'll do the same for other people, just to make things even. I thought of going to that policeman who came with you that day. But he was so rude and suspicious that I don't like the idea of going near him again. Now you were different, Mr. Brand. I could feel you were sympathising with me then. And, as I said, it's you that got me into this mess by poking your finger in at the start. So I made up my mind I'd come to you and tell you something and then you can use it the way you used the other information you got. And while you're at it, I wish you'd talk over the wireless to my neighbours—mentioning no names—and tell them just what I think of them."

"Perhaps they don't listen to me," suggested The Counsellor with unusual modesty.

"Well, someone would tell them about it, no doubt."

"First of all, though," said The Counsellor, "you might tell me these facts that you want me to know."

Mrs. Campion shifted her chair slightly nearer to him, as if to suggest secrecy. She laid her hand palm downwards on the desk in the best position for displaying the stones in her ring.

"I told you before," she began, "that Vin—Vin Hawkstone, I mean, though he called himself Merlin to me—didn't let me know who he really was or where he lived. But he did talk to me about some of his affairs, just casually, now and again, as it happened to come up in conversation, you understand? I remember sometimes I chaffed him about being a married man. He'd let out that he was married, you see? And sometimes I'd say: 'Now, Vin, what would your wife say to this?' And he used to laugh at that and say: 'Don't you worry, Lorna. Not on that account, anyway. She's got her own amusements, same as we have.' Or else he'd say: 'My partner's quite ready to keep her from feeling lonely, any time.' Things like that. They just happened to stick in my mind, because they made me feel I wasn't doing her any harm by seeing Vin."

"I understand," said The Counsellor as she paused expectantly.

"Well, there it is," continued Lorna Campion. "Here am I, being treated like a curiosity in the Zoo just on account of doing what that stuck-up-looking woman was doing herself. And she gets all the sympathy and all I get is a lot of mud thrown at me and goodness knows what rows and trouble when Percy comes back from America, over the head of it. It's not fair! It isn't, really! And I've been thinking things over, now and again, and I've seen something that almighty-clever policeman doesn't see yet, so it seems, smart and all as he thinks he is."

She hitched her chair a shade nearer the desk and dropped her voice to a confidential undertone.

"You heard all that evidence at the inquest about the money and the firm? I heard it, but I didn't pay much attention to it at the time. But I kept all the newspapers, with reports of the inquest, and I've been reading them carefully, and I've been putting two and two together, I can tell you. And made more out of them than that policeman did. He's so busy being rude and cruel that he's got no time to use his brains, I expect, if he has any. Well, I'll tell you what I made out of it. That lawyer man made out in Court that he stood to lose £15,000 over this affair, didn't he? And everybody swallowed that like a penny ice, didn't they? But just you think, Mr. Brand. Now that Hawkstone's out of the way, what's to hinder that lawyer marrying my fine lady, Mrs. Hawkstone, an eligible widow and not bad-looking? He's keen on her, from what Hawkstone let out to me. And if he marries her, he doesn't need to pay out any money. It all stays with his old firm, doesn't it? And she's got some money of her own, I've heard tell. So she wouldn't be a bad match, apart from her clothes and her looks, which really aren't so bad, though not in a style that I much admire myself, I must say. Now what do you think of that, Mr. Brand? A nice ending to a little romance it would be, wouldn't it? I don't know exactly how far things went between the two of them while Hawkstone was alive; but I do know that he wouldn't have cared a rap no matter how far they'd gone. He was clean off his wife. I knew that well from things he dropped now and again. So there's no saying . . ."

She paused; but The Counsellor refused to fill the gap, so she continued.

"It's very convenient for them, Hawkstone dying like this; that's all I say. A nod's as good as a wink to a blind horse. . . ."

"Thanks for the compliment," interjected The Counsellor, who had heard as much as he wanted.

"Well, there it is," said Lorna Campion. "I'm not saying anything. Those that live longest will see most. But if those two get married, don't say I didn't give you a plain hint quicker than that ugly policeman managed to do. You'll see," she concluded with a would-be portentous nod. "You'll see, Mr. Brand."

She seemed disappointed to find that her communication fell apparently flat. The Counsellor had his own axe to grind in this interview, however, and he felt that it was time to bring it out.

"Heard from your husband since he left?" he enquired, as if the subject had just come into his mind.

"No," answered Lorna, with something like faint discomfort in her tone, "I haven't had a line from him since he went away. Usually he sends me a postcard, just a word or two to let me know he's landed safely at his journey's end; and I expected one from him this time, specially, seeing he was going off on the ship. But he sent nothing. It's a bit funny, isn't it?"

"He left home exactly a week ago, on the 14th, didn't he?" enquired The Counsellor. "You said so in your evidence at the inquest, I remember. On the morning of the 14th. And he was going to do some business in Liverpool before he went on board the liner. It sailed on the 17th. Plenty of time to scribble a p.c. But it must have slipped his memory; and once the liner left port it was too late to write to you."

"Still, it's worrying," Lorna insisted. "You see, he promised to send me a card. It was the last thing he said, before he went off to the station that morning."

"You can always send him a message by wireless," suggested The Counsellor.

"That costs money," said Lorna Campion with a gesture, as if pushing the proposal aside. "A lot of money, from all I've heard. I wouldn't do that, especially as he'd have to spend more money answering me. We're not all as rich as you, Mr. Brand."

"Perhaps—if you're really anxious about it—I could make an enquiry about him," The Counsellor suggested. "But I'd need a description of him, you know."

"I can tell you all that," Lorna replied at once, evidently relieved to find that she could get something for nothing. "He's got a small brown moustache—sort of tooth-brushy. Blue eyes and brown hair going thin on the temples. He was wearing a dark blue suit with a white pin-stripe. And a dark tie to match. And a blue-and-white shirt with a soft collar. Dark blue socks and black shoes. . . ."

"What height was he? About the same as Mr. Hawkstone, say?"

"Just about it. And no jewellery."

"Teeth?"

"He's got nice white ones. Very proud of his teeth, Percy is. The only time he ever had to go to a dentist in his life was when he got his left front tooth stopped with gold. So he always boasts."

"Regular in his habits?" demanded The Counsellor.

"Pardon?"

"Not inclined to be rackety?" The Counsellor paraphrased.

Lorna Campion hesitated a moment or two before answering the question.

"Well, he's apt to get gay sometimes," she admitted. "I mean, he likes a whisky and splash and sometimes he takes as many as are good for him, if he gets amongst men in a bar. And he likes company at times, Percy does. He's a good mixer, I'm told, when he's on the road, though he's on the quiet side when he's at home. But that's only natural, you see. A commercial gentleman has got to make himself popular and well-liked, if he's going to do much business. Dismal Jimmies don't cut much ice in his line of business. And if the buyer for a firm happens to be a girl, I expect he'd take her out for an evening and have a bit of fun, just as I do, and put her in a good mood for doing business with him next day. I never got jealous over that kind of thing, myself; though he's a fair, seven-tailed Bashaw, so to speak, sometimes when it comes to my having a spree on my own."

The Counsellor pulled a scribbling pad towards him and made a note or two. Then he turned again to his visitor.

"What firm does he work for?"

"Collyer and Hanway of Castle Place. It's a big firm, you know."

"And what liner did he go away in?"

"His passage was booked on the *Meteoric*," Mrs.

Campion explained. "That's one of the best in that Line. First class, he went. All expenses paid, of course. They say you can't hardly sit down in a deck-chair without a steward coming up and asking you if you want a banana or a cup of coffee, no matter what hour of the day it is. I expect he'll come back as fat as a seal, unless he's careful."

The Counsellor added a jotting to the pad before him, tore off the leaf, rang a bell on his desk and handed the note to the boy who came in answer to his summons.

"That's for Miss Rainham," he directed.

He pushed away his scribbling pad and turned back to Lorna Campion.

"Well, I'll see what can be done," he said cheerfully. "Most likely, though, he's just forgotten to write. If I pick up anything, I'll send you a wire, just to relieve your mind. I've got your address."

Lorna did not trouble to thank him. She rose from her chair with a certain reluctance; but as she did so, The Counsellor halted her with a gesture and she sat down again without protest.

"Just a moment," he said, as though the point had just occurred to him. "I remember hearing somewhere that you're a friend of Mr. Richard Barrington. You do know him, don't you?"

"I don't know where you've picked that up," said Lorna Campion with a sharp and rather suspicious glance at The Counsellor. "It's true, though. I have come across him once or twice, if that's what you mean. Vin introduced him to me once; and after that I went to Caplatzi's two or three times with him. What about him?"

"So he didn't meet you under a *nom de guerre*?"

"Pardon?"

"I mean he used his own name. Didn't call himself Binks from Borneo or anything of that sort?"

"Why should he?" asked Lorna, reasonably enough. "He's a bachelor and doesn't need to think about difficulties, the way Vin Hawkstone had to."

"Do you like him?"

"Do I like him?" repeated Lorna reflectively, as if the matter had not occurred to her before and she had to think it over before answering. "Well, not specially. He's free-handed, I must say, and ready enough to stand any amount of cocktails. And he always gave me a box of chocolates to take home with me, which was thoughtful in a way. But he was all out for himself, if you understand me. He did the generous to please himself, not to please me. He liked to feel open-handed and that kind of thing. Really, behind it all, he was casehardened. Callous, you know. Real hard-hearted. I once told him I'd lost my kittie and found some beastly boys had taken and hanged it to a tree along the road. I was awfully cut up about it. It was such a nice little thing and so trustful. I told Mr. Barrington about that, and I'm sure the tears were in my eyes for I was fond of the kittie. And he just laughed. Thought it was a great joke, he did, and roared. Now that wasn't nice, was it, with me so distressed over the poor little thing? Amn't I right to say he's callous?"

"Quite. Quite," agreed The Counsellor sympathetically. "Callous is the word."

"I can see you're quite different, Mr. Brand," said Lorna gratefully. "And now, I suppose, I must be going. It's getting on, and now I'm up in Town I want to go to a show before taking the train home. Are you doing anything to-night, Mr. Brand?" she ended with a glance which screamed the unspoken invitation.

"I'm afraid I am," said The Counsellor hastily. "Some other time, perhaps."

"I'll remember that," Lorna declared archly. "And now I must really be going."

The Counsellor did not detain her. When she had gone, he spent a few seconds in speculating what sort of companion she would recruit instead of himself. He could hardly imagine her going alone.

Chapter X

STANDISH, *ALIAS* WATSON

WHEN Lorna Campion had gone, The Counsellor rang a bell and gave a curt direction to the messenger who answered his call:

"I want Mr. Standish."

In a few minutes Wolfram Standish, his manager, came into the room, looking none too pleased at being disturbed in whatever work he had been doing.

"Well, what is it, Mark?" he demanded rather irritably. "I'm busy. We can't all sit around and think great thoughts, you know. *Somebody* has to keep this business running."

The Counsellor waved him into a chair and pushed the cigarette box across the desk.

"Meaning yourself?" he said, indulgently. "I know. I know. You're devilish efficient, Wolf. You don't lose a moment, suffer no grass to grow under your feet, and improve the shining hour. Hustle, in fact. But I happen to require your personal services at this juncture. I need a listener. . . ."

Standish shifted uneasily in his chair. The movement did not escape The Counsellor, who continued blandly:

"A listener, to sharpen my wits on. A Watson, in fact."

"O *Lord*!" ejaculated Standish in dismayed protest. "You want to jabber about this blazing car case? Tell me all about it, in every detail, eh? Thanks so much. It may be news to you, Mark, but it's been discussed *ad libitum, ad infinitum* and *ad nauseam*—as you would put it, in your learned way—by the whole office staff, from the messenger boy up to Sandra. You can't tell me anything about it that I don't know already."

Standish disapproved of The Counsellor's excursions into criminology and made no concealment of his views.

"A bit of a wet blanket, you are," said The Counsellor critically. "But you relieve my mind in one respect. I see I shan't have to go over the details of the case with you. I can take 'em for granted and go straight on to higher flights."

"Well, make it snappy," said Standish, resignedly.

"Snappy or no, it'll probably be slanderous. So don't let my remarks go any further. I've chosen you as a confidant, Wolf, because Sandra knows some of the people mixed up in the business, so I can't let myself go all out in front of her without running the risk of rasping her feelings."

Standish ostentatiously consulted his wrist-watch.

"To business, then," said The Counsellor, taking the hint. "This is how it is, Wolf. Begin with the body found in the blazing car. It was either Hawkstone's or else it wasn't. That covers all possibilities. If it was Hawkstone's body, then either he committed suicide or else someone put his light out. If it *wasn't* Hawkstone's body, then . . . But let us proceed step by step."

"Like Euclid?" said Standish. "Ending up with Q.E.D.?"

"Eventually, if not now, I hope," retorted The Counsellor. "But to proceed. You claim to have all the sordid details of the evidence at your finger-ends. You don't know the Stop Press News, but let that pass for the present. Motives are what I have in my mind at the moment. Now the Coroner prefers the simplest explanation of the affair. He plumps for plain suicide by Hawkstone. What's the motive to account for that? Well, Frobisher received certain letters from interested parties. They suggest that Hawkstone got into trouble with various women; which doesn't seem out of character. Compare, further, the evidence of the saturnine Barrington brother, who discussed the same subject with Hawkstone at that interview just before the balloon went up. One may readily admit that Hawkstone had got himself into a tight place. Possibly he felt that *felo de se* was the only way out. So that's that."

"What's what?" demanded Standish, waking up suddenly. "Pure guesswork, I call it."

"Guess again, then. As follows: Second possibility. Remember the Rouse case? Chap who got mixed up with so many women at once that he didn't know what to do. Like the Old Woman Who Lived in a Shoe in the nursery rhyme. So he planned a get-away by murdering some poor devil and burning him in Rouse's own car. The idea being to have the body mistaken for Rouse himself, while the said Rouse departed to fresh woods and pastures new. Milton. Usually misquoted as 'fresh fields' owing to the catchy alliteration. Hawkstone must have known about the Rouse case—so like his own fix. So he may have copied Rouse; but gone one better by making a clean get-away, which Rouse failed to do."

"It's possible," Standish admitted, with a faint show of interest. "You haven't a scrap of evidence for it, of course."

"Wait-a-bit, as the South African thornbush is said to remark when it catches your bags. The Stop Press News hasn't reached the staff outside yet, so you don't know the whole tale. Nor do I myself at the moment. But I expect to, very shortly."

"Sensation!" interjected Standish ironically.

"These hypotheses I've just laid before you represent the case of Hawkstone as an active agent," The Counsellor continued. "Now we turn to other possibilities. My friend Inspector Hartwell has his solution on tap: Hawkstone was murdered by some person or persons unknown. It remains to be seen who murdered him."

"Job for the police, that," said Standish. "Not *my* business—or yours either, Mark."

The Counsellor ignored this last thrust.

"No murder without a motive," he continued oracularly.

"Except when a homicidal maniac commits it," grunted Standish.

"We'll rule that out, except in the last resort," declared The Counsellor. "No murder without a motive. *Ergo*, if this is a murder, there must be a motive in the background. Euclid couldn't put it fairer than that. What is this motive?"

"Well, what is it?" demanded Standish impatiently.

"Women, cash and revenge are at the back of all reasonable murders in this country, either singly or in combination with each other. I doubt, myself, if revenge comes in here at all, except in conjunction with a woman. Hawkstone may have tampered with some damsel who'd been already marked down by some other man. I don't know the particulars of the Coroner's budget of correspondence, so leave it aside. But this dame Lorna Campion is never tired of telling her friends and the public how jealous her husband is. And Campion might possibly doubt her story that her dealings with Hawkstone went no further than hand-holding and a kiss or two. In which case, he might have felt seriously aggrieved against Hawkstone. That's a possibility. And it's worth considering. Which we'll do later on, when the Stop Press News comes in."

The Counsellor pulled the box back across the desk and helped himself to a cigarette before continuing.

"Cash is another factor. Hawkstone was a solicitor. Solicitors have a good chance of embezzling clients' securities. . . ."

"But the victim never hears about it till the game's up," objected Standish. "And I haven't heard any evidence of a public exposure yet in Hawkstone's case."

"Agreed," said The Counsellor, promptly. "But now's the time for me to become slanderous, I think. There are two partners in that firm: Barrington and Hawkstone. Either—or both—may have been doing some quiet embezzling. Suppose that Hawkstone was the embezzler unknown to Barrington. The trade goes on for a while; but finally Justice or Nemesis comes clumping along, *pede pœna claudo*, as Horace puts it; and the game's up. Barrington spots what's been going on, at long last. Hence a somewhat heated interview between him and Hawkstone, as per evidence but on a different subject from the one stated by Barrington. Fine old firm going to be disgraced, etc. Barrington would naturally want to save the firm's name if he could; and doesn't want to split. If he splits, Hawkstone goes to gaol. But suppose Hawkstone funks gaol and prefers suicide?"

"Then Barrington would have to cough up the amount of the deficit out of his own pocket if he wanted to save a scandal," said Standish.

"Not all of it, perhaps," explained The Counsellor. "This is Stop Press News which you haven't been able to pick up in your gossiping with the underlings in the office. Barrington holds an insurance policy of £15,000 on Hawkstone's life. That's a simple business precaution, because on Hawkstone's death Mrs. Hawkstone can demand the return of the £15,000 that Hawkstone paid for his partnership. So by Hawkstone's death, the firm is £15,000 in pocket over that insurance; and this sum, plus anything Barrington can stump up himself, might cover the deficit, provided that Mrs. Hawkstone can be persuaded to draw an income instead of demanding £15,000 cash. And, by the way, she comes in for £10,000 herself over her husband's death, under another life policy."

"Does she?"

"She does, according to my inside information. Now on this basis, it would be essential to keep the whole embezzlement business dark, for obvious reasons. So if Hawkstone goes off and commits suicide in his car, Barrington has to devise some tale about that last interview which is very different from the truth."

"You saw him give evidence; I didn't," said Standish. "You should have some idea whether he was lying or not."

"I'm damned if I have. That's the bother," confessed The Counsellor ruefully. "You might as well ask me what made Mona Lisa smile. I just don't know."

"As usual, you're a whale at theory, but weak in practice," said Standish. "That's why I'm down on all this clue-hunting stunt."

"If he were lying, you couldn't prove it by talking about his facial expression," said The Counsellor sulkily. "So we can leave that out. Try again. I've given you the hypothesis based on embezzlement by Hawkstone. But now turn the thing the other way round. Suppose Barrington's been embezzling and Hawkstone discovered it lately. Barrington would have to shut Hawkstone's mouth, wouldn't he? By murder, if necessary. And by murdering him he would rake in

£15,000 which (under the conditions I explained already) might be enough to square the books of the firm and cover up the deficit."

"Slanderous seems well-chosen," commented Standish. "You could hardly find a better word. You won't mind my pointing out that Barrington has an absolutely cast-steel alibi supported by two maids and a G.P. Think again, Mark."

"Every murderer with any sense is sure to fake up an alibi," retorted The Counsellor. "And the ones who get away with it don't get hanged. But enough of this foolery! Let's widen our angle, look further afield. Hawkstone wasn't the only man who died—if he did die—in that neighbourhood about that time. You've heard of Earlswood, Sandra's pal of the cataleptic trances and the fear of being buried alive?"

"See Office Gossip, *passim*," said Standish. "He's come to my notice, never fear."

"Well, here's a possibility," said The Counsellor. "Earlswood was well provided with property. His solicitors were the excellent firm of Barrington and Hawkstone. Earlswood had trouble in his jaw. Who was his dentist? Richard Barrington, brother of the solicitor. A surgeon was called in and operated. Who was the surgeon? One Wyndcliffe, who inherits the bulk of Earlswood's estate. Now, let's suppose, for the sake of argument, that these three are birds of a feather. Bird No. 1, Barrington senior, has been embezzling some of the Earlswood cash and can't replace it. Discovery stares him in the face, looking very ugly. He calls in Bird No. 2, his brother, and Bird No. 3, Wyndcliffe. They arrange between them to get Earlswood out of the way."

"How?" interjected Standish.

"Ha! I interest you? That's so nice. This is where

I become technical, having consorted with a medical expert on the subject. Septic tooth, followed by trouble in the maxillary antrum, which is a hollow inside the upper jaw-bone, technically known as the antrum of Highmore. Now there's a channel through which infection can pass from the antrum to the brain, thus-wise. A vein drains the blood from the mucous lining of the antrum. This vein communicates with the pterygoid plexus of veins, which in turn communicate with the cavernous sinus, situated in the base of the skull, close to the pituitary body. If you get infection travelling along that channel to the sinus, then the patient gets cavernous thrombosis. A clot in the blood there and his death within a few days is a dead cert. So my expert tells me."

"Yes, I saw you reading that last bit off his notes," said Standish, drily. "Boiling it down and leaving out the polysyllables, it simply amounts to this, that given a septic tooth and bad faith in the dentist and surgeon (or even accident and bad luck) a man might get trouble somewhere in the brain and die. Hope I don't get antrum trouble."

"Oh, it's very rare in practice, my expert tells me. Cheer up. Even if you get trouble in your antrum, there's only the slightest risk of that complication. But it does happen, once in a blue moon. Well, making the assumptions I made, how do the three confederates stand after Earlswood dies? Wyndcliffe comes out pretty well, as he gets the Earlswood estate. He can be sure of this beforehand, since Barrington would have drawn up Earlswood's will and could say definitely that Wyndcliffe was being made the heir. Barrington senior would get off with the proceeds of his embezzlements, if there were any left, and get a sponge rubbed over his little delinquencies in the past. Wyndcliffe would be willing enough to pay that commission on his inheritance. Also, Barrington junior might expect a few shekels for his services in the affair. Though it's quite on the cards that he didn't come into it guiltily, but merely was persuaded by his brother to call Wyndcliffe in when surgery was needed."

"Then you're assuming that they just took advantage of the septic tooth when it turned up. They didn't necessarily plan the thing beforehand to a fixed date?"

"How could they? You can't tell when a man's going to have toothache, in the ordinary way. No need to complicate the affair further than's necessary."

"Quite right," said Standish, approvingly. "Especially when you've invented such a devil of a lot of complications, anyhow. I think it's mere rubbish, Mark, whether you ask my opinion or not. And, now I come to think of it, you seem to have wandered away from Hawkstone altogether. What's all this got to do with him?"

"Well, he may have discovered the embezzlement before Barrington could cover it up. Naturally they couldn't have *that* advertised, at that stage of the game. So that would entail sending Hawkstone to follow Earlswood, purely to make things safe."

"I can't deny that you've got inventive powers, Mark. But except for that, I haven't a good word to say for all this stuff of yours. Bunkum, if you ask me candidly."

"There's more to come," said The Counsellor, ruthlessly. "I'll just point out that by Hawkstone's death Mrs. Hawkstone comes in for £10,000 from an insurance policy on Hawkstone's life. Stop Press News again, so fresh to you, Wolf. And rumour goes that Mrs. H. and Barrington senior are not unfond of each other and might make a match of it now that Hawkstone's out of the road. So Barrington had the double incentive of cash and a woman."

"I can guess why you didn't choose Sandra as your victim for this talkee-talkee," said Standish. "She'd have gone off like a Catherine wheel if you'd told that tale to her about a girl she likes. So I suffer. You've got a ghastly mind, Mark. Likewise a low one."

"There's more to come," said The Counsellor as Standish rose from his chair. "The next bit's something different. The Dunecht . . ."

"Tell it to yourself, then," Standish advised. "You won't tell it to me. I know when I've had enough. Send out for one of these stuffs you see advertised—Rinsit or Clean-O or whatever it is—and give your mind a good wash-up, Mark. It needs it."

He moved towards the door, but just as he did so a messenger boy entered with a note. The Counsellor glanced at it, dismissed the bearer, and arrested Standish on the threshold.

"Sit down, Wolf. This isn't speculation. Plain facts. Sandra's been phoning up about Mr. Percy Campion and his doings and this is the result."

"Wise of her to jot it down and send it in to you instead of coming herself to see you give your imitation of the Ancient Mariner," commented Standish. "Well, since it's facts and not vain imaginings, I don't mind listening for a few seconds more. But you won't catch me again in a hurry, I warn you."

"This is it," said The Counsellor. "Percy Campion is employed by Messrs. Collyer and Hanway of Fernhurst-Hordle as a traveller. On the morning of Friday, April 14th, he was to leave for Liverpool where he had arranged to board the liner *Meteoric*, which sailed on the 17th. Sandra rang up the shipping firm and luckily they have a note of the passengers who actually embarked. Campion didn't go on board, although his berth was booked. Sandra rang up Collyer and Hanway also. They haven't heard of Campion since he left here. He was to do some business for them in Liverpool before he sailed. It hasn't been done. Summarising the above: Campion disappeared when he left his home on the morning of April 14th and hasn't been heard of since—like James James Morrison's mother. Conclusion: it's a rum start."

"At long last, Mark, you seem to have got hold of something," Standish admitted. "What do you make of it, now you've got it?"

"I say it's a non-negligible item of information," declared The Counsellor with deliberate moderation.

"What you really think is that either Hawkstone murdered Campion or Campion murdered Hawkstone," said Standish. "So the body may have been Hawkstone's or Campion's. Were they about the same build?"

"They were, according to Mrs. Campion, who ought to know."

"H'm! It's interesting. That is, if the two disappearances are really connected. What do you propose to do next?"

"Ring up my pal the Inspector, and also put an enquiry in the next broadcast. Something ought to emerge. I'm a bit sceptical, though. There's an item that doesn't fit, here."

"What's that?" demanded Standish.

"Something that *ought* to have been amongst the car débris, but wasn't there. Think it out, Wolf. It's all in plain sight."

Chapter XI

INFORMATION WANTED

"Don't mind my dropping in for a few minutes?" enquired The Counsellor jauntily, when he got access to Inspector Hartwell next day. "Got a fact or two more for you about the Hawkstone affair, if that makes me any more welcome."

"Thanks. I can do with them," the Inspector returned.

From Hartwell's expression, The Counsellor gathered that the Hawkstone mystery had not grown much clearer since their last meeting.

"Well, here's a start. Glance at these two letters. Handwriting the same in both? Good. One was written by the cove who wanted the cipher ads. solved by my Problem Department. The other, as you see from the signature, was penned by our friend, Mr. Richard Barrington in answer to an enquiry of mine about the habits of tench. So between them they help to clinch his connection with that episode in the business."

"I dare say," admitted the inspector, gloomily. "But we knew already, from that girl clerk's evidence, that it was Barrington who inserted these ads."

"Granted. But now we know that he stirred up my Solutionist to get them unravelled. Doesn't that strike you as quaint, *outré* and possibly remarkable? Here's a cove making up a cipher message, putting it into the ad. column of a newspaper, and then writing to me to find out what it means. Sounds like rats in the garret or bats in the belfry, surely."

"Perhaps he was only a messenger," suggested the Inspector. "Somebody else wrote the cipher ads. and asked him to push them over the counter. By and by, Barrington gets curious about them, wants to know what they were about, and writes to you on the subject."

"Brilliant!" declared The Counsellor. "Only . . . no good, really."

"It's possible," admitted the Inspector. "But I don't yet see any need for this delayed-action stunt, as you call it."

"Well, I didn't when I saw you last. But I do, now. From information received, as you say when you want to be mysterious and deep. Would it surprise you to know that the Hawkstone man was insured for £25,000?"

"Was he?" demanded the Inspector, obviously surprised by the sum.

"He was. Sydney Barrington scoops in £15,000 when the death's established. Mrs. Hawkstone gathers up £10,000. *Now* do you see why it was essential to get the body's identity proved? Without that, no insurance money."

"That puts a fresh light on things," said the Inspector ruminatively.

"No, it doesn't. It simply turns it on a bit stronger. Makes the delayed-action idea a cert."

"A nod's as good as a wink to a blind horse," said the Inspector, unconsciously plagiarising Lorna Campion. "But I'm not so blind, yet. I'll think that over."

"When you've got your thinking-cap on," said The Counsellor, you can meditate on something else as well.

This is it. Remember Mr. Percy Campion? Middle name, Othello, according to his spouse. Jealous as a Barbary pigeon, which they say gets high marks in such competitions. Well, he's vanished."

"Vanished?" echoed the Inspector, evidently completely at a loss. "Gone to America, you mean?"

"Gone, but not to America, so far as I can make out," said The Counsellor. "He didn't embark on the liner. Nor does he seem to have done any business in Liverpool, as he was expected to do."

"He left here the morning before the night of the blazing car," said the Inspector thoughtfully. "At least, she said he did. . . ."

"Thought-reading experiments, No. 1," said The Counsellor. "It's the Rouse case that's crossed your mind. Or ought to have done."

"Maybe," said the Inspector, admitting nothing.

"That £25,000 of insurance would cut up not badly, even if two or three people had to get a share out of it," mused The Counsellor. Quite enough to let a bright young man get a fresh start in life after committing a murder. Question is: Who's the bright young man."

"You mean: Is the body Hawkstone's or Campion's?" demanded the Inspector, all alert.

"I leave it to you, partner. Campion may be walking the earth in perfect fettle at this moment for all I can tell. All I know is that he isn't on the road to America. I suggest that you race me for the first news. You set the Liverpool wires to work and consult your opposite number in that city. I'll set the ether quivering tomorrow. We'll see which of us breasts the tape first. It ought to be you, for I'm giving you a twenty-four hours' start, if you get busy as soon as you can."

"I'll take you on," declared the Inspector. "We've got a few notes about Campion already which will help."

"Go to it, then. But don't use up all your energy on it, because I've got a suggestion or two further to make in the matter of lines of investigation. First of all, could you find out if the Barringtons leave their garage doors open in the daytime when their cars are out?"

"I'll see about that at once," said the Inspector, getting up and going out of the room.

In a couple of minutes he returned again.

"I've put an enquiry through," he explained. "We'll hear very shortly."

"Right!" said The Counsellor. "Now here's another point in that field, but it'll take more trouble. D'you think you could find out, somehow or another, if any peculiar noises were heard in the Barrington garage on the night of the 9th?"

"What sort of noises?" demanded the Inspector.

"Call 'em noises, just, and leave it at that," said The Counsellor. "Better not to make it too definite or you may get a lot of people swearing they heard exactly what you ask about, screams, groans or what not. Say 'peculiar noises' and take what replies you get. Some maidservant's bedroom window may look out on the garage from the next house. You might get a tip that way."

"I'll see what can be done," said the Inspector in a rather doubtful tone. "I see your point, but . . ."

"But you'd like to know what I'm after? Sorry, I think it will be best if you yourself aren't biased in the business by knowing what I'm thinking about. As a matter of fact, it's a long shot and I doubt if you'll rake in anything. Because I may be on the wrong tack, you see," admitted The Counsellor brightly.

He delved into his pocket once more and produced a sheet of paper on which a newspaper cutting was pasted.

"I suppose you searched back through the files of the

Courier and the *Herald* for the rest of that series of cipher advertisements put in by Hawkstone and Mrs. Campion. I left you at the *Herald* office, I remember, last time we met. You didn't find anything peculiar about the previous communications, I take it?"

"No," said the Inspector. "There were a few, just as she admitted; but they were just making appointments for a night out and that kind of thing."

"I looked them up myself," explained The Counsellor. "Both these papers have London offices and I turned up the files there. As you say, it was all quite innocent stuff. But I pursued my researches among some of the other ads. and in both papers issued on April 7th, I found an ad. that interested me. You've got a local evening paper, haven't you?"

"The *Telegraph*, yes."

"Well, I found that out, too, and I searched its columns in that day's issue and found the same ad. there. Here it is."

He passed his sheet of paper to the Inspector, who read:

"WANTED IMMEDIATELY. Garage or good shed to hold one car. State terms per week.—Box E.341."

Hartwell stared at the cutting, obviously without being able to see its importance. Evidently he suspected some cipher, for The Counsellor could see him making efforts to get at an underlying meaning. At last he took pity on Hartwell.

"No hanky-panky," he explained. "It's all in plain sight and means just what it says. Somebody wanted a garage or shed in a devil of a hurry. Bought a car, perhaps, and then remembered it needed a roof over it at night. Anyhow, it interests me. Another long shot, I admit. Care to enter for another race? I'm going to make an enquiry about it in to-morrow's broadcast. But I guess you'll be able to beat me hollow by simply questioning your constables or setting them to make quiet enquiries. All I can tell you is that I think it might be a winner, if we can pick up some news about the matter. Have a dash at it, will you?"

"You want to know if anyone let a garage or a shed as the result of this ad.? Anything else?"

"Anything else you can pick up: situation of garage, neighbours, name of person who leased it, name of new occupier—things of that sort."

"I'll look into the matter," said Hartwell. "Anything more up your sleeve, Mr. Brand?"

"There's one thing I'd like to know a little more about," The Counsellor confessed. "At the inquest, that chemist fellow gave the results of an analysis of some white deposit found near the body amongst the car débris. Tell me some more about it, will you?"

"There wasn't much of it," the Inspector explained. "About a teaspoonful or so, altogether, when we'd got it gathered up. It was a fine powder, different from the rest of the ashes on which it was resting—the remains of the seat—so I collected as much of it as I could get and handed it on to the analyst. But there was nothing in it, so far as I could see. You heard what he found: chlorine and calcium. It might have been something from a packet in one of his pockets, for all I know. Anyhow, it didn't throw any light on the affair."

The Counsellor apparently took his word for that and pursued the subject no further. He passed at once to something else.

"What sort of gate was that beside the place where you found the number plates?"

"An ordinary wooden gate, painted white. Fairly newly painted, if I remember."

"And there was a mark on it as if something had slid down and scraped the paint, I think you said at the inquest?"

"That's so."

"Well, if I were in your shoes, Inspector, I think I'd cut that bit off the gate and preserve it carefully."

"Not much use doing that," said Hartwell sceptically. "It's just a mere scrape, if you see what I mean. You couldn't do anything with it, even if you had it."

"Not alone, I admit," The Counsellor conceded. "But if another sample of that paint turned up, a young friend of mine could do more than you suppose. He's strong on this micro-analysis stunt that's come in not so long ago. Give him enough of a stuff to make an ant sneeze and he'll do you an analysis of it quite accurately with this technique. So don't despair because the quantity's minute."

"I'll take your advice," said the Inspector with no great show of belief.

"It may amount to just nothing," admitted The Counsellor candidly. "Still, it might come in useful. One never knows. By the way, what colour was the streak?"

"Black," said the Inspector. "The same colour as ninety per cent. of bicycles."

"Some cats are black and so is coal," The Counsellor pointed out. "But that doesn't mean that cats and coal are the same thing."

"They didn't teach logic at your school, evidently," said the Inspector sardonically. "It's a hobby of mine: logic. Do you know Lewis Carroll's one about the lizard? 'No bald person needs a hair brush. All lizards are bald. Therefore no lizard needs a hair brush.' That's the model for you, sir, when you begin to put things logically."

158

"Lobsters are bald," retorted The Counsellor, "but if you'll look up *Alice in Wonderland*, you'll see a picture of a lobster with a hair brush in its hand. So don't you trust too much to Lewis Carroll, Inspector. He'd pull your leg as soon as look at it."

"Is there anything else you'd like to talk about?" asked Hartwell, consulting his watch ostentatiously.

"Is there?" said The Counsellor thoughtfully. "Oh, yes. You went through that débris carefully, I suppose?"

"We put most of it through sieves when we were on that wild-goose chase after match-heads which you so kindly set us on," said the Inspector a trifle tartly. "You can take it that we missed nothing bigger than a pin's head, and perhaps not even that."

"Did you, now?" retorted The Counsellor with obviously feigned admiration. "I do like to see thoroughness—in other people, of course. So I may take it that the catalogue of finds you gave at the inquest represents the total bag of all sorts?"

"You can."

"H'm!" said The Counsellor ruminatively. "Then the most important thing of the lot is the thing you *didn't* find."

"I'll bet we missed nothing," declared the Inspector rather hotly. "If anything was there to find, we found it."

"That's just what I mean," said The Counsellor with a grin which irritated the Inspector, who had got rather confused by the last few sentences. "But I saw you looking at your watch. I mustn't trespass on your time. Tell you what. Come and lunch with me at 1.30 p.m. Same place as before. I'll meet you in the vestibule. And bring with you the news about Barrington's garage, if you can. I'm really interested in that point."

The Inspector, with memories of The Counsellor's

earlier hospitality, accepted readily. When he made his appearance at the restaurant, his host was awaiting him; and as they met, The Counsellor cocked his eyebrow interrogatively.

"I haven't got all you wanted yet," said Hartwell, answering the silent question. "It'll take some time to get hold of these maids and so forth in the adjoining houses. But I'm sure of the other matter. The constables on the beat could tell me that. That garage is left with its doors open all day and most of the night, too, for one or other of the brothers is always out late, often well into the small hours; and the garage is never shut up until the last of the cars comes home for the night. What's more. They hire a jobbing gardener who comes four days a week, and he keeps some of his tools—the lawn-mower and so forth—at the back of the garage beyond where the cars stand. And he's in and out of the place at all hours. So if you're looking for something mysterious about that garage, sir, I guess you'll have to try again. It's all open and above-board."

"Well, that's that," said The Counsellor, lightly. "And that reminds me of something else I want to know. Find out, if you can, whether the Barringtons are still keen on fish courses at dinner. You can easily get one of your men to chum up with their cook and worm that out of her."

"One of your jokes, Mr. Brand?" queried the Inspector, who obviously saw no point in the jest.

"One of my jokes," confirmed The Counsellor with an austere expression. "Still, I'd like to know."

"Think it's too difficult for me?" retorted the Inspector. "We'll manage it, if it isn't just a leg-pull. I suppose you shrink from asking for news on the point in your next broadcast and so you have to fall back on the stupid police, eh?"

The Counsellor ignored the slightly nettled tone.

"That's it in a nutshell," he admitted. "Fish are said to contain phosphorus. There was a trace of phosphorus on the fragments of that poison-bottle found in the burned car. Phosphorus is said to be good for the brain. Care to join me in a sole when we go to lunch? Might brighten us both up a lot, perhaps. Stimulate the grey matter. But, before I forget, I'll see you next Tuesday. Eleven o'clock, say. I hope to have the next thrilling instalment worked out by then."

Chapter XII

THE GARAGE

On the following Tuesday, The Counsellor journeyed down once more to Fernhurst-Hordle and paid his promised visit to the Inspector.

"Any news?" he demanded after they had greeted each other.

"There's no news of Campion," the Inspector confessed. "The Liverpool police know nothing about him."

"Not been run over in the street and taken to hospital with concussion or anything?"

The Inspector shook his head.

"No. I got them to comb the hospitals for unidentified patients. There's nobody answering to his description in any of them. Had you any better luck, sir? I heard you enquiring in your Sunday broadcast for someone answering to his description, though you didn't mention his name."

"I didn't care to go *that* length," said The Counsellor, "for obvious reasons. But it's a dead heat, Inspector. Neither of us has got any news about him."

"It's very queer," mused the Inspector, rubbing his nose thoughtfully. "I certainly expected to find him in hospital. It's about the only way one could reasonably account for his disappearance. And street accidents happen often enough nowadays."

"They'd have found some identifying papers in his pockets if he had been knocked down in the street," objected The Counsellor. "That cock won't fight. We'll have to find another one that will. But don't bother about it just now. What about any noises in the Barrington garage?"

"I've nothing about that, either, so far," confessed the Inspector rather ruefully. "But there's still a chance. The most likely person to have heard anything is a maid in the house next door to the Barringtons. Her bedroom window overlooks the garage. But she's on holiday at the moment, it seems, or gone sick. Anyhow, she's away and won't be back for a day or two. And she's left no address, so we'll just have to wait till she gets back again."

"Have you collected that paint-scrape from the gate?" asked The Counsellor.

"Yes, I've got that. I did it myself. Cut a complete sliver of wood away, with the mark on it; and I've got it safe inside a bottle."

"Good!" said The Counsellor. "Don't lose it, whatever you do. It's a long shot, that; but it may well come in useful later on. And now," he added with a grin, "what about the Barringtons' diet? Have they been taking an extra allowance of phosphorus for their grey matter?"

The Inspector laughed, as though the joke was on his side.

"Not in the form of fish, anyhow," he declared. "They haven't had a fish course in the last fortnight, I discovered. Usually they seem to have it once a week at least."

"They aren't Roman Catholics, are they?"

The Inspector shook his head.

"No, it wasn't a case of fasting," he said. "They didn't have it on Fridays regularly. I asked about that. Or rather, I put my man up to ask about it. He's good at worming information out of people without making them suspicious."

"What luck did you have in the matter of the garage advertisement?" demanded The Counsellor, coming abruptly to the subject which seemed to interest him most.

"Not bad," said the Inspector. "I've found the place that was let in answer to that ad. It's a small, brick-built affair in Fletcher Street, and it was taken on a weekly tenancy."

"I've got a shade more information in answer to my broadcast," explained The Counsellor. "Cast my net a bit wider than you had to do, and raked in some extra news. What I got were the names of three or four places which had tried to catch the advertiser, but didn't manage it. Also the Fletcher Street address, of course. If you've got an hour to spare, Inspector, I don't think it would be wasted in having a look at these places. They might suggest something to an enquiring mind like yours."

Inspector Hartwell evidently did not relish this last dig, but he was growing to rely on The Counsellor's aptitude for producing fresh evidence, so with as good a grace as possible he agreed to go round and look at the various buildings. They went out to The Counsellor's car and began their tour.

The garage at the first address selected by The Counsellor was only a garage by courtesy. It was a rather decrepit wooden shed standing in a weed-grown patch of ground beside an undeveloped building-plot. The Counsellor got out of his car, walked round the neglected edifice, stared in through the dirty window, and then inserted his finger into a crack between two of the boards.

"Not very attractive," he declared, turning to the Inspector. "I'm not surprised that the advertiser let a bargain like that slip through his fingers. We'll try the next one."

The second garage was a shade better. It was a rough-cast erection, with a good solid door, and was well lighted by two moderate-sized windows on one side.

"That looks a sound enough place," commented the Inspector, as he mechanically tested the fastenings of one of the windows. "I see nothing wrong with it. The rent may have been too high, perhaps."

"Perhaps," echoed The Counsellor as he went back to his car.

The third call was at a well-built wooden semi-temporary garage which seemed in first-class condition. The Counsellor lifted himself on tip-toe, gazed in through the windows in the upper part of the doors, and announced that he could see a stand-pipe.

"Water laid on for washing a car. It's a well-built place," said the Inspector ruminatively. "The rent may have been too high, though. Some people expect a fortune."

"A good, sound article," The Counsellor admitted. "But it didn't suit, apparently. Let's try again."

The fourth call brought them to a very spick-and-span double-doored garage, red-tiled, which stood in a little patch of ground adjacent to the garden of a trim villa. They looked in at the windows and noted a hose and stand-pipe inside, as well as a series of shelves along the wall at the back.

"That's the one I'd take myself, out of those we've seen, so far," said The Counsellor. "Nice neighbour-hood, too. Wonder why it didn't suit. We'll see, per-haps, when we come to the one that was actually rented. It's our next port of call."

Fletcher Street proved to be a rather down-at-the-heel thoroughfare which had evidently seen better days; and the building which the advertiser had finally chosen was simply an old coach-house, with rather battered and decayed doors and a slate roof which would have been none the worse for some attention. The Counsellor's eye was caught by a brand-new staple and padlock which had been screwed on above the older fastening.

"So this is the advertiser's dream, is it?" he said reflectively, as he cast his eye over the building's rather woebegone exterior. "Tastes differ. One has to admit it. Perhaps it was the rent that turned the scale. It's got a good concrete floor evidently," he continued, stooping down to examine the bottom of the door. "No way of getting a look inside, apparently. I'd like to see some more. Who owns the place, do you know?"

"The people in that house across the way," explained the Inspector. "They could tell you something, perhaps, if you're very interested."

"I am, somehow," retorted The Counsellor. "So let's try."

When they rang the door bell, they were confronted by a shabbily dressed, tousled girl of about sixteen, with sharp, inquisitive eyes and a suspicious manner. From the promptness of her appearance at the door, The Counsellor felt little doubt that she had been watching their previous doings from behind the window curtains.

"Is your mother in?" demanded the Inspector.

The girl shook her head, keeping a hand on the door as though in readiness to close it in their faces.

"No. She's not. What do you want?" she asked in a mistrustful tone.

"Merely to ask whether that garage over there is to let at present," explained The Counsellor.

An expression of uncertainty crossed the girl's face.

"It is, and it isn't," she answered doubtfully. "You'll need to wait till Mother comes home if you want an answer."

"Quaint way of putting it," commented The Counsellor with a smile. "Can't you make it sound less like a puzzle? Try."

A reluctant smile shaped itself at the girl's mouth-corners and her suspicions seemed to diminish a little as she glanced from the burly, official-looking Inspector to the much less impressive Counsellor.

"Well," she explained, "somebody rented it and paid a week's rent in advance, but we've had no more out of him and we don't know his address. He owes us for last week and he hasn't shown up or sent any money. Could we let it to somebody else, with things that way?"

Her glance appealed to the Inspector as the more weighty of her interlocutors.

"Did he arrange to pay weekly?" demanded Hartwell.

"He didn't arrange at all," explained the girl. "We answered an advertisement in the *Telegraph*, saying we'd let the place for five shillings a week. It hasn't been let for over a year, you see, and we were glad to get any offer for it. Back came a letter, with a five-bob postal order inside, saying he'd take the garage and this was a week's rent in advance and would we have the place clean and tidy and leave the door open so that he could get into it when he needed to. So we did that."

"What name did he give?" asked The Counsellor, in the tone of a man asking an idle question.

"He didn't give any name, just said 'the advertiser,' " explained the girl, with a quick return of suspicion to her eyes. "Is it all right? Anything amiss about it?"

The Inspector, at a quick glance from The Counsellor, took upon himself to deal with her. He ignored her final questions.

"Paid one week's rent and then defaulted, did he?" he said weightily. "In that case, he's got no further claim on the premises, since you had no means of giving him notice even if you'd wanted to, not knowing his name or address."

"I think I'll take the place myself, if you like to let it," The Counsellor broke in. "Care to accept me as a tenant? I'll take it for a month, anyhow, and pay in advance. Probably I shan't want it for longer. If you get a permanent tenant in the meanwhile, I don't mind clearing out."

"I can't say anything till Mother comes home," explained the girl with obvious regret. "She ought to be here in a minute or two now. She's just gone shopping."

"You've got a new fastening and padlock on the door, I see," said The Counsellor. "Can you give me the key, so that I can have a look at the place?"

The girl shook her tousled locks decidedly.

"No, that's the padlock *he* put on. We haven't any key for it," she explained.

"H'm! We can always wrench the hasp off," said The Counsellor. "That is, if we can come to terms with your mother."

"Here she is, now," cried the girl in a tone of relief, pointing to a stout, middle-aged woman, obviously of the lower middle class, who had just turned the street corner. She came up to them in leisurely fashion, weighed down by a market-basket on her arm which seemed loaded with vegetables and other goods.

"What's your name?" demanded the Inspector, turning to the girl.

"Mamie Taylor."

"What's your father?"

"He's dead. There's just Mother and me at home. We keep lodgers since father died." Then, as her parent came up, she hailed her.

"Mother! These men want to hire the garage."

It took a little persuasion to overcome Mrs. Taylor's doubts about her duty towards her previous tenant; but finally the prospect of at least one pound in hand outweighed any remaining scruples left after the argument, and she consented to give The Counsellor immediate access to the premises. The Inspector borrowed a case-opener; and he and The Counsellor, after some rather aimless conversation, went across the road to the garage, accompanied by Mamie, who was evidently determined that nothing should escape her curiosity. The new fastening was a sound one, but the case-opener, in the hands of the Inspector, proved more than a match for it and the doors soon were free. Before opening them, however, The Counsellor turned again to the girl, with the air of making idle conversation.

"You never set eyes on the fellow who rented the place? Don't you keep your eyes about you? He must have come here to fix that hasp and the padlock."

"We've all got to sleep sometimes, haven't we?" retorted the girl rather angrily. "If you kept lodgers, you'd be glad enough to get some sleep when you can, I can tell you. Bed at ten o'clock and up early to get the men's breakfasts, that's how we do. I didn't see that padlock put on because it was done after we'd gone to bed. It wasn't there one evening, and it was fixed up and locked by the next morning. I thought it was funny, myself, doing things that way, and I mentioned it to Mother, just in passing, but she said: 'Don't you worry. We've got the money in advance, and he can't put the garage in his pocket and take it away with him.' Mother's like that. She never bothers her head about things till she has to. But I'm not that sort myself. I get curious about things; can't help it. And I was a bit surprised that no car seemed to come to the garage at all, not for three or four nights. Then one night I happened to be awake later than usual, and my bedroom's at the front of our house, and I heard a car reversing in the street below, trying to get into the garage, which is a bit awkward, you see, since the road's narrow."

"Remember what night that was?" enquired The Counsellor with no sign of curiosity.

"It was a Wednesday, I remember, because I'd been at the pictures and saw a Ginger Rogers film, and I was a bit late in getting home because I went for a walk with a boy afterwards."

"Last Wednesday?"

"No, not last Wednesday. It must have been the week before."

"Oh!" exclaimed The Counsellor. "Then if the car's still here, I'm afraid my bargain about the garage is off."

"Oh, but it isn't," explained Mamie, eagerly. "It didn't even stop that night, for next day I got a bit curious to know what sort of a car the man had, and I went over to the garage to have a look. There's no windows to see through, but I managed to find a bit where the doors didn't meet tight, because it's an oldish garage and the wood's got a bit warped. And when I looked in, there was no car there. There was nothing at all, except a bundle done up in some old sacking with a rope round it, lying in one corner at the back, so far that I couldn't rightly see what it was except that it *was* a bundle of stuff all packed up."

"A biggish bundle?" enquired The Counsellor.

"A biggish bundle would about describe it," Mamie affirmed. "About as big as me, or a bit bigger. Looked like a bundle of bamboo canes, like they use in garden for propping up plants, or something of that sort. And there were two petrol tins standing beside it, against the wall."

"Sharp eyes, you must have," said The Counsellor approvingly. "It must be pretty dark inside there. Where's this crack in the door? I'd just like to see how much I can make out, myself."

Mamie pointed to the crevice and The Counsellor solemnly put his eye to it.

"The bundle must have been in the right-hand corner," he said as he lifted his head. "That right?"

"Yes," the girl confirmed, pointing in the direction he had guessed.

"Now, would you mind telling your mother I'd like to see her in a minute or two, please. I've got to pay my rent, you know. And I'd like to see that note from your last tenant, if she can find it, just to be on the safe side."

The girl obediently went off on her errand, and as soon as her back was turned The Counsellor pulled a flash-lamp from his pocket, opened the doors and went inside the garage. The Inspector followed him, stepping gingerly in response to a muttered direction, and The Counsellor drew the doors together, leaving only enough space to let in a small beam of light from outside.

"Better stand still for a moment or two till I've had a look over the floor," suggested The Counsellor.

He went down on hands and knees while, with the aid of his flash-lamp, he searched the concrete floor, foot by foot, with the greatest care from the doors onward. At last he rose to his feet again and dusted the knees of his trousers.

"Now, step carefully," he directed. "Put your right foot here. Now your left foot—there! Stand fast. Watch this."

He threw the beam of his lamp on the floor and in its circle of light the Inspector saw a small stick, apparently a piece of firewood.

"You can pick that up. Careful, for Heaven's sake! Catch it by the end and don't knock any of that stuff off it."

He held his lamp so that the Inspector could examine the find.

"Looks as if somebody with an uncommonly dirty boot had trodden on it," commented Hartwell, as he scrutinised the stick. "There's a regular blob of mud on it."

"Here's an envelope," said The Counsellor. "Shove the stick inside it, without rubbing off that mineral deposit if you can help it. You'd better number these envelopes; there are more to come. Now put your right foot here and your left one there. Steady on your pins? Right. Now look at this. See some more of that mud on the concrete? Then watch me sweep it up in true C.I.D. style with this camel-hair brush. Now it's in the test-tube. A cork, a label, and I hand it over to you for numbering. If you ask me, someone came in here with that mud on his boot, sticking between the front edge of his heel and the flat of his sole; and when he stepped on that stick, the stuff got loosened. Some of it stuck to the wood and the rest got detached when he made his next step, and so it was left on the concrete. Now you can step along here to the back of the garage. See these splashes of white powder? Looks like lime, or something. We want a sample of them, too. But before you start, just notice this one. See the triangular cut into it? My idea is that there was a petrol tin standing there, when the powder got spread about; and the tin shielded the floor at that spot. This is the corner where that girl saw the tins, you remember. Don't disturb that pattern when you dig up samples; and if I were you, I'd get a photo taken at close quarters to show just how the thing looks."

"Anything else?" enquired the Inspector when he had finished this task and brushed some of the powder into one of The Counsellor's envelopes.

"Have a sniff over the patch," advised The Counsellor.

"Chloride of lime," was the Inspector's verdict. "I know that well enough."

"*Alias* bleaching-powder," The Counsellor amplified. "Now just three more specimens, and I think we're through." He brought his flash-lamp close to the ground and pointed to something in its beam. "See that fibre? We want it. Here's a test-tube and a label. Bit of coarse stuff, isn't it? Hemp, or jute, or whatever it is they make sacking out of. Confirms that damsel's tale about seeing a bundle of bamboos or something tied up in sacking. And now we want some oil from that patch there. Dripped out of the crank-case of a motor, obviously, and moderately fresh. See if you can scrape some of it up and get it into this test-tube. . . . That's good; there's enough for the purpose, I think. The crank-case must have been pretty leaky if that dripped out of it in a short time. And now, here's positively the last find. See that little bit of black stuff there, where my finger is? About half the size of my finger-nail, and flattish. Scoop it into this test-tube. Here's a label. And a cork. Now, I think, that finishes the job."

"You'd have had a better light if you'd opened the doors," grumbled the Inspector as he rose to his feet and dusted the knees of his trousers.

"And given all the kids in the street a free show: two able-bodied gentlemen crawling around on their stomachs. Bound to draw a crowd, especially in a neighbourhood like this. Fact is, Inspector, the less talk about this episode the better. That's why I tactfully got rid of the young damsel at the start of our performance."

He gave a last glance over the floor as though looking for something still undiscovered.

"Looking for anything more?" queried the Inspector, who had by no means relished the purely subordinate part he had been playing.

"Yes, I'm looking for the thing you didn't find amongst the débris of that car," answered The Counsellor, with a crooked grin. "But it isn't here either. Never mind. Let's drop across and see Mrs. Taylor. Meanwhile I'll send my chauffeur to get a fresh hasp and padlock for this door, while we're having our chat. We don't want *hoi polloi* blundering into that garage as soon as our backs are turned."

He ushered the Inspector out, closed the garage doors, and gave some instructions to his chauffeur. Then he led the way across the street and handed the borrowed case-opener back to Mrs. Taylor, who awaited him at her front door.

"I can't find that letter nowhere," she confessed at once, as The Counsellor came up. "I must have burned it, seeing it had no name and address to it. I've a sort of recollection I did burn it, now I come to remember. Anyways, I can't find it."

"It doesn't matter, really," said The Counsellor carelessly. "Typewritten, I suppose?"

"Yes, it was typed, I remember," Mrs. Taylor confirmed. "But anyways I'm sure enough about what it said about taking the garage by the week, with payment in advance. I don't forget things that's really important, like a matter of business as it was."

"Right! Then I'm taking it for a month from to-day," said The Counsellor, drawing out his note-case. "Here's the rent. And if you get a chance of letting it before the month's up, drop me a note—here's my card—and I dare say we'll be able to arrange for the new tenant to get in whenever he wants to. By the way, when you let it last time, did you clean it out for your tenant?"

"We gave it a clean-up, certainly," Mrs. Taylor explained. "You see, we used to keep a lot of odds and ends and things in it, when it wasn't let: old chairs and firewood and things like that. But when we got it let, we had to clear all that out of the place; and then the floor was a bit untidy, as you can imagine, so we gave it a swill with water and brushed it over with a broom, just to make it right for the car coming in."

"Very thoughtful of you," said The Counsellor approvingly. "I noticed how clean-swept it was."

Evidently, he reflected, some of the firewood had been removed after the cleansing had been done; and one stick must have dropped out of the bundles unnoticed as they were being carried away.

"Your last tenant doesn't seem to have made much use of the place," he continued, apparently idly. "Ever see him?"

Mrs. Taylor evidently had a love of gossip. She seemed loath to let her visitors go.

"I never set eyes on himself," she admitted. "But I did see his car, once, backing into the garage. A big green Hernshaw-Davies, it was. Not that I know many makes by sight myself, but I do happen to know that one, with the heart-shaped radiator front and the bird mascot they put on top of it. I just happened to be coming up the street, one night, when the car passed me just as I was almost abreast of the garage. So being curious to see what sort of car was using our place, I stopped and had a look at it."

"See the number, as it passed you?" interjected The Counsellor.

"Not to remember. No. I just took a glance at it before it began to back towards me, reversing to get round into the garage. It ended in 56, I remember, because my house-number's 56 and it struck me as a queerish coincidence. And the letters were XYZ, for that's easy enough to keep in mind, too, whether you need it or not."

"What night was that?" asked The Counsellor without betraying too much curiosity.

Mrs. Taylor pondered for a moment or two.

"Lemmesee," she said at last. "I was out extra late that night. My sister's been ill, and when I went to see her that evening she asked me as a favour to sit up with her, because she couldn't sleep and she'd do anything for company to save lying awake in the dark. She's no great reader, you see? And it's lonely when you can't sleep in the night, all by yourself in the house. So I stayed on with her and didn't get back home until just after one in the morning, which is unusual late for me. Now that was a Friday."

"Last Friday?"

"No, the week before."

"That would be the 14th, then?"

"Would it? It was Friday, anyhow. I'm sure of that."

"Or one o'clock in the morning on Saturday, eh?"

"Yes, that's what I mean," Mrs. Taylor agreed. "One o'clock on Saturday morning, it was."

To disarm any suspicion, The Counsellor stayed for a few minutes longer, chatting to Mrs. Taylor. His

176

chauffeur, meanwhile, had procured a new door-fastening for the garage and had screwed it into place.

"You can take the old padlock if you think it's worth while," said The Counsellor to the Inspector as they recrossed the road. "But I doubt if you'll get much off it in the way of finger-prints."

"I'll take it, anyhow," said Hartwell.

"Now, just one thing," said The Counsellor impressively as they got into the car and drove away. "Don't you go handing these specimens to any of your ordinary analytical chemists for examination. They'd most likely make an unholy mess of the job. Here's the address of the man you must send them to."

He took a slip of paper from his pocket and passed it to the Inspector, who glanced at it and stowed it in his notebook.

"You've got me a bit out of my depth with all this garage affair," Hartwell confessed rather sourly. "But I'll do as you say, sir, and hope for the best. All I can see in it so far is that Hawkstone's car was in that garage or calling at that garage an hour or so before it went afire at the Cross Roads; and it's on the cards that these petrol tins were picked up from this garage, if that mark on the floor amounts to anything. So far, that's plain enough. And now I come to think of it, there was that chloride of lime on the garage floor, and there was that white powder we found in the car débris, the stuff our chemist detected calcium and chlorine in. That means chloride of lime, one would think."

"Chloride of lime is a trade name. The chemical name is calcium hypochlorite," explained The Counsellor learnedly. "Calcium chloride is a different stuff altogether. But that's merely to be pedantic, Inspector, I admit. I'm quite with you in the matter of the two white powders. What you found in the car is just some traces of the garage stuff after it had been through the furnace. And that rounds off the evidence neatly and makes it practically a cert that Hawkstone's car was in that garage sometime between his leaving Barrington's house and the final flare-up at the Cross Roads."

"You don't think the Coroner's right after all, do you?" demanded the Inspector anxiously. "I mean, that it was really suicide? It begins to look almost like it, with this new set of facts. And yet, somehow, I can't see it so. Have you any notion, sir?"

"Between ourselves," retorted The Counsellor, "I'm not much struck by the Coroner; his brain-power. I'd want some better evidence before jumping to that conclusion, though it's always possible."

"And when do you expect to get any better evidence?" asked the Inspector in a tone tinged with despair. "Out of this analytical chemist of yours? What's he likely to do for us? I ought to know, seeing I'm giving him this work to do more or less on your say-so, sir."

"He'll tell you more or less what you know already; but he'll be able to go into the box and swear to it. He'll tell you the white powder's bleaching powder. He'll swear to the character of that fibre, whatever it is, hemp or what-not. He'll go through that bit of mud with a small-tooth comb, or at any rate with all the latest gadgets like ultra-violet lamps, microscopes, centrifuges, and Lord knows what, and tell you all about it. And he'll perhaps be able to tell us a thing or two about that oil. Finally, he may enlighten us about that little bit of black stuff I gave you. It looked like a fragment of sealing-wax, you remember. He'll tell us all about it in detail."

"That'll make a pretty bill," said the Inspector,

rather aghast. "We're not millionaires when the expense account comes in, you know."

"He's a friend of mine," said The Counsellor, soothingly. "I'll see he gives you special terms, if necessary. Don't you fret. This looks like a good newspaper case, and it'll do him good to be in it."

"Well, I'll do as you say, sir, and hope for the best. I'm a bit out of my depth in all this chemistry and stuff, I quite admit. But it didn't take me out of my depth to enquire into something else," he concluded with a slight recrudescence of self-satisfaction in his voice.

"What was that?" enquired The Counsellor.

"You remember how I identified Richard Barrington as the man who handed in that cipher ad. about Mrs. Campion offering to spend a week-end with Hawkstone? Well, I went to him, and put it to him straight . . ."

"The devil you did!" ejaculated The Counsellor in a curious tone which made the Inspector glance sharply at him. He suspected that The Counsellor's sense of humour had got the better of him.

"I did, devil or no," he retorted stubbornly. "And he told me that it was Mrs. Campion herself who asked him to do it for her, one night she was out on the spree with him. She wanted to get it into the paper as soon as possible, and it was past post-time. She'd forgotten about posting it till it was too late. His dentist shop is quite near the newspaper office; and she asked him to pass it over the counter in the morning as he was going to business. So that's that. And now we know what Mrs. Campion is. A poor liar, just as I always thought."

"That's a damned interesting bit of work," declared The Counsellor with unfeigned enthusiasm. "You've scored a winner there, Inspector, by the look of it.

Congratulations. And now, there's just one more thing I want you to do for me before we part. I've got an appointment with Sydney Barrington shortly, so I'll cut the cackle. Can you produce somebody—a thoroughly reliable man—who has leisure enough to spend a day wandering about the countryside with me and making a careful note of what I do, so that he could swear to it afterwards in the witness-box?"

"What *are* you going to do?" demanded the Inspector rather blankly.

"Dig up the county by instalments with a trowel," said The Counsellor impishly.

"Ah! Geologising, may be? Then I've got a friend, a retired schoolmaster, who'd suit you to the ground, for his hobby's geology. Or mineralogy, it may be. I never can remember which is which."

"He'll do, first-class," declared The Counsellor. "Just jot down his address in my notebook, will you? And fix it so that I can pick him up on his door-step to-morrow morning, please. About eleven o'clock, say. Right!"

"What are you going to hunt for?" demanded the Inspector in a tone of slight exasperation.

"Hunt for? Diatoms, may be. Foraminifera, perhaps. It just depends. Merely a scientific excursion, Inspector. I hadn't heard so much as the names of diatoms until a day or two ago. I mean to do better, though. Much better, once I get really enthralled with the subject. But I mustn't weary you with my hobbies. I know what a layman feels like when an expert gets started. I suffered from that in the graveyard the other day when young Mr. Barrington began to discant on fishing. Devastating, I assure you. Positively devastating. I spare you, in memory of that. Let's chat about something easier. Ships and shoes and sealing-wax, and cabbages and kings. Take your choice."

Chapter XIII

THE DIVORCE CASE

SYDNEY BARRINGTON's private room in his firm's office was a big high-ceilinged apartment, furnished soberly and with an eye to solid comfort. A tidily arranged desk and tiers of white-lettered deed-boxes on the walls were the only indications of its business character. As The Counsellor was ushered in, Barrington rose deliberately from his desk chair and greeted him with a pleasant smile in which The Counsellor seemed to detect something both quizzical and ironical. With a gesture, the solicitor invited The Counsellor to seat himself in a big well-padded, leather-covered armchair at one side of the hearth, and then busied himself with offering cigarettes and cigars to his guest, before seating himself in his turn in the corresponding chair on the opposite side of the hearth. He had taken a cigar from the box he offered to The Counsellor, and as he used his piercer, he examined his guest in silence for a moment or two, as though he were considering how to begin conversation. He had the rare knack of keeping silence without seeming discourteous. The Counsellor, determined not to make the first move, waited patiently for his host to begin. At last Barrington broke the silence with an unexpected remark, the apparent rudeness of which was tempered by the humorous twinkle in his eye.

"I hope you won't take offence, Mr. Brand; but don't

you think you've been a bit of a busybody in this Hawkstone affair?"

"No offence at all," declared The Counsellor blandly. "It's my chosen profession: being a busybody and interesting myself in other people's affairs. I'm not ashamed of it."

"So I imagined," said Barrington, smiling outright. "Otherwise I wouldn't have risked even a semblance of discourtesy, after asking you to call on me. I know all about how you bring comfort to Jilted Jennie, Puzzled Peter, and the rest of them. But these people, I believe, bring their little bothers to you voluntarily."

"They do," confirmed The Counsellor.

"And by so doing," Barrington continued, still smiling, "they give you a free hand to meddle with their affairs if you choose. But this Hawkstone business seems on a rather different footing."

"Not at all," The Counsellor pointed out. "I hadn't the least interest in it until the Coroner asked for my help. I was dragged into it without any seeking on my part."

"That's strictly true," conceded Barrington pleasantly. "Frobisher tells me that you gave him some assistance. My point, however, Mr. Brand, is that you didn't stop there. Forgive my saying it, but you've been poking your nose into the business on your own account. I've no special knowledge. But this is a gossipy town, and you're a well-known person. Naturally people discuss your doings. Some of that talk comes my length without my having to go out and seek it."

"Well?" said The Counsellor, wondering what all this might be leading up to.

Barrington leaned forward in his chair and held up his hand.

"I'll put my cards on the table," he said frankly.

"You, Mr. Brand, have gone into this business as an intellectual amusement. I think that's correct? I'm not finding fault, not in the least. *But*, your intellectual amusement may have consequences quite other than you expect, consequences which I'm sure you'd regret if you produced them. . . ."

"Sounds almost as if you were threatening me," commented The Counsellor with a quick frown.

"Threatening you?" said Barrington in obvious surprise. "My dear sir, such a thing never crossed my mind. What I was going to say, when you interrupted me, was simply this. There are things in the background of this affair which you don't know. And therefore you can't guess the amount of harm and distress you may cause to some quite innocent people by raking up things which are better left alone."

He paused for a moment, and The Counsellor noted that the initial half-chaffing tone had gone from the lawyer's voice and had been replaced by something much more serious.

"That being so," Barrington continued, "I've thought very carefully over the matter, which is a ticklish one. I've come to the conclusion that I'd better tell you a thing or two which may throw more light on the situation. I don't like doing it," he added, with convincing earnestness, "but I don't see any other way of managing the affair. It's a damned awkward position."

There was something very like a flash of temper in the last sentence and The Counsellor wondered if Barrington really felt altogether happy, now that he had made up his mind, as he said, to put his cards on the table.

"Very well. Go on," said The Counsellor, who knew when to be concise.

Barrington did not accept the invitation instanter. He fiddled with his cigar, as though dissatisfied with the way it was burning. Evidently he found some difficulty in putting his statement into words, and was glad of even a momentary respite.

"My trouble in this conversation," he said at last, "is that I'm forced to tell you something about the private affairs of another person, a person for whom I've a considerable friendliness. What I'm afraid of—I'm speaking quite bluntly, you see?—is that you'll merely take these fresh facts as so much extra grist to your intellectual recreation mill. You won't be content with what I give you. You'll insist on poking your nose further into the affair. And, as a result, out will come the very things I don't want made public. If they are made public, they're going to cause unnecessary pain to the person I mentioned."

"I have some decent feelings," said The Counsellor frostily; "though you may not credit it."

"That relieves my mind," said Barrington without a trace of irony in his tone. "On that basis, I'll go on."

The Counsellor made no attempt to amplify his statement, though Barrington seemed to expect something of the kind. After a slight but perceptible pause, the lawyer continued.

"I knew Mrs. Hawkstone when she was quite young, long before she was married—before Hawkstone appeared on the scene here at all, in fact. We were good friends, though I was some years older than she was; and at that age a few years count for more than they do later on in life. Don't go building up any romantic pictures on that foundation," he advised with a cautionary gesture. "There was nothing of that sort. Her father and mine were old friends, so naturally she and

184

I saw a good deal of each other. That was all. If I were to insist on the point any further, you'd probably say I was protesting too much. But the point's important, as you'll see."

He knocked the ash from his cigar before continuing. The Counsellor refused to help him by any interrogation.

"My father died and left me in charge of this firm," Barrington went on. "He'd been named as an executor under Mrs. Hawkstone's father's will; and I was put into his place. Soon after that, her father died; and I was one of the trustees for his estate. It wasn't a particularly big one, but the income was enough for her to live quietly on. Then Hawkstone turned up in this neighbourhood. He seemed a decent fellow, for all we knew; and he made himself so well liked that in a very short time there was an engagement."

The Counsellor had been watching for some betraying change in Barrington's voice when he reached this point in the narrative, but nothing of the kind was detectable. Barrington continued his story in the same tone, evidently striving to be clear and yet concise.

"As her trustee, my duty in these circumstances seemed clear enough. First and foremost, to safeguard her capital; secondly, to insist on his making the best marriage settlement that I could extract from him. That, from my point of view, as her lawyer and her friend, seemed to me an obvious precaution. Hawkstone was only a chance acquaintance, so far as I was concerned. It was she, in fact, who introduced him to me. And although he was quite open about his financial status, I meant to take no risks. I've seen too many sad cases arising through taking things for granted.

"Hawkstone, to do him justice, didn't raise the least objection. He was a lawyer himself by training, though his practical experience was small. Negligible would perhaps be a better adjective for it. He had a certain amount of capital, about £30,000; and I made him tie up £10,000 of it in his wife's name. That, as things went in those days, gave her about £500 a year in addition to her own little income, no matter what happened. I'm very glad now that I insisted on that. As you may know, he didn't turn out altogether satisfactory as a husband. But I'll come to that later."

"Go on," said The Counsellor as Barrington seemed to expect some interruption.

"I don't want to bore you with my own affairs," Barrington continued, "but it chanced that about that time I was rather hard pressed for a not inconsiderable sum of money."

The Counsellor had little difficulty in surmising how this had come about. Probably that rackety brother had got into some serious scrape and required money to extricate himself. It must have been a pretty serious business if the amount was big enough to cause embarrassment to Sydney Barrington's finances.

"Mrs. Hawkstone wished to remain in Fernhurst-Hordle after the marriage," Barrington continued. "Hawkstone had a very small practice in his native town. I doubt if he made more out of it than paid the rent of his premises. And I'm sure, after years of experience of him, that he wouldn't have expanded it as time went on. He wasn't in any way zealous. Far from it. And he didn't mix with the right people, from the expansion point of view. It was Mrs. Hawkstone who saw the possibilities of the situation. She knew about my broth . . . I mean, she knew about my temporary financial difficulties. She wanted to tether Hawkstone to Fernhurst, so that she wouldn't have to leave her friends here and go away amongst strangers. So she suggested that I should take Hawkstone into partnership, where there was a ready-made connection waiting for him."

"Very satisfactory," said The Counsellor, adding, as if by an afterthought, "on the surface."

"On the surface," repeated Barrington with a telling intonation. "Quite true. Had my hands been free, I'm not sure I'd have cared for Hawkstone as a partner. Even at that stage, I'd noticed a thing or two which didn't recommend him. But I was in a difficult place and couldn't be too particular. I agreed. But I made my own terms. He put £15,000 into the firm, and that I regarded as a kind of caution for his good behaviour. If he made himself a nuisance or behaved in such a way as to discredit the firm, that sum was to be forfeit. I didn't intend to enforce that except in some very grave situation, you understand? It was simply meant as a rein on his behaviour. And in the case of his death, that £15,000 was to be repaid to his wife as part of her separate estate."

"And you, as her trustee, would see that he didn't touch it?" interjected The Counsellor.

"Exactly. My idea was to safeguard her in every way I could," Barrington explained candidly. "Naturally, I had to safeguard myself as well. I don't profess to be a philanthropist any more than my neighbours. So to cover the risk of his death, I took out an insurance policy on his life for £15,000 with the Condor and Chiltern Insurance Company. At the same time, I suggested that he should insure himself with the same Company for £10,000 and make the policy payable to his wife if he predeceased her. He took my advice."

"Just a moment," interrupted The Counsellor. "Let's see if I've followed that. Suppose Hawkstone died. You had to pay Mrs. Hawkstone £15,000 out of the firm's assets or some equivalent in income. You got in £15,000 from that policy on his life. So over all you came out more or less square?"

"More or less," agreed Barrington.

"As to Mrs. Hawkstone," continued The Counsellor. "She had the £10,000 from her husband's life policy and also a claim on you for £15,000 from the firm's assets: total £25,000. That's right?"

"That's correct," Barrington confirmed.

"On the other hand, if Hawkstone fell into disgrace in some way and discredited the firm, without dying, Mrs. Hawkstone got nothing and you were £15,000 in pocket. At least, you didn't legally need to pay back his £15,000 to him or anyone else. That's so, isn't it?"

"That is so," Barrington admitted.

"In that case, Mrs. Hawkstone could have stuck to the £10,000 which he settled on her, you could have stuck to his £15,000, and he'd have been left more or less stranded?"

"More or less," Barrington confirmed, "unless she chose to let him live on her income."

"I see the state of affairs. Go on," said The Counsellor.

"I had to give you these facts," Barrington proceeded with a certain deliberation, "to put the matter in perspective. Now I come to the kernel of the business. You heard the evidence I gave at the inquest; I saw you there. That evidence was correct in every item, and it was quite sufficient to enable the jury to arrive at their verdict eventually. It wasn't the whole story. Perhaps you've guessed as much. But the rest of the story is the part which I do not wish to see dragged into publicity if that can be avoided. It throws no fresh light on the affair. But if it comes out, it'll be painful to Mrs. Hawkstone. There'll be a lot of ill-natured tittle-tattle, in a place like this; and there's been quite enough already, without adding more to it. That's what I particularly wish to avert, for Mrs. Hawkstone's sake. If you persist in these enquiries of yours, Mr. Brand, that gossip will start and spread. That's why I decided to take the bull by the horns and tell you the facts. When you've heard the whole story, there'll be no need for you to pursue certain lines of enquiry which are sure to set people talking. You'll have the facts in your possession without having to go and look for them. You see my position?"

"I understand it," said The Counsellor noncommittally.

Barrington hitched himself forward in his chair as though to emphasise that they were speaking confidentially.

"I'd better begin with an analogy," he said. "Suppose you put a jar on one pan of a balance and a heavier weight into the other pan. Then you begin to drip water, drop by drop, into the jar. You see no noticeable result for a while. But suddenly, with the addition of one final drop, the whole beam of the balance swings over. That last drop of water is no different from the rest. It's just because all its predecessors have each exerted its weight as it dripped into the jar that this final droplet turns the scale. Nothing to do with any special characteristics of the last drop."

"The last straw that breaks the camel's back?" condensed The Counsellor.

"Yes, that's what I mean," Barrington agreed without betraying any annoyance. "Now, you're something of a psychologist, Mr. Brand, or you wouldn't have taken up this Counsellor business. Substitute for my drops of water a series of little incidents, each almost negligible in itself, but each contributing to a cumulative effect. The last of these incidents may be no different from the rest, and yet, because of all its predecessors, it produces a decisive effect. It is, as you say, the last straw, even if it's only a straw. Have another cigarette?"

He passed the box across to The Counsellor, who helped himself.

"The Hawkstone marriage wasn't a success," Barrington continued. "Hawkstone, as I soon discovered, was a sordid little Don Juan of the suburban type. He'd secured a wife who was much better than he deserved: clever, good-looking above the average and with plenty of character. You've seen her at the inquest, and you must have formed your opinion of her from what you saw there. Something rather uncommon, obviously. But Hawkstone didn't find her enough, it seems. They'd hardly got back from the honeymoon before I found he was running about after cheap conquests: shop-girls, typists, anything that would look at him twice. He used to pick them up in tea-shops or at the pictures; and I suppose some of them were faintly flattered by his higher social status. How do I know all this? Because I've had him watched by a private enquiry agent for a good while back."

"Indeed?" interjected The Counsellor, suddenly interested.

"Yes, I'm coming to that," Barrington continued with the faint suggestion of a rasp in his voice. "He was an insensitive beast himself and he credited other people with an equal thickness of skin. As a result, Mrs. Hawkstone eventually began to surmise what sort of man she'd married. The discovery came gradually, and by the time she was quite sure about the state of affairs, I suppose she had got accustomed to the idea, in a way. I mean, it wasn't a case of the knowledge coming on her like a bolt from the blue. There was some trouble, though, and I was called in to mediate between them as best I could. Hawkstone was a poor creature under his thick skin. When he found he was detected, he promised reform and amendment—very profusely. That sort of thing was to stop, once and for all. It was a most uncomfortable interview for me, as you can imagine; and it must have been even more uncomfortable for her. By that time, the gilt was off the gingerbread, so far as she was concerned; and she agreed to a formal reconciliation, not because she particularly wanted to have him back, but merely because it seemed the simplest way out of an unpleasant affair. . . ."

Barrington broke off for a moment and stared at the end of his cigar as if it were some curio which he had just picked up.

"Well, of course, a man of that sort never does reform," he continued. "She soon found that he was up to his tricks again. He was quite hopeless, and a liar into the bargain. I didn't discuss the business with her, naturally. But from the outside it looked as if she were simply shrugging her shoulders, rather contemptuously, over his peccadilloes and not paying much attention to them so long as he didn't thrust them directly under her eyes. But it seems that all the time, each fresh indiscretion of his was adding its little weight to the balance-pan in her mind. No outward sign of the effect, but a steady mounting up of the total, one drop after another. And, finally, there came this affair with that woman Campion. It was no different from a dozen that had gone before it, but it turned the scale, suddenly. Mrs. Hawkstone had had enough."

"I begin to see your drift," The Counsellor confessed. "This is what was kept back at the inquest?"

"Of course it was kept back, as far as possible,"

Barrington admitted, quite candidly. "And having kept it back, naturally we don't want it to come out now. It can do no good. And Mrs. Hawkstone has no desire to see her private affairs chattered about by every loose-lipped gossip in town. It could have been kept completely out if it hadn't been for your efforts, Mr. Brand. You dug up the history of Hawkstone's car that evening; that dragged the Campion woman into the limelight; and our hands were forced, up to a point. We could not keep the whole affair dark after you'd intervened; but we did what we could to minimise the damage."

"We?" queried The Counsellor.

"Mrs. Hawkstone and I," Barrington elucidated. "She's consulted me in the later stages of the business —not as a lawyer, of course, but merely as an old friend."

"Of course," agreed The Counsellor, drily. "She could hardly make a professional matter of it when you were her husband's partner."

"To cut a long story short," Barrington went on, "Mrs. Hawkstone decided to divorce her husband, using the Campion woman as co-respondent. I can't say I was sorry when I heard her decision. It seemed overdue, if anything. There's a certain petty humiliation in a husband's unfaithfulness, even when his wife has ceased to care anything for him. Personally, I had no scruples in the matter; and I was growing a little tired myself of his manner of living. It did the firm no good, to put it moderately. I'd made up my own mind quite definitely that when this divorce case came on, I was going to get rid of the fellow—clear him out of the firm under our agreement."

"I see. That gave you an independent motive for going into the matter," interjected The Counsellor shrewdly. "You weren't in charge of Mrs. Hawkstone's interests; but that didn't hinder you from looking after your own. That's it, isn't it?"

"Exactly." Barrington agreed, without a smile. "And so I was able to import myself into the business without acting as Mrs. Hawkstone's client. I needn't go into details. My brother was of some assistance to us in various ways. He had no great difficulty in scraping an acquaintance with the woman Campion and finding out one or two things which we might have missed without his help. He put us on to these cipher advertisements which Hawkstone and the woman Campion used in some of their communications. You know about them?"

The Counsellor nodded without explaining further. It was no business of his to give information.

"Yes," continued Barrington. "You got to know about them, I believe. That was a blunder of my brother, made off his own bat without consulting me. At the time, he thought he was making a rather clever stroke by sending these advertisements in to your Problem Department. He's inclined to be impulsive, and he didn't appreciate that by doing what he did he was bringing you dangerously near to the divorce affair—the very thing which we wanted to keep quiet, if possible. But for that bright idea of his, I doubt if you and your friend Inspector Hartwell would have guessed exactly what the state of affairs was, even after you'd run down the Campion woman by tracking Hawkstone's car."

"That's quite likely," conceded The Counsellor. "But go on."

"Through my brother," Barrington continued, "we'd picked up a certain amount of information about Campion's affairs. I knew he was going to take this trip to America. It seemed hardly fair to him to let him go off out of the country unwarned about what was coming. It was a rather awkward position, for I didn't care about asking him to come and see me at my office. . . ."

"Hawkstone might have run into him?" suggested The Counsellor.

"Exactly. So I arranged another meeting-place. An old servant of mine is married. I arranged that she and her husband should go out for the evening of the 11th and leave me in charge of their house; and I rang up Campion and asked him to meet me there next night, alleging some business or other which would bring him without fail. Naturally I did not give him details over the phone. He kept the appointment, and I told him plainly what was in the wind. At first he refused to believe me. However, I showed him the cipher advertisements. My brother's interested in that sort of thing and had explained to me the system of the cipher. Campion is a puzzle-maniac—as my brother had discovered from Mrs. Campion—so he saw the thing at once when I showed it to him. That convinced him, or did more than anything else to convince him. He was frantic when he finally realised what had been going on. A violent man, that, I'm afraid. I was surprised at the bitterness of the jealousy he showed to a stranger like myself. In fact, I had considerable difficulty in preventing him from going straight home and accusing his wife, there and then, which might not have suited our plans. I staved that off by asking him if he had any means of checking his own movements in the past, so as to see how his absences from home fitted in with the facts, so far as we had ascertained them, about the association between Hawkstone and Mrs. Campion."

"What night did you meet him?" demanded The Counsellor.

"On the night of Wednesday, April 12th," Barrington explained. "But as I was saying, when you interrupted, I asked Campion then if he had any diary, or a pocket-book showing his engagements: anything which would let us verify his movements and so prove that he had been out of town or out of the house in the evening at certain crucial times. Fortunately, it turned out that he kept a diary, a fairly full one. So full, in fact, that he deemed it safest to keep it in cipher—the rail-fence cipher, he called it—so that no one would be much the wiser if they happened to pick up the volume by accident. From which I inferred that Campion, too, might have his own little amusements, despite his furious jealousy where his wife was concerned. Anyhow, I arranged with him that he was to bring this precious diary back to my old servant's house the next night; and I arranged with her that the place was again to be left to me. I'm afraid I made a slip in that business. I'd let out to Campion my real name, and he showed that he knew I was Hawkstone's partner. It made him suspicious, for he was very suspicious by nature, I found. However, I managed to quieten him as best I could. Then he wanted to arrange the date of our next meeting. He proposed to come to my own house on Friday night, the 14th. I wanted to get that side of the unpleasant business over as quickly as possible, so I refused and told him I couldn't have him about my own house while this sort of thing was in the wind. My position was already delicate enough without that. Besides, I explained to him, Hawkstone was coming to see me late in the evening and I certainly didn't want to run any risks of them meeting on my doorstep or inside. Finally, he seemed to fall in with my scheme, and he turned up the next evening at my ex-maid's house with his diary. I'd got my brother to post me about this rail-fence cipher, so that I could check the actual diary without having to depend on Campion's interpretation of his gibberish. One has to take precautions in a matter of that sort, as you can guess."

"Obviously," said The Counsellor. "I remember the rail-fence system. It wouldn't give you much trouble."

"It didn't," said Barrington with a smile. "A childish affair, once it's explained; though I don't say I'd have unravelled it if I hadn't the key. However, that's not to the point. I went over the necessary dates with Campion and he showed me enough of his entries to enable me to check the state of things. Undoubtedly she had been using his absences from town to play the fool with Hawkstone. When Campion realised that, I had considerable difficulty in calming him down. He wanted to go straight home and speak his mind to his wife on the subject, just as a beginning. I talked to him for a long while before I could persuade him that his best course was to keep a quiet tongue until we had all our evidence complete and ready for use. He saw it at last; but he left me in a state of anger which made me wonder if he would be able to meet his wife without giving the show away."

"When did he leave you?" interjected The Counsellor in an indifferent tone.

"He came fairly late, after my old servants had gone to bed. They're early birds. Say about 11 p.m. And he went off again shortly after midnight, I should say. I didn't note the time, of course."

"Nothing in it, anyway," The Counsellor decided, after a moment's pause for reflection. "Go on."

"Next night, I'd arranged for Hawkstone to come

and see me. It was hardly the kind of thing I wanted to discuss at our office, with clerks about the place and the chance of high words which might have been overheard. So I asked him to come to my house. You heard my evidence at the inquest. It was all perfectly true, but naturally I suppressed the pending divorce case affair, on Mrs. Hawkstone's account. It added nothing that the jury needed to know, so far as their verdict was concerned. I did say that Hawkstone told me Campion was furiously jealous by nature and that Hawkstone thought he'd grown suspicious of the intrigue with his wife. That's quite correct. Whether he had any grounds for it or not, Hawkstone was undoubtedly perturbed about Campion. He told me so, before I even mentioned the divorce affair. I think he was afraid that the Campion woman, after that row at Ranger's Copse, might get careless and say something which would put her husband on the alert. And I have a notion, too, that she had been dropping hints about her husband suspecting something already. Her type *would* do that, with the idea of making herself interesting and raising her value. 'See what I'm risking for you, with a jealous husband like that at my heels.' That sort of thing."

"Something in that, perhaps," The Counsellor admitted. "How did Hawkstone react when you sprang the divorce affair on him?"

"Lost his nerve completely," said Barrington, grimly. "I don't know that the threatened divorce alone would have shaken him up so badly. He wasn't the kind of man to feel much shame or contrition or whatever you choose to call it. But I coupled the divorce affair with our partnership agreement, and I made no bones about the fact that I intended to kick him out as soon as the divorce case came into the public eye. He had enough wit to see what that meant to him financially, quite apart from the moral question. He didn't exactly go on his knees to me; but short of that he did everything he could do to turn me from my decision. But once my mind's made up, I don't turn. And I'd had long enough to think the thing out in all its bearings. I told him so. He's dead now, so there's no use telling you all his pleadings and promises of reform. They didn't move me in the slightest. He was a miserable creature, really. In the end, he was so unnerved that I had to give him a stiff drink to pull him together, though to my mind he'd had enough on board already. Perhaps I wasn't in the best mood for compassion. As I mentioned at the inquest, I was feeling far from well that evening; pretty sick, in fact, with my head swimming a bit. So possibly I was more brutal than I need have been. Not that he deserved anything better."

"The Coroner thinks he went off and committed suicide," said The Counsellor in a tone which showed neither assent nor dissent.

"Considering his state of mind when he left me, I shouldn't be surprised if he did," said Barrington in a bitter tone. "He was a weakling, and quite probably that was the easy road for him out of his difficulties. If he did commit suicide, I don't feel it on my conscience."

The Counsellor, examining the frowning countenance before him, felt he could well believe that.

"Campion's missing," he said. "I suppose you know that?"

"What?"

If Barrington's surprise was not genuine, it was an extremely clever piece of acting.

"Missing, you say?" he continued. "He's gone to America, of course."

"No, he hasn't," retorted The Counsellor. "He's just plain missing. Disappeared, vanished, *spurlos versenkt* and left not a rack behind. Trust me. I've gone into the matter."

Barrington seemed to think hard for a few seconds before he spoke again.

"That alters the case," he said at last, speaking in a dubious tone, as though he could not quite find his bearings. "If your tale's true, then I'm not quite so certain as I was about siding with the Coroner."

"You mean Campion murdered him?"

"Or he murdered Campion and disappeared afterwards," Barrington mused, as though thinking aloud. "You didn't see the remains of the body they took from that car? No? I did. I was specially careful in my evidence at the inquest, and I'm glad now that I was careful. No one could have recognised any particular person in these remains. All one had to go by was the probable height of the man when he was alive. And Campion and Hawkstone were just about the same height and the same build. I wonder . . ."

He fell silent and seemed to be turning the problem over in his mind.

"Didn't you say you'd blurted out to Campion that Hawkstone was coming to see you on that Friday night?" demanded The Counsellor, who had little patience with other people's reveries.

"That is so," Barrington confirmed in an absent-minded tone, as if his mind were elsewhere, perhaps engaged on weighing his two hypotheses against one another.

"Well, I must be going," said The Counsellor, rising from his seat. "Thanks for telling me all this."

Barrington suddenly waked up, apparently.

"You'll remember why I told you it?" he questioned,

rather anxiously. "I don't want Mrs. Hawkstone to be worried by this affair coming to light. You won't go and question her about it or let her know that you've got hold of it? That was more or less understood, you know, before I said anything."

"I have some decency," said The Counsellor curtly. "Besides, I don't think it throws much light on the affair, really. You gave the main facts at the inquest. Certainly I'm not going to bother Mrs. Hawkstone with questions. Make your mind easy about that."

"Thank goodness!" Barrington said with a faint but quite audible sigh of relief. "I took a risk in telling you anything at all. But I was pretty sure I'd sized you up accurately and that you wouldn't make it any more difficult for her, once you saw how things stood. I don't want her to be badgered with questions. She's had enough to bear already without that."

"That's all right," said The Counsellor awkwardly. "And now, if you've no more to tell me, I'll go."

A few minutes later, The Counsellor was in a public call office, ringing up Inspector Hartwell to make a second appointment for that afternoon.

Chapter XIV

THE DIARY

THE COUNSELLOR had no objection to weighing up moral problems when they were put before him by his clients; but he disliked them when they came any nearer home. As he walked down the steps of Barrington's office, he mused over the one which the solicitor had set him by implication.

"After what I said, I can't go and put questions to Mrs. Hawkstone. That's that. But if I pass Barrington's tale on to the Inspector, then he'll go and question her. Which is probably worse than if I did it myself, so far as her feelings go. And if I simply sit tight on this information, I may be impeding justice by my inertia. Curse that man Barrington! He's passed the news to me, so he can always say that he didn't conceal it. And by doing so, he's landed me with the responsibility for it, whether I like it or not."

A way out of the apparent impasse presented itself to his mind.

"I can always question Mrs. Campion about her husband's affairs. She consulted me about them. And by working that line, I can ask to see this diary, if he hasn't taken it with him. It might throw some light on things. In any case, it'll confirm Barrington's tale, if I can lay hands on it. Or disprove his yarn, perhaps. I don't need to tell Campion's wife what the entries mean, if they happen to be awkward. She'll never be able to read them herself, if they're in cipher. It's worth trying, anyhow. There's seems nothing else I can do."

He gave his chauffeur the address in Savernake Park, where he was lucky enough to find Mrs. Campion at home.

"Oh, it's you, is it?" she greeted him when she came to the door. "You haven't brought that Inspector with you, have you? Well, I am glad! I can't stand that man, with his continual questions. Come in, please. You'll just have to take me as you find me," she concluded with her characteristic feeble titter.

"I haven't been able to find out anything yet about Mr. Campion," The Counsellor confessed frankly. "Have you had any news?"

"Nothing," Lorna Campion said, with a slight down-twitching of her mouth corners. "I'm getting worried about Percy, really. I was hoping you'd brought something fresh about him when I saw you on the doorstep."

"He didn't go aboard the *Meteoric*," The Counsellor informed her. "I've ascertained that quite definitely. And he doesn't seem to have paid any of the visits in Liverpool that he meant to make. It's queer."

"It is, indeed," Lorna agreed. "It's worrying, too, for me. I just don't know what to make of it. Percy may have had his faults, like most men, but he's never done anything of this sort before. You can't do anything more, can you, Mr. Brand?"

"There's just a chance," The Counsellor answered slowly, as if he thought the chance a poor one. "Did your husband keep a diary or a note of his engagements or anything that might give us a hint?"

"He kept a diary," she admitted grudgingly, "but it wouldn't be much good to you even if you got it. He kept it in some queer sort of cipher stuff of his own. Just one of his little peculiarities, it was. He was always a bit of a puzzle-fan, you know, Mr. Brand." She tittered half-apologetically.

"I'm something of a puzzle-fancier myself," said The Counsellor with an engaging smile, "so don't be too sure I couldn't make it out if I had a look at it. Could you find it, do you think? Or has he taken it with him?"

"He keeps it here," Lorna explained, stepping over to a small cupboard in the wall and opening the door as she spoke. "All of it. Don't you wonder at any man having the patience to write as much gibberish as that, Mr. Brand?"

"All of it" seemed to mean a number of uniform volumes. The Counsellor moved to her side and pulled down the final one of the series: a fat quarto loose-leaf.

"Let's see," he commented as he opened it. "Yes, this is the most recent one. Right up to date. Last entry labelled 13/4/39. One would have thought he'd take it with him on his travels, to write up as he went along. Most likely he bought a fresh volume to take with him, though. When he got back, he could transfer the leaves into this case."

"Likely enough," agreed Lorna. "But just look at it, Mr. Brand. You'll never make head or tail of stuff like that. Welsh is plain English compared to it, if you see what I mean. The dates are the only thing in it that make sense. Look at that, there," she ended, putting her finger on one entry:

"11/4/39. OfcauuliieWxoLdpneBoaduenCPoerm Brigoslctraigpt 3 p W d t 2 hp tnto cleeigihonfiessa Vstdal wt Secr r sn J n adah nfo Sarntnoiiomknap9omea1SesoS TSaavnnwtLra."

"Seems a bit cock-eyed, doesn't it?" said The Counsellor with a slightly dismayed expression, assumed for her benefit. "Still, one never knows. It might be simple, after all, once one gets down to it. Mustn't neglect any chance."

Lorna Campion seemed to have little interest in the diary problem.

"About Percy," she said, ignoring The Counsellor's remarks. "Could he have got into some accident, do you think? Got knocked down by a motor, or something like that? You know how easy these things happen, nowadays, Mr. Brand. He might have been knocked unconscious and taken to hospital and perhaps they haven't troubled to find out who he is or to let me know about it. That seems about the only thing that would account for it."

The Counsellor shook his head regretfully.

"I'm afraid it's not that," he said kindly. "The Liverpool hospitals have been tried, and they know nothing about him. He may, of course, have met with an accident before reaching Liverpool; but if anything had happened to him here in Fernhurst, we'd have got news of it at once. They'd have rung you up as soon as his identity was discovered."

Up to that point, Mrs. Campion had evidently refused to allow herself to look on the darker possibilities of the case; but suddenly she seemed to find it impossible to blind herself any longer.

"You mean he's disappeared?" she asked incredulously. "Gone off somewhere without leaving any word?"

"I'm afraid it looks rather like it," The Counsellor had to admit. "We've no news of him, of any sort, since he left here."

"Well, I just don't understand it," said Lorna Campion tonelessly, letting her hands drop to her sides as she spoke. "It just can't be. You've made some mistake, I'm sure of that. Percy was on business, this trip; and there's nobody more conscientious in business than he is, nobody. I know that. He'd never go gallivanting off on his own and miss the liner at Liverpool. It's not his style at all, that, Mr. Brand. And I *know* he hasn't been embezzling or anything of that sort. Percy'd never do a dishonest thing, with the firm trusting him the way they did. He had his faults, had Percy, but they weren't that sort of fault. He was a good, straight man where business was concerned. I simply don't believe all this, Mr. Brand," she ended with a flash of anger. "You're just trying to frighten me. Though why you'd want to be so cruel, I can't think."

"I'm not trying to frighten you," declared The Counsellor in a tone so convincing that she seemed at last to take the matter seriously.

When she perceived that he was in earnest, her reaction to the idea was characteristic enough.

"But what am I to do, then?" she asked, half-whimpering. "The firm won't go on paying his salary if he's gone off on his own hook. I'll be left stranded for money; and there's the house-rent to pay and the instalments on the vacuum-cleaner. He was to have been back quite soon, and now if he doesn't turn up there'll be no cash. It'll mean my going back and being a typ— I mean a secretary, again. That is, if I can get a job, nowadays. But it can't come to that. It just *can't.*"

The Counsellor thought it kindest to divert her attention for a moment.

"Did you notice anything out of the way in his manner before he left?" he enquired. "Did he seem worried or anything like that?"

Lorna Campion knitted her brows while she considered this question, which evidently suggested something she had overlooked.

"Well, now you come to mention it," she answered slowly, "I do call to mind that he seemed a bit off colour somehow, just before he left. Sulky and snappy-like, in a way, which wasn't his usual. I said something about it; told him he wasn't his usual self and asked if he'd got a headache or if he'd eaten something that didn't agree with him. He just put me off and said he'd got a touch of neuralgia, like he sometimes used to have now and again; so I thought no more about it. But now you mention it, I certainly do remember that he was different from his usual. But if he's gone off like that and left me in a fix, I'll never forgive him. I don't know what I'll do. I do not, indeed. I don't want to go back to work in an office, taking dictation and copying letters. I had enough of that, before. But it can't come to that. It just can't."

The Counsellor did not need much cynicism to notice that these lamentations sounded more genuine than what had gone before; and his sympathy declined markedly.

"Well, I'll see if there's any help in this diary," he said, picking up the volume from the table, where he had placed it. "If I find anything, I'll let you know. And, of course, I'll let you have the book back, in any case."

"You're not staying in Fernhurst to-night, I suppose," Lorna Campion said fishingly as she accompanied him to the door. "I haven't the heart to go to a show alone, somehow. And it'll be so dreary, sitting about in the house and thinking what's come to Percy. Nobody seems to drop in and try to cheer me up these days. It's in times like these that one gets to know what people really are. You'd hardly believe it, Mr. Brand, but since that inquest I've been regularly oysterised."

For a second or two The Counsellor had to puzzle

before he succeeded in interpreting the last word into "ostracised." He had no intention of staying in Fern-hurst-Hordle for the evening; and he made that clear to her as tactfully as he could, while taking his leave. When he got back into his car, he gave his chauffeur orders. Then he pulled a scribbling-tablet from one of the door-pockets, took out a pencil, and opened Campion's diary. The rail-fence cipher, he knew, was a simple affair for both ciphering and deciphering. To encipher a message, one wrote down its first letter; then put the second letter in a line below, then wrote the third letter alongside the first one, the fourth letter in the second line, the fifth on the top line again, and so on to the end. Then one wrote the letters of the top line one after another till one reached the end of them; and thereafter one added the letters of the second line in their order. That was all. To decipher the message, one broke off the series of letters in the message in the middle and then treated the first half as the top line section and the second half as the lower line section. This done, one could read the message in a zigzag.

"Now, let's see," he said to himself. "It was on the 11th that Barrington said he rang Campion up for the first time. Let's see if Campion refers to that in his diary entry made that night."

He counted the number of letters in the entry, finding 136 in all. Each "line" must therefore contain 68 letters; so the "top line" must begin with "Ofcau..." etc., and end with "... gihon"; whilst the "lower line" must begin with "fiessa..." and end with "... wtLra." He began writing the letters as indicated by this:

        O f c a u u l i i e W x o L d . . .
          f i e s s a V s t d a l w t . . .

This was enough to show him that he had got on the

right track, for the message obviously began: "Office as usual. Visited Waxlow, Ltd. . . ." The Counsellor scribbled industriously and soon had deciphered the whole entry:

"11/4/39. Office as usual. Visited Waxlow, Ltd., Spencer Bros., and June and Co. Phone from Barrington, solicitor, making appt. 9.30 p.m. Wed. at 12 Shepstone St. To Scala in evening with Lorna."

The visits were evidently trade calls, The Counsellor inferred. But the important fact was that Barrington's tale was here confirmed up to the hilt by unimpeachable evidence. When he wrote that entry, Campion could have had no idea of what was coming. And the entry was obviously genuine, since the handwritings in each entry different slightly, but unmistakably, from each other, showing that they had been written at different times, as in any diary.

The Counsellor took the next entry and deciphered it in turn, with the following result:

"12/4/39. Saw S. Barrington, 9.30 p.m. Informed me Mrs. Hawkstone bringing divorce action, Lorna as co-respondent. Showed me documentary evidence, very black, including arrangement for her to spend week-end with H. as soon as I leave for Liverpool. Can hardly believe it. B. asked me to check some dates from this diary. Cancelled our engagement with Stevens to-morrow night. Meeting B. instead. Cannot believe Lorna would do such things. B. warned me against letting her suspect I know. Must keep stiff upper lip and not show anything. If that swine H. has been playing tricks with her, I'll make him smart for it. Lorna is too easy with men, but I've always trusted her not to go whole hog. Cannot believe it. If true, will make him pay for what he's done, up to hilt. He'll be sorry before I've finished with him. Cannot concentrate my ideas, so knocked out by news."

The ultimate entry in the diary betrayed how further knowledge affected the writer:

"13/4/39. Saw B. again to-night. Evidence seems conclusive. Never dreamed Lorna would have done it. Can hardly swallow it yet, in spite of everything. B. says divorce case certain. Mrs. H. not going to change her mind. Meanwhile, I'll be away in the States for some weeks, leaving H. with free hand to do what he likes with Lorna. The very thought drives me frantic. And the whole tale will be dragged out in Court, every detail. Our office staff will be reading all the evidence in the local papers and grinning at me behind my back. Damnable. And then I'd have to choose whether to divorce Lorna myself or not. Can't bear the idea of losing her. Don't blame her as much as H. All right, if men would only leave her alone. But to think of her like that. Damnable affair. If H. were out of the way, it wouldn't be so bad. I could bear it better then, I think. Why can't a man like that be struck dead? That would clear up everything. No divorce case then. No fear of his getting round Lorna if I did forgive her. I'd have an easy mind then. And she'd have got a lesson she wouldn't forget. But things don't happen so by accident. Why can't a car run over him and . . . I'd like to see him smashed up and lingering in hospital for a day or two before he petered out. Best thing for him, swine that he is. 'Something lingering, with boiling oil in it,' as it says in *The Mikado*. That would really fit the case. Must remember B.'s warning and not show anything to Lorna. But to go off to the States and leave her with him to do as he likes with. Just the sort of beast who'd chuck her over as soon as trouble comes, I expect, from what B. told me. Damn him."

The Counsellor closed the diary and replaced his scribbling pad in the door pocket.

"Now, if I show that to Hartwell," he ruminated, "the first thing he'll do will be to post off and question Mrs. Hawkstone about this divorce affair. Can't have that, if I can avert it. I more or less promised Barrington not to drag her in on the strength of what he told me. So I'll need to keep my thumb on this diary for the time being. Bit of a responsibility to take. Still, I'll risk it. Then another point. Campion's vanished, and wherever he's gone to, he must have had a fair amount of cash in his possession when he went, in view of this U.S.A. trip. So either he *or somebody else* has that cash now and can pay his way without going to his bank. Might serve to keep the Inspector busy in the meanwhile. Anything else? Oh, yes, the motor oil; he can tackle that easier than I could. And he'll be able to tell me if he's fixed things up with his geologist pal for to-morrow. And I'd better enquire about that thief, just to be on the safe side. H'm! Quite a lot of subjects for a chatty conversation."

The Counsellor's telephone call had forewarned Hartwell, and he was waiting when the car arrived at the police station.

"I've fixed things with that ex-schoolmaster," he explained to The Counsellor. "He'll be waiting for you to-morrow morning, as you wanted. Dunbar's his name. Here's his address; I've written it down."

He handed over a slip of paper which The Counsellor placed in his pocket-book.

"Right! Thanks for troubling," he said in acknowledgment. "Anything fresh?"

"Not since I saw you an hour or two ago," said Hartwell, rather sulkily. "What do you expect?"

"Nothing much," said The Counsellor ambiguously. "But I've had a bright thought or two. For instance, could you find out how much cash Campion had in his possession when he vanished? He must have some dibs, going on a journey like that. The bank might tell you; they certainly wouldn't tell me."

"We have our methods," admitted the Inspector grudgingly.

"Try 'em out, then," advised The Counsellor. "Somebody must have that money. Perhaps it's traceable. Probably not. Still, I'd have a dash at it if I were you. And now the next article. Are you really good thief-catchers in this part of the country? Remember telling me about some practitioner who got away with a lot of odds and ends—piping and what not—from some house in your jurisdiction? Did you ever lay hands on him, for example?"

"No, not yet," admitted the Inspector, rather crossly.

"Still on the job, eh? Never drop a case, like the C.I.D. Well, just a word in your ear. In your shoes, I'd have another look over the premises and take samples from the broken ends of all the pipes where they were cut off. Straight tip for you, that. You see, before long you'll be educated up to employing my friend the micro-chemist, on jobs of that sort. Nothing like beginning early. I'm serious," he added with a complete change of tone.

"Oh, well, if you're *serious*," said the Inspector, "I'll

see about it. But we've no time to waste over futilities, remember."

"Dead serious," declared The Counsellor. "Another long shot, but I think it should be worth the bother eventually. And now there's another thing. You remember that sample of oil we took from the garage floor this morning? Well, I want other samples for comparison with it. Could you get them without calling out the town-crier to help you? On the strict Q.T., I mean."

"I might," said the Inspector, rather doubtfully. "But why don't you get them yourself? Any garage would give you oil samples."

"Because I want rather special ones," explained The Counsellor. "I want them from the crank-cases of cars belonging to the following people: Mrs. Campion, the Coroner, the two Barringtons, Miss Glenarm, Dr. Wyndcliffe, and . . . what's his name? . . . Jelf. Friend of the Barringtons, if I remember. That should identify him for you. And, further, I want to know the date on which each crank-case was last drained and refilled with fresh oil. The owner's garage people ought to be able to tell you that in each case easily enough."

"I dare say," admitted the Inspector unenthusiastically. "Anything else, while you're about it, sir?"

"An easy one. Which of these cars has an oil-drip from the crank-case. You'll get that, I expect, by looking at the saw-dust tray or the garage floor in each case, if you can make some excuse for visiting."

"Can't you give me some notion of what you're after, sir?" demanded the Inspector. "I'm taking a bit of responsibility, spending time over all these notions of yours. Have you really got an idea at the back of your mind?"

"Heaps of 'em," said The Counsellor flippantly.

"Question is, which of 'em is right. One is, I'll guarantee that. Just you take me on trust for a few days more, and then I'll give you something that'll make Frobisher blink, anyhow. And probably more besides. Much more. Look here, Inspector. I'll lay you £1,000 to a bob that you'll be satisfied with what I give you. Take it?"

"I will!" said Hartwell emphatically. "And we'll have it in writing, if you please."

"Done, then!" said The Counsellor, much to the amazement of the Inspector, who had regarded the offer as a mere rhetorical flourish. "I'll put it in writing now," he added, pulling out his notebook and scribbling duplicate statements of the bet. "Here's your copy, just in case you don't trust me. And if I win, remember, I'm going to collect that bob without fail. I mean to put it in my museum."

He watched the Inspector stowing the paper in his pocket and then continued:

"Now, here's something else for you. It came to me in the form of Information Received—as you people phrase it—and to some extent I'm not a free agent in the matter. But I don't feel comfortable, sitting on it. So I pass it to you to make what you like out of it. Only, don't come back asking me questions. Then you'll be told no lies. See? Well, this is how it is. There's a married couple living at 12 Shepstone Street. Recently, as a favour, they were asked to go out for the evening and leave their house—and the coast—clear for somebody else. All I want to know is: on what dates did this happen. I'm just checking some points. Likely enough there's nothing in it. Anyhow, I leave you to make what you can out of it; and I'd be glad to know the dates, if you can discover them."

"These African witch-doctors could take twenty yards and a beating from you, Mr. Brand, when it comes to mystery-mongering," said the Inspector in a tone showing no admiration for this aptitude. "No use asking questions? From you, I mean. No? Well, I've no powers to extract information from you if you won't give it. But I wish I had."

Chapter XV

FAIR EXCHANGE

THREE days later, The Counsellor had secured sufficient data for his next move. Then, by a judicious use of persuasion, flattery, veiled threats, cajolery and bluff, he succeeded in making the trustees of the Earlswood estate so uneasy about their position that they were prepared, though very reluctantly, to fall in with the proposal which he made to them. The Coroner proved unexpectedly pliable, owing to his belief that the results would discredit the police; and having obtained his agreement, The Counsellor had no scruples in using Frobisher's official position as an argument to bring the others into line. Finally, it was agreed that the investigation should be carried out in presence of Frobisher, Sydney Barrington, Wyndcliffe and Hartwell, who were already familiar with the state of affairs in the Earlswood vault. The Counsellor, who could not resist playing the mystery-man, refused to say beforehand what he proposed to do, beyond assuring them that it entailed neither desecration nor illegality.

He had arranged to pick up the Inspector *en route* to the cemetery, and Hartwell, waiting for him at the door of the police station, was surprised to see a second car pull up behind The Counsellor's.

"What's all this about?" demanded the Inspector when he had taken his seat beside The Counsellor. "You've kept me more in the dark than I care about, sir. I suppose you know you can't do anything that counts as exhumation unless you've got a special permit from the Home Secretary? If you begin anything of that sort, I shall have to forbid it."

"Right!" said The Counsellor. "To exhume means to dig out or to unearth. Looked it up in the dictionary myself, just to be on the safe side. Now the entrance to that vault isn't covered in yet, under Earlswood's will; so there'll be no digging out there. And there's no earth inside the vault, so one can't unearth anything in it. That's plain enough. As to the coffin . . ."

"You can't open the coffin, sir. That would be exhumation of the body."

"Would it? Not in plain English," retorted The Counsellor. "But as I was saying, the coffin is plain oak, I'm told, not lead-lined. . . ."

"In plain English, sir," demanded the Inspector in a nettled tone, "what are you proposing to do?"

"I? Oh, merely to establish the identity of the body found in that blazing car we've been so interested in lately," explained The Counsellor innocently. "It wasn't Hawkstone at all, of course. Didn't you guess that? If you hadn't been in such a devil of a hurry to bury the remains, I could have proved it beyond a doubt. But that would mean exhumation, now. A real digging out or unearthing, which needs the kind permission of the Home Secretary. I'm taking an easier way round, that's all."

The Inspector was no dullard. He jumped at once to his conclusion.

"You mean to say that it was Earlswood's body that was burned that night? Is that true?"

"Truth is always relative, Inspector," said The Counsellor lightly. "But if it *was* Earlswood's body, then both you and our friend the Coroner have been barking up the wrong tree. A dead man can't commit suicide. So much for the Coroner. You can't murder a corpse. So much for you. There you are. And where are you?"

The Inspector tilted his hat forward and rubbed the back of his head with an air of perplexity.

"You have us there," he admitted at length. "If you're right, that is. But the thing's impossible. We're long past the days of body-snatching."

"Thinking of Burke and Hare's period?" queried The Counsellor. "A bit out of date in your instances, Inspector. Never hear of the Dunecht case in 1881? Not so long ago, that, as crime stories go."

"No, I never heard of it," admitted the Inspector, slightly taken aback.

"Quite a Society mystery," explained The Counsellor. "The twenty-fifth Earl of Crawford died and his body was placed in a special mausoleum under the family chapel at Dunecht. The entrance to this crypt was closed by huge horizontal slabs of granite, made secure with lime at the interstices. Then earth was spread on top; and grass, flowers, and shrubs were planted over the spot. Nobody suspected anything, in spite of a warning letter received by the family solicitor; but in the following December it was found that the vault had been entered and the late Earl's body had been removed. It was discovered buried in a ditch on the estate, and the perpetrator of the outrage got five years' penal servitude eventually. So don't you be so sure, Inspector, that the resurrection men haven't found successors."

"What was the man going to get out of it?" demanded Hartwell.

"A reward for finding the body eventually, it's thought. It wasn't a case of any ill will against the Crawford family, apparently."

217

"Is this stuff about Earlswood's body just a wild guess on your part, sir, or have you any sound evidence in support?" demanded the Inspector rather anxiously.

"Remember our last visit to this cemetery?" asked The Counsellor. "Call to mind our friend the Coroner doing a fancy dance when he slipped on some clay that had fallen over the edge on to the steps of the stair? You do? Good! Recollect the piece of sticky soil that had stuck to the bit of firewood in the garage? Fine! Well, that was the evidence, mainly."

"Not much in that," said the Inspector, shaking his head in doubt. "Clay soil's common enough. What's to prove that the stuff in the garage came from this cemetery—which I suppose is your point."

"What's to prove it? Expert evidence, of course. My friend the micro-chemist got a sample of the garage clay from you, and I sent him, myself, a sample of the clay from the steps down to the Earlswood vault. That was on my own hook, but I'm prepared to swear to the identity of the sample. Now I'm no expert on chemical, mineralogical or pedological investigations; but I can understand the results, once they've been got. Here's how it is. The expert starts by sifting out the material and estimates the relative percentages of sand, silt, clay, etc., in each sample. They tallied closely in the two samples we're talking about. So that's Point One. Next, the expert separates off in each case those particles with a definite size, say less than 0·002 millimetres in diameter. He then estimates the ratio of silica to mineral base in these particles. The ratios tallied in the two samples we're talking about. So that's Point Two. Then he applied X-ray examination and worked out the form of the crystal-lattice—the arrangement of the atoms in space—in the case of each sample. They tallied also. So that's Point Three. Finally, the character of the original soils showed that they came from water-bearing strata. My expert turned on the microscope and found both diatoms and foraminifera present, tiny creatures found in some soils. By using ultra-violet light, he made counts of the relative numbers of diatoms and foraminifera in each sample and found that they tallied here also, which is Point Four. And when you get agreement on all these four points, it would be pretty nearly a miracle if the two samples hadn't come from the same source. See?"

"I see," the Inspector declared. "And so that's what you were after when you talked about digging up the county by instalments, was it?"

"Not exactly," The Counsellor explained. "What's wanted is a set of samples of other clays, from other graveyards and places like that, so that my expert can swear that they differ among themselves and that none of them is identical with the Langthorne Cemetery stuff. That should clinch the thing in the mind of a jury."

"Well," the Inspector admitted frankly, "you've got ahead of me there, Mr. Brand. It's a very neat bit of work. Very neat. Thanks."

"Thank my expert friend and his staff," said The Counsellor. "They must have worked like niggers to get the results in that short time. But you can trust 'em."

"Let me think this out a bit," suggested Hartwell, and he relapsed into silence for a minute or two before speaking again. "I think I see it," he continued after this pause. "This means that somebody took Earlswood's body out of its coffin in the vault; shipped it to that garage, where it lay wrapped up in sacking—that would be the bundle that girl saw, I suppose—and then shoved it into the car and burned it at the Cross Roads."

"After dressing it in Hawkstone's dress suit and

putting his ring on its finger," added The Counsellor. "And the white deposit was obviously bleaching-powder to preserve the body as well as possible. Some of it got spilt in the garage and some of it clung to the sacking and appeared in the car débris. Then there's another thing. Remember that bit of black stuff I picked up on the floor and handed to you? My expert tells me that it's common black sealing-wax. There were seals placed on Earlswood's coffin, weren't there? Was black wax used for them? You ought to know. I don't."

"It was black wax, right enough, sir," the Inspector confirmed. "But wait a bit! When I visited the vault on the 21st, I examined the seals on the coffin. They were intact then. But that was at least a week after the body had been removed, according to your ideas."

The Counsellor made an impatient gesture.

"Anyone can take an impression of a wax seal and reproduce the design in fresh wax. Nothing in that," he said rather contemptuously. "I could do it myself at a pinch. That's not important. Now, just to finish, there's another matter in connection with that garage. Remember the petrol tins that girl saw when she peeped through the crack in the door? And the corresponding clear space on the floor where the bleaching-powder had got scattered about? Now reason it out. The clay samples show that somebody went from the Earlswood vault to that garage. The bleaching-powder was accidentally taken by someone from the garage to the burnt-out car, where it appeared as a white deposit containing lime and chlorine lying near the corpse on the remains of the seat. Therefore, someone took something from the garage to Hawkstone's car. My view is that this 'something' was Earlswood's body. I hope to prove half the story this morning; and we can prove the rest of it as soon as you get permission from the Home Secretary."

"H'm!" said the Inspector in a non-committal tone. "Very nice, Mr. Brand. I see what you're hinting at. The keys of that vault were in charge of Barrington and Hawkstone. So was the seal for sealing the coffin. Hawkstone had access to both of them. So, if he decided to disappear for reasons of his own, he simply took Earlswood's body out of the vault, shoved it into his car, and faked the flare-up to prevent any identification of the body. And so he had a clean sheet for his getaway, seeing that the Earlswood body was supposed to be his. Is that it?"

"You're missing out the garage," The Counsellor pointed out. "He had to have a quiet place where he could dress Earlswood's body in his own evening clothes, assuming the rest of the tale's correct. And that brings me to the thing which set me on the track of the substitution first of all. I mean the thing you *didn't* find in the débris of the burnt car."

"Well, what was it?" demanded the Inspector, unable to hide his eagerness.

"What do you wear under your visible garments?" enquired The Counsellor rhetorically. "A set of gent's underwear, no doubt. And what is that fastened up with? Buttons, usually. Made of shell, or brass covered with linen, or bone, eh? Even the bone ones would stand heat fairly. And yet you found not a single trace of anything of the sort. Why? Because a corpse doesn't wear pants and so forth in its coffin. Therefore, no buttons discovered, except those on Hawkstone's evening shirt and suit which had been shoved on to the corpse to manufacture some evidence of identity: gold studs and singed broadcloth and what not. See? As soon as I heard that evidence at the inquest, I knew there was something fishy. And that's why I persuaded you to have an extra special goose-chase through the remains of the car, looking for match-heads. I knew that you'd then find buttons, if buttons there were. But there weren't. And the evidence was all the better, since I hadn't put you on the real track, but merely asked you to hunt for something smaller than any button."

The Inspector's face exhibited signs of a series of emotions succeeding each other in quick succession as The Counsellor made his explanation. Surprise first, then a gleam of vexation, then a reluctant admiration for The Counsellor's acuteness, and, finally, more vexation as he realised that he had been sent—as The Counsellor admitted—on a wild-goose chase after something that mattered little in comparison with the main facts.

"Thanks," he said in a very dry tone when The Counsellor had concluded his explanation. "You fairly led me up the garden there, certainly. I'm not denying that it sounds plausible. But you've still got to prove two things: that Earlswood's body has been lifted from under our noses; and that it's really the one that was found in the burned car. Ah! Now I see what you were after when you asked if there was a leaden shell in Earlswood's coffin! You can't open it, so you're going to use X-rays to see if it's empty. The bones will show, if the body's there. That's it? I thought so. And this second car's got the apparatus aboard it? Quite so. Well, I was a fool not to think of all that myself."

The Counsellor agreed with this last statement, though he refrained from saying so.

"I'm not going quite so far as that," he said. "I can't guarantee that the coffin's empty. In fact, I don't feel sure that it is. But I doubt if Earlswood's in it, dead or alive. By the way, how are you getting on with your enquiries about that man Campion? Is he still missing?"

"Yes, he is, so far as I'm concerned," the Inspector admitted grumpily. "He drew a fair amount of cash before he vanished. That's all I can tell you; and you needn't repeat even that, please. I don't mean he'd embezzled, or anything of that sort. But he did draw some cash out of his private account; and, of course, he got a fair amount of expenses money from his firm, which he'll have to account for when he turns up. So he has enough in hand to turn round comfortably. His firm haven't asked us to charge him with anything—not yet, anyhow. Old and trusted employee, and all that kind of thing. When the scent's stone cold, they may expect us to begin a hunt for him. And by that time, the cash will all be spent."

"Ah, well," said The Counsellor, pretending to yawn behind his hand, "those who live longest will see most. I hope to live for a day or two yet. One can see quite a lot in a week. Quite a lot. . . ."

"Have you squared the Vicar over this business?" the Inspector demanded coarsely.

"I've come to an amicable arrangement with him, if that's what you mean," answered The Counsellor with more dignity than usual. "He saw the matter in a proper light when I explained it to him. He was much shocked at the very idea of the desecration of the dead, and is only too anxious to have the matter sifted to the bottom. So there's no kick coming from him," he ended, with a reversion to his normal vocabulary.

The car drove past the main entrance to the Cemetery and a little further on it turned in through the ivy-grown gateway of Langthorne Church. The second car followed, and drew up before the church steps, where a verger-like person was awaiting them. The Counsellor and the Inspector alighted and were joined by the X-ray expert. The Counsellor greeted the man on the steps, who evidently had got his instructions from the Vicar; then he turned to the expert.

"You'll want current, of course? There's a lamp in the porch. You could plug in there, if you take the bulb out. The verger will switch on for you. That's the entrance to the vault down there"—he nodded towards the mounds of clay beside the stairway—"so you'll need a cable long enough to reach there, and perhaps thirty feet beyond."

The expert, obviously a taciturn person, merely nodded and began making his preparations. As he did so, other cars appeared, and within a few minutes the assembly was complete. Hartwell, having learned what was afoot, showed no particular interest at the moment. Wyndcliffe glanced through the window of the second car as he came up the drive and his nod of recognition showed that he had grasped the nature of the apparatus. Barrington betrayed very little of what was in his mind, but that was his normal way. He seemed merely slightly curious as to the procedure which was to be adopted. Frobisher, though last to arrive, showed an immediate desire to take complete charge of the operations and began making suggestions which the taciturn expert ignored completely as he went about his task. The verger and the two chauffeurs hovered uncertainly in the background, obviously intensely inquisitive. Under Frobisher's direction, Barrington produced his keys and opened the door of the vault, and for a few minutes the expert busied himself with installing his apparatus.

"That's ready," he said concisely when he had finished.

"Then we'd better go down," suggested The Counsellor, leading the way, much to Frobisher's annoyance.

"Close the door, to keep the daylight out," directed the expert when they were all in the vault.

He produced a powerful electric hand-lamp which lit up the rows of coffins resting on stone shelves around the chamber.

"This is the coffin which concerns us," said Frobisher fussily, pointing to one easily distinguished from the rest by its comparative freshness. The stone shelves were broad enough to hold two or even three coffins on each, but this coffin fortunately was the only occupant of its shelf, as The Counsellor saw with some relief.

"You'd better examine the head, first of all," The Counsellor suggested.

The expert nodded curtly and proceeded to install his X-ray tube in the proper position at the back of the shelf, behind the coffin. When he had satisfied himself about his connections, he took a big fluorescent screen from its case, switched off his lamp, and switched on the X-ray tube. A pale apple-green glow suffused the space behind the coffin, and then, as the expert held up his screen between the coffin and the audience, it also glowed vividly green. Unconsciously, they all moved nearer, to see better.

"Don't crowd," ordered the expert sharply. "You'll get a bad shock, if you don't take care—or trample on my apparatus," he added in an even more dictatorial tone.

There was really no need for them to push nearer. The big glowing green oblong of the fluorescent screen was clearly visible to them all in the darkness. On it they could see the shadow of the coffin structure, with the sharply defined black images of the coffin nails and brass bindings. But beyond that, they saw nothing. The coffin was empty. Hartwell, standing next The Counsellor, heard a slight intake of breath as though his neighbour had not seen quite what he expected. It was drowned by louder gasps of surprise from the darkness as other onlookers realised what the picture on the screen implied.

"No body?" ejaculated Frobisher in the tone of a man who can hardly credit his eyes. "What? What? You gave me a hint, Mr. Brand, that things were not quite as they should be; but certainly I did not expect to find your hypothesis verified so strikingly. Where *is* the body, if it isn't here?"

"I think Inspector Hartwell knows," said The Counsellor, who felt that the Inspector deserved some kudos in return for his work even if this particular increment was unearned.

"I'm not certain yet," Hartwell broke in hastily.

Barrington saved him from his embarrassment by intervening.

"This is very awkward," he declared, turning to The Counsellor. "From the purely legal point of view, in connection with Earlswood's will, we seem to be deprived of means to fulfil our obligations. As the body has disappeared, we have no certain proof that Earlswood is dead."

"Oh, he's dead, undoubtedly," said The Counsellor soothingly. "Quite dead. The Inspector will explain it all, once he's been able to secure one final piece of evidence. In the meantime, I suggest that we complete this investigation." He turned to the expert again. "Can you shift the tube along until it's opposite where the hands should be? That's where the electrical gadget is placed inside the coffin, isn't it?" he asked, glancing at Barrington.

"Yes. It's there, so that he could give the alarm voluntarily if he waked up."

The expert rearranged his apparatus and they saw

on the screen the heavy shadows of some bits of mechanism.

"No bones, you see," The Counsellor pointed out. "The body's obviously gone. Just run the rays right along the coffin, please. You see? Not a sign of a skeleton. You're all satisfied? Right! Then we needn't prolong this."

The expert switched off his current and turned on his hand lamp once more. The Counsellor picked it up and took it near the coffin.

"Seals all intact," he pointed out. "And the wires are tight in the exterior binding-screws. Whoever took away the body had only to release these wires as a first move; and then the alarm wouldn't sound, even if the mechanism was disturbed as the body was being taken out of the coffin."

"What about the seals, though?" demanded Barrington, who had examined them over the Counsellor's shoulder.

"Oh, anyone can counterfeit a wax seal," retorted The Counsellor airily. "There's a whole flock of low-melting alloys, like Wood's metal. They give sharp casts and you could melt them in hot water in a thermos flask. They'd take a sharp impression of a wax seal without damaging it; and you could use that impression to make a fresh wax seal if you didn't jam it on until the wax blob had cooled down a bit. That's easy enough."

"This is disturbing. Very disturbing," the Coroner broke in. "You'll need to look carefully into the legal position, Mr. Barrington. On the surface, it certainly appears as though we had not fulfilled—or at any rate cannot now fulfil—the conditions of our trust under the will; and in that case we cannot honestly accept the honorarium provided. Not that this matters to me personally. But it may mean a relatively considerable loss in one case."

He stared at the Inspector as he ended, as though he were not sorry to see that unfortunate man threatened with the loss of what was, in his case, a considerable sum of money.

"I think the Inspector will be able to prove clearly enough that Mr. Earlswood is undeniably the late Mr. Earlswood," said The Counsellor quietly. "And I suppose that will be sufficient to cover the case. And now, as we seem to have finished our work here, I think we may pack up and go."

He set an example by moving towards the entrance, and the others followed him, leaving the expert to collect his apparatus. The Coroner, Barrington and Wyndcliffe formed a little group at the head of the stairs and began a low-voiced discussion. The Inspector followed The Counsellor to his car and got in beside him. In a short time the expert had carried his apparatus to his own car and packed it for transit. Then he came across and leaned on The Counsellor's window.

"O.K.?" he asked concisely.

"Quite O.K., thanks," answered The Counsellor. "You took a set of photographs after that gang cleared out? Right! Just as well to have a permanent record. You might let me have a set of prints from the negatives some time."

The X-ray expert nodded and turned away to his own car. The Counsellor seemed to have nothing further to do in the cemetery. He gave his chauffeur a signal to drive back to the town.

"Satisfied?" he demanded, turning to the Inspector.

"You seem to have hit it," Hartwell confessed. "But I noticed you were surprised, somehow, when that coffin showed up empty. What else did you expect?"

"I thought there might have been a body in it—not Earlswood's, but somebody else's."

"Hawkstone's?" queried the Inspector. "Gad, I never thought of that! That would have been a neat dodge. No one would ever have thought of looking for it there, especially with all these committee meetings in the vault over the catalepsy business, and the electric gadget and all. It would have been as safe as houses."

"Time's moving," The Counsellor pointed out. "I've got a few words to say to you before we reach town. First of all, what about these oil samples I asked you to get. Did you manage that?"

"I got some of them," the Inspector answered. "Wyndcliffe has just bought a new car and there was no sign of any drip from its crank-case, when one of my men examined it while it was standing in the street outside a nursing home. Miss Glenarm's car's almost new. It left no drip when she parked it while she was getting her hair waved; so we can rule it out, too. The Coroner isn't so up-to-date; his car's a two-year-old and drips a bit. I've got a sample from it. Straight out of the crank-case by turning the drain-tap. I took it that you'd want it uncontaminated with road dust if possible."

"That's smart," said The Counsellor heartily. "As a matter of fact, it's just what I did want, only I forgot to mention it."

"Barrington the solicitor has a new car with no drip," Hartwell continued, evidently pleased by the tribute to his thoughtfulness. "I got a small sample out of his crank-case while his car was standing outside some-body's house the other night, when he was playing bridge inside. That man Jelf you asked about, he had a smash on the 10th of this month, and his car got badly scuppered. It's still in the hands of the repairers, with the engine dismantled; so I drew blank there. Barrington junior's car is old and has a bad drip. I've got a sample from it. But you can rule it out. He had it down at his bungalow at the time of the Cross Roads affair and left it with the local repairers to get cleaned and greased. He didn't need it while he was at the bungalow. He spends all his time there fishing and uses his car only to drive up and down from town. Then there's the Campions' car. It's got a bad drip. I took a sample from it. I've got the lot in test-tubes at the station, labelled; and you can have them now, if you want them. Though what you expect to get out of a lot of samples like that, I can't see myself. Once oil's gone into an engine, it gets pretty well chewed up, and what can you make of the results? Nothing much, I'd say."

"Oh, one never knows," said The Counsellor vaguely. "By the way, did you find out from the garages when each of these cars was last filled up with fresh oil in the sump?"

"Yes, I did. It's usual to drain off the old oil and put in fresh stuff every two thousand miles or so," explained the Inspector, ignoring the fact that The Counsellor was a car-owner. "Campion used his car a lot; and his garage says he had fresh oil about a week before the Cross Roads affair. The Coroner doesn't drive for pleasure; he got his oil changed a month or more ago. Barrington the solicitor bought a new car ten days or so before the Cross Roads business and hasn't had any new oil put in. His brother had fresh oil put into the sump of his car on the 9th. Wyndcliffe's car is new, as I told you; and he hasn't needed any fresh stuff. Miss Glenarm, ditto. Jelf we needn't bother about. That's all, I think."

"Right!" said The Counsellor. "Now, just to play fair with you, have you ever heard of a stuff called Dag? You haven't? So sad. But you can always find out by asking. That's what a tongue's for. By the by," he added, to escape the question which obviously was on the Inspector's lips, "how's Mrs. Hawkstone taking things?"

"Pretty well, I'm told," Hartwell answered. "She's not inconsolable, if that's what you mean. In fact, by common gossip, Mr. Barrington—the solicitor one—seems to be doing all the consoling she needs. He's often round at her house and he stays pretty late."

"*Honi soit . . .*" said The Counsellor. "Meaning you. They're old friends."

"Maybe," retorted the Inspector cynically. "And likely to be close relations—by marriage—before long, if all tales are true. She's a fine woman and he's not a bad-looking man, if you like that style. I shouldn't be surprised myself."

The Counsellor seemed to have a distaste for this kind of gossip; and he turned the conversation by putting yet another enquiry:

"What about the house at 12 Shepstone Street? Did you find out anything?"

"I did," the Inspector admitted. "The people who live there—name of Keeton—were asked to leave their premises empty on the evenings of Wednesday, April 12th, and Thursday, April 13th. They were a bit reluctant to say who asked them to do it; but I got it out of them. It was Barrington, the solicitor. Keeton's wife was an old servant of the Barringtons; so he'd no objection to doing what he was asked. Now, I wonder . . ."

It was plain enough what he wondered; but The Counsellor had no intention of helping him, so he

231

remained silent and ignored the invitation of the Inspector's aposiopesis.

"You won't say?" Hartwell went on, after a pause. "Well, then, I can always ask Barrington himself about it."

The Counsellor ignored the veiled threat.

"Of course you can. Why not?" he retorted.

After all, he reflected, it was Barrington's business, not his. The solicitor had no right to unload awkward confidences upon him and expect him to shoulder the responsibility of suppressing them. Let him do his own explaining to the Inspector, since he'd been so free with his talk about Mrs. Hawkstone's schemes.

"I've a good mind to," said the Inspector, though there was more than a hint of indecision in his tone. "These were the two nights before the murder. . . ."

"Do you see any connection?" asked The Counsellor flatly.

The Inspector scratched his chin as though that might give him some inspiration.

"No," he admitted dubiously. "I don't quite."

"Well, then, what excuse are you going to make for prying into his private—or possibly business—affairs? Take my tip. You find out first of all what Dag is. That reminds me, Inspector. Did you ever play a game when you were a kid. Somebody hides something and then tells you 'Hot' or 'Cold' as you come near it in your hunt or move away from it. You ought to be pretty hot under the collar at the present moment, and you may be boiling when you find out what Dag is. In the meanwhile, in your shoes, I'd hold my hand for a couple of days until we get my chemical pal's views on these oils. That's a tip straight out of the horse's mouth for you. I'll give you the news as soon as I get it myself. This is about the last lap, if I'm any judge. Or, to vary the symbolism, it's just about time the balloon was going up."

"They used to have hot-air balloons at one time, I've heard," the Inspector retorted with intention.

"They went up, though. Don't forget that," advised The Counsellor with a grin.

Chapter XVI

ALL IS FISH THAT COMETH TO NET

THE COUNSELLOR had made pre-arrangements with Hartwell by telephone; but he had not mentioned that Standish was coming with a second car.

"What do you want two cars for?" the Inspector demanded as he came forward. "The two constables and I could have got into the back seats of your car easily enough."

"Could you?" queried The Counsellor with a grin. "If you take a glance through the window you'll find some rather knobbly parcels in the back. Sit on them if you wish. I'm all for people enjoying the simple pleasures they long for. But I think your men would prefer plain seats, which they can get in Mr. Standish's car. Mr. Standish is my manager. That's to relieve your mind, Inspector. I saw you giving him a nasty look as if you didn't care for his butting into this expedition. Quite O.K., I assure you. He suffers from pauciloquy. A bad case of obmutescence, in fact. Or, in plain language, he can keep his jaw shut when that's necessary. You needn't think he'll give us away."

"Oh, if you vouch for him, sir. I suppose that's enough," said the Inspector rather grudgingly.

"I do. So that's that. Your men will hop into his car. So will my chauffeur. You will sit with me in front here. We can have a pleasant chat on the road. In you get."

The party distributed itself as he directed; and

although the Inspector cast an inquisitive glance at the parcels in the seat behind him, he refrained from immediate questions.

"We've a loose end or two on our hands," began The Counsellor as he drove off, followed by Standish's car. "I passed these oil samples on to my chemical expert, to see if he could identify the car which left the oil-drip in that garage. Probably you didn't notice at the time, but I made a rough trial with my finger-tip and it made me wonder if there wasn't some graphite in that oil. That's why I chaffed you about Dag. I suppose you've found out what Dag is, by this time?"

"Trade name for Deflocculated Acheson Graphite, so I'm told," said the Inspector.

"Yes. Quite so," said The Counsellor. "Colloidal graphite. You can get it into the cylinders either by mixing it with your petrol or by adding it to your lubricating oil. They say it cuts down wear. Now you remember that out of the list of cars I gave you, only three had any drip from the crank-case. I put my expert on to see if he could identify the car which dripped oil similar to that sample we found in the garage. I don't profess to know all about what he did, but amongst other things he took the specific gravities, the Redwood viscosities at different temperatures, the closed flash-points, the carbon residues and the sediment insoluble in carbon disulphide. The figures for two of the oils were far out, especially in the carbon residue figures. The third sample concorded very well with the garage specimen. So that's that. But to be on the safe side, you'd better find out from the garage Hawkstone patronised whether he used Dag in *his* car. Now another loose end. What about that maidservant who was on holiday or on the sick list when I asked you about noises in the Barrington garage?"

"I've got hold of her since," explained the Inspector. "It's a good while since the 9th, and in the ordinary way I wouldn't have expected her to remember clearly about that particular date. But we've had a bit of luck, there. It seems the girl had a bad tooth which produced an abscess. That kept her awake most of the night, and she could be sure of the date, because she remembered all about her sore jaw and about going to see a dentist. Lying in pain, like that, her nerves were all on edge and the noise next door irritated her more than a little. She said it was like a big rat gnawing and gnawing away, and once when she was just dropping asleep it waked her up again. She remembers it all right, no doubt about that. I've been thinking about that, sir. A sound of filing would fit the case. But the date's all wrong for that. The Cross Roads affair didn't happen till the 14th. That's four or five days later."

"Right!" agreed The Counsellor. "But just a word in your ear, Inspector. That was the night when Wyndcliffe took the late Hawkstone home in his car owing to a breakdown of Hawkstone's own motor."

"Trying to fix it on Barrington?" demanded the Inspector in a sceptical tone. "No good, sir. Barrington's got an alibi that simply can't be broke. You must see that yourself."

"I'm not trying to fix it on anybody," said The Counsellor gently. "That's the police way of doing things. I'm trying to get at the truth, which sometimes isn't the same thing. And since you've mentioned an alibi, I'm inclined to ask: An alibi for what? Just you think that out, Inspector. It's worth the bother. But don't let's start arguing. I see you casting inquisitive glances at the back seat. These parcels excite you, eh? Like a kid on Christmas morning wondering what's inside the wrappings. I'll relieve your mind. The big one is a little outboard motor, the kind of thing you can fix on to the stern of a rowing-boat with a clamp or two. I'm a believer in making machinery do the work if possible, instead of using brawn and muscle. The other package contains some fishing equipment: lines, hooks, and so forth. Having kidnapped you, I'm going to turn you into a poacher, no less. And now, if you don't mind, we'll each plunge into our reflections for a while. I don't want to talk till we get to our destination, which will be in another twenty-five minutes or so."

"I can guess where you're going," said the Inspector, who had a good knowledge of the local roads. "The Barringtons' bungalow, isn't it?"

"It is," The Counsellor confirmed rather testily.

"What do you expect to find there?" demanded Hartwell. "Remember I told you that the younger Barrington's car was in the local garage in the next village, getting fixed up, at the time the Cross Roads business happened."

"Calm yourself, Inspector," snapped The Counsellor. "I'm not looking for his car. It's probably in town, like himself. I've taken the precaution to flood him out with patients to-day, so that he won't come bothering us down here. There are plenty of folk with sore jaws about, who're glad enough to take ten bob and a dentist's fee if one asks them. Young Barrington's practice, on the whole, wasn't aristocratic, so he won't think anything of it if some of them are a bit shabby."

"Well, what are you looking for?" persisted the Inspector, determined to satisfy his curiosity.

"A bicycle. And some other things."

"Oh? A bicycle? Well, I hope you'll remember that we can't go breaking into locked premises in search of it. I've no search warrant."

"I'm not going to break in."

Even yet the Inspector was not silenced.

"A bicycle?" he ruminated. "That's the bicycle that left those tracks near where we found the number-plates of the car, eh? What makes you so sure of finding it at the bungalow?"

"I'm not sure. Or, rather, I'm pretty sure we won't find it at the bungalow. Did you remember to bring that inflator with you, as I asked?"

"I've got it," the Inspector assured him. "And a bit of the lead piping, too. You wanted that as well."

"A regular Universal Provider, eh?" snarled The Counsellor, whose nerves were on edge. "Just give me a little peace and quietness now, and that'll finish my shopping."

The Inspector suddenly fell silent, pondering over the implications of what he had heard. It did not take him long to guess that The Counsellor expected to find the missing bicycle in the little lake beside the bungalow. The outboard motor was there to fit on to Barrington's rowing-boat. And here the Inspector gave The Counsellor a well-deserved good mark for forethought. Barrington would keep his oars under lock and key when he was away from the bungalow, to prevent stray poachers from using his boat during his absence. It might have been impossible to get at the oars without house-breaking; but the little motor on the back seat would serve instead.

"He's got his wits about him," the Inspector admitted to himself. "But he seems in a bit of a temper this morning. I wonder why."

If he could have seen inside The Counsellor's mind, he would have found that there was no ill temper there. The Counsellor was on the edge of a gamble which might turn out successful or else, if futile, might make him slightly ridiculous after all his airs of omniscience. He had no wish to look ridiculous; and he wished that the episode was well over. Hence the edge on his nerves.

At last they turned up a by-road and in a few minutes reached a rather neglected-looking little bungalow standing near the edge of a tiny lake. Tied up to a decrepit wooden jetty was a small rowing-boat. The Counsellor got out of his car, opened the gate of the drive up to the bungalow, then, taking the wheel again, he drove on to the lake-side, followed by Standish's car. When he pulled up, he began to busy himself with the parcels in the back seat, calling Standish to his assistance.

"Here, Wolf. You take the motor and screw it on to the stern while I get the rest of the truck ready."

The next item puzzled the Inspector, who could not guess what use could be made of a yard-long square wooden tube with a glass plate at one end.

"It's a water-glass," explained The Counsellor, who seemed to have recovered his spirits now that the time of action was at hand. "You stick the glazed end under the water and glare down the open end. Gives you a clear sight of the bottom, with no surface ripples to bother you. See?"

"I see," admitted Hartwell, again impressed by The Counsellor's forethought.

"Then we start. Your men can wait here. Mr. Standish will do the steering. You'll look over one side of the boat and I'll look over the other. That'll keep her in trim."

"You're looking for that bicycle?"

"Wrong. I'm looking for weeds."

"Weeds?" said the Inspector, rather puzzled and taking this as one of The Counsellor's jokes.

"Weeds, of course," retorted The Counsellor. "If you wanted to hide anything under water, would you choose a place with a nice sandy bottom? Give the man credit for some brains, Inspector. Of course, if he wanted to hide a cycle or anything else, he'd dump it into the weediest patch he could find. The fronds would cover it up nicely. See? Oh, Wolf! Here's your map. Keep us on the lines I've marked, just as I explained to you this morning. The sailing-marks have got circles round them on the map. You've only got to keep them in line."

He handed over an unfolded sketch, evidently constructed partly from a large-scale Ordnance map and partly from personal charting.

"You've been down here before?" queried the Inspector.

"Of course," admitted The Counsellor. "I didn't leave anything to chance. These lines will take us within sight of most of the lakelet's bottom. Your job is to hang overside and shout, 'Weeds on the port bow, Captain,' or 'Weeds abaft the binnacle, Commodore,' when you sight any. But perhaps it'll be safest if you just say, 'Weeds!' as soon as you see any within ten yards of your side of the boat. Mr. Standish will then jot down the cross-bearings on the chart. And so, eventually, we shall learn where the weed-patches are. Then we can try 'em out, one by one, with the fishing-tackle."

It took time to locate all the weed-beds in the lakelet; but as the work proceeded, the Inspector realised that this thorough and systematic method might save time in the end, as against mere dragging at random.

"Now we can start fishing," said The Counsellor, when they had finished the allotted task and Standish's rough map was complete. "We can begin with that patch there."

The "fishing-tackle" proved to be an ingenious arrangement of small grapnels attached to a long bar and towed from the stern of the boat.

"Just quarter that weed-patch over yonder," The Counsellor ordered Standish. "I'll hang on to the fishing-line and tell you if it fouls anything worth mentioning."

The first three weed-patches yielded no results; but as they traversed the fourth, The Counsellor gave a sudden exclamation and Standish turned the boat towards the near-by shore. When they came to shallower water and a weed-clear bottom, The Counsellor drew the boat back above the object they had been towing and examined it through his water-glass.

"Got it!" he ejaculated, jubilantly. "Go ahead, Wolf. Beach her, and then we can haul in from *terra firma*. We might upset the boat if we hauled up here."

"What is it?" demanded the Inspector. "The bicycle?"

"Yes, the bicycle," The Counsellor assured him with something that sounded like a sigh of relief. "Bull's-eye, after all."

In a few minutes they had dragged the cycle ashore.

"See the inflator-clips?" said The Counsellor, pointing. "Now just try that inflator in them and see if it's the right length."

The Inspector did so, and found that the inflator clipped neatly into its place.

"Not conclusive, but fairly good evidence," declared The Counsellor. "I haven't wasted your time, anyhow, Inspector; and that's something off my mind."

He stared thoughtfully at the rather rusty cycle for a moment or two, then took out his penknife and opened it.

"This isn't likely to be a bull's-eye," he warned them, as he stooped over the bicycle. "Still, one ought to be thorough. There's just the chance that this machine was re-painted. It certainly looks a bit amateurish—

not the real stove-enamel surface." He scraped some of the paint away carefully and then invited them with a gesture to see what he had disclosed.

"Aluminium paint underneath the black," said the Inspector, with a nod of satisfaction. "You can call it an inner, anyhow, Mr. Brand. An aluminium bicycle's noticeable; a black one isn't. That's a bit suspicious on the face of it. And it's amateur re-painting right enough, as you say."

The Counsellor showed no excessive elation over his score. He rose erect, put away his pocket-knife and glanced at his watch.

"I think we'll get the luncheon-basket out of the car now and revive our energies for the next job. Perhaps we won't be so keen on food after it, if I'm on the right lines."

"What do you mean?" demanded the Inspector.

" 'Thus bad begins, and worse remains behind,' " quoted The Counsellor. "That's from *Hamlet*, Inspector. But, of course, you remember; you had *Hamlet* at school, as you once mentioned. Come on. I'm hungry. There's enough for six in the basket; not to mention 'this cordial julep, here, that flames and dances in his crystal bounds.' Milton. Makes me thirsty to quote it. Though the other one's better, about the wine of Egypt. 'See how it pours, thick, clear, and odorous.' That's Beddoes. And I bet you didn't have *him* at school."

"No," admitted Hartwell, "I hadn't. I suppose it was *crème de menthe* he had in mind. Sounds like it."

"I hadn't thought of that," confessed The Counsellor. "Perhaps you're right."

Despite The Counsellor's sinister hint, the party enjoyed its picnic, for the host had not stinted his hospitality. The Counsellor himself was now in high spirits, enlivened by the success which he had already scored in his "fishing." He even delayed them by insisting on a quiet smoke before resuming work, though the Inspector was obviously growing impatient. He tried to extract from The Counsellor his reason for pursuing the search now that the bicycle had been found, but here he came up against a stone wall.

"I believe in being thorough," was all he got in reply to his questions. "We'll find something—or else nothing."

The laborious dragging of the weed-beds was resumed, but for a long time the searchers drew blank and the Inspector began to think that the cycle was to be their only catch that day. Then, suddenly, something weighty was caught by the grapnels, and the boat was turned shoreward, dragging heavily at the submerged object. The Counsellor picked up his water-glass and stared down into the depths through it as the boat drew clear of the weed-bed. The ripple on the water-surface concealed the lower strata from the Inspector, and he had to content himself with watching The Counsellor's face as he peered down through the water. Suddenly he saw a flash of triumph cross its features, to be succeeded by an expression of nausea and repulsion. The Counsellor suddenly sat back in the boat, making it roll violently, and then he handed the water-glass to the Inspector with a gesture inviting him to look for himself.

"Hawkstone!" ejaculated Hartwell as he caught sight of the object entangled with the grapnels. "Oo! The fish have been at him!"

The Counsellor passed his handkerchief across his lips.

"They have," he agreed. "Now you can guess why Mr. Richard Barrington's lost his taste for fish-courses —at least, if they came from this water. 'A man may fish with the worm that hath eat of a king, and eat of the fish that hath fed of that worm.' *Hamlet*, again, Inspector. But they had stronger stomachs in those days, no doubt. Obviously, Mr. Barrington, junior, couldn't rise to their heights, so he cut fish off his menu. I almost feel inclined to do the same after this. It's . . . not pretty."

The Inspector had met a good many disagreeable sights in the course of his duty, and his nerves were not particularly sensitive. This corpse was all in the day's work.

"It *is* Hawkstone," he decided.

"How do *you* know?" demanded The Counsellor, glad to find some vent for his feelings. "You didn't know Hawkstone when he was alive, did you? And even if you did, I don't see how you could swear to him on the strength of *that*." He pointed over the side of the boat. "As a matter of fact, I don't think it *is* Hawkstone. Campion's more likely. Wait till we get him ashore and I think I can tell you definitely. But that body's wearing the kind of suit Campion was wearing when he disappeared. His wife described it to me. You'd better call up your men, Inspector. We'll leave them the job of getting him ashore once we've got the boat grounded. I don't envy them the task myself. Ugh!"

Standish showed no desire to use the water-glass when the Inspector politely offered it to him in his turn. The dialogue which he had just heard was sufficient to put a bridle on his curiosity for the moment. They beached the boat and retired a few paces while the constables brought the body ashore.

"My notions seem to be turning up trumps to-day," The Counsellor pointed out. "See these coils of lead piping wound round the body to serve as a sinker? Just compare them with your sample from the empty house that was robbed. There's green paint on the coils round the body. Your specimen's got paint on it also? Put them side by side and see if they look the same."

The Inspector took a piece of piping from his pocket, went forward again, and compared it with the coils which were twisted round the body.

"They look much the same," he reported, "except that the one lot has been down in the mud at the lake bottom for a while."

"My chemical friend will tell us definitely if they're the same or not," said The Counsellor. "And another thing, Inspector. Don't forget to uncoil that piping and measure its exact length. You'll be asked about it at the trial, obviously. For present purposes, here's some twine. Just wind it round the body the same number of times that the piping goes round, will you? . . . Thanks. Cut that bit off, please. Now measure it; here's an inch-tape. How does that compare with the lengths of piping stolen from that house? . . . Only about half the length? H'm! Then it's worth while going on with the fishing. And, by the way, take a look at the dead man's teeth, the front ones, will you?"

"There's some gold stopping in the left front incisor," the Inspector reported.

"Then in all probability we've found Campion. His left front tooth was gold-stopped, his wife told me. Come along! We've still got to find Hawkstone and the rest of that lead piping."

They resumed their search of the weed-beds and, after drawing blank several times and once being disappointed by securing a sunken log, they hooked a second body girdled with lead piping. Once they got it clear of the reeds, The Counsellor examined it with the water-glass.

"Nothing but underclothing on it," he announced. "This is Hawkstone—or what's left of him. Beach her, Wolf."

When the boat reached the shore and they had disembarked, The Counsellor seemed to have had enough sensations for that day.

"We'll leave you to it," he said to the Inspector. "No need for us to wait, is there? Mr. Standish will take me in his car. I'll leave you my car and my chauffeur, so that you can summon assistance and some sort of van to take the bodies to the mortuary. I'd rather they didn't go in my car, if you don't mind."

"I wasn't thinking of it," declared the Inspector indignantly.

"Neither was I," retorted The Counsellor. "I wouldn't think of it at any price. Now, another thing. You'd better scrape some paint off that cycle and send it, along with the sample you cut off that gate near the Cross Roads, to my chemical friend. . . ."

"But what we got off the gate was just a trifle," protested the Inspector, "far too little for an analysis."

"You don't realise what microchemistry can do nowadays," said The Counsellor. "Just take my tip and follow it."

He reflected for a moment or two.

"Post all the stuff to my chemical friend to-day. And, by the way, you'd better get Campion's dentist to look at that gold stopping and see if he recognises his handiwork. Nothing like certainty. Mrs. Campion will be able to tell you who did the stopping. And, of course, you'll have to break the news to her some time. Better wait till you're dead sure it *is* Campion. In fact, I don't know that I'd be in too much of a hurry to publish our doings and results. The news might make Barrington junior prick up his ears. He's down on trespassers on his property, I believe. No need to irritate him till things are all squared up."

He paused again, evidently making some mental calculation.

"Let's see," he resumed. "Give my expert friend three days to do his stunt. Come and dine with Mr. Standish and me, at my house in Town on Friday. That suit? I'll send my car for you and pack you back in it that night so you won't be away long. And when you send on these samples, tell my chemical friend to send his first results addressed to you at my house in Town. That'll save time in the post and yet keep you officially all right. By that time, I hope to have everything squared up and ready for you. And, by the way," he added with a broad grin, "don't forget to bring a bob in your pocket to pay your bet with. You're going to lose, so it's well to have everything shipshape on the night."

"I think I see my way through it now, more or less," said the Inspector. "Largely thanks to you, sir," he added gratefully.

"Well, there's someone else who ought to be thankful to both of us," said The Counsellor. "And that's the Coroner, since he dotes on inquests. We've given him two more now; and he'll have to begin all over again with the current one, since it's pretty clear that he and the jury are sitting on a body which has been already buried in proper order, with death certificate complete. I don't know how the law stands in a case like that."

"That'll be Mr. Frobisher's look-out, sir," said the Inspector, grinning unashamedly. "It'll be a nice little problem for him. Not our affair. He'll find it hard to prove that a dead man committed suicide in a burning car, anyhow," he added unsympathetically.

"Well, we'll see you later in the week," said The Counsellor, summoning Standish with a nod as he turned away and walked towards the cars.

Chapter XVII

GALLIMAUFRY

"BETTER let me tell it in my own way," suggested The Counsellor, pushing a cigar-box towards the Inspector. "Ask questions as I go along, if you like. Mr. Standish will do that without my asking him to."

Standish, engaged in lighting his pipe, succeeded in giving a nod of confirmation. Then, putting down the stub of his match, he took his pipe from his mouth.

"Naturally I shall," he said. "I haven't heard more than a few bits of the story so far. They didn't seem to me to make much sense as they stood."

"Well, this is how it is," began The Counsellor hurriedly, as though to stifle any further remarks. "Start with that burned-out car at the Cross Roads. Inside the remains of it you found a cracked blue glass poison phial, a body minus one tooth, the detached missing tooth, the remains of a dress suit with a complete set of the corresponding buttons, gold sleeve links, a waistcoat buckle, and studs from a shirt and a signet-ring with the stone seal badly cracked and incomplete. That's the complete catalogue, isn't it?"

"All that matters, I suppose," admitted the Inspector.

"What wasn't found in the car," continued The Counsellor, "was the man's latch-key for one thing; and any vestige of buttons from underclothing, for another. Also, the search drew blank in the matter of a matchbox or cigarette-lighter."

"Hawkstone was a non-smoker," interjected the Inspector, turning to Standish.

"At this stage," continued The Counsellor, "our friend here parted company with the Coroner. Frobisher took the presence of the blue glass phial to indicate that the deceased—whoever he was—had poisoned himself; and he wanted a verdict of *felo de se*. The Inspector, here, couldn't fit that in with the displaced tooth which was found in the car débris and which fitted the gap in the jaw of the body. He guessed it was a murder case. The Coroner's notion got a bad shock when no carbon particles were found in the post-nasal space of the body's skull, which proved that no breath had been drawn after the fire started. To fit that in, you've got to assume that the poison was almost instantaneous in its action and yet gave time for the man to set the car afire after he'd swallowed his dope from the blue bottle. Possible, but far from likely. On the other hand, if one takes the Inspector's side, that phial could only have been put there as a blind by the murderer. No poison was detected in the body's stomach; and the only things detected on the fragments of the bottle were traces of sulphur and phosphorus; and phosphorus isn't a quick-acting poison—far from instantaneous, anyhow. Further, the medical expert produced no evidence of violence, unless you include the displaced tooth under that head. The hyoid bone was intact, and it would probably have been broken if the patient had been strangled in the course of a struggle. So, as far as that part of the show goes, there we were, and where were we?"

"Up a gum-tree," suggested Standish unkindly.

"I proceed," said The Counsellor, ignoring the interruption. "Two witnesses actually saw the car blaze up, and there seems no doubt from their evidence that nobody was near the car when it went up in flames. That looks like a point for the Coroner's notion and a snag for Mr. Hartwell's idea. *But*, yellow phosphorus dissolves in carbon disulphide. And when the solution evaporates, it leaves the phosphorus so finely divided that it takes fire spontaneously in the air. Compare the chemical evidence about the blue glass. Not absolutely conclusive, I admit. Still, it suggests that that blue glass phial did contain phosphorus solution and that somebody sprinkled the liquid about the inside of the car and then cleared out. The time taken by the carbon disulphide to evaporate might be half a minute or more, which would give time for that somebody to make his getaway before the witnesses came near enough to spot him in the dark."

The Inspector gave an appreciative nod.

"I believe you've hit it," he said. "And I suppose the blue glass bottle was left behind to suggest suicide— as it did to Mr. Frobisher."

"The next thing that struck me was this," The Counsellor continued. "Looking at the whole of the facts, I got the notion of delayed action. I mean the underlying idea seemed to be that the body shouldn't be identified straight off, and yet there was enough evidence left about to ensure that it *could* be identified eventually. For instance, the engine and chassis numbers had been filed off. That meant one couldn't identify the car merely by writing to the makers and giving these numbers. *But*, the actual number-plates of the car had been removed, apparently to baffle identification; and yet these number-plates weren't taken clean away but were hidden fairly near at hand in a place where they were pretty sure to be found, once there was time for a really thorough search of the ground. Then, again, take that signet-ring. It was cracked to suggest that the fire had split the stone in it. But there was enough of it left to identify it if anyone could produce an impression that had been made by it before it was deliberately smashed. There wasn't enough left to enable a stranger to use it as a means of identification. It was no use to you, for instance, Mr. Hartwell. But there was enough of it there to establish identity by someone who had known the intact seal, if he chose to come forward later on, when it suited him."

"That's mere hypothesis, Mark," said Standish judicially. "Still, I admit that you lend it an air of probability. Go on."

"There was one thing that Hawkstone habitually carried about with him," The Counsellor proceeded, "something which would have furnished an immediate clue to his identity and which was fire-resistant as well: his key-ring. On it, he had one of those metal insurance tabs offering a reward of five shillings to the finder if he took the keys (in case of loss) to the Chief Police Station in Fernhurst-Hordle. The tag's numbered, and the police are in touch with the insurance company. That tag would have established Hawkstone's identity in quick time. Curiously enough, that key-ring was not in the débris of the car. It turned up at Hawkstone's office and the assumption was that he'd happened to leave it behind there, that evening, after opening the strong-room. Sydney Barrington handed it over to the Inspector here eventually."

"That's so," Hartwell confirmed.

"Put all these facts together," continued The Counsellor, "and they suggest not only a murder case, but something else as well—what I called 'delayed action.' The murderer didn't want immediate detection of the dead man's identity. No. For then any possible witnesses would have their recollections of important details fresh in their minds. Therefore it was a good tip to postpone identification as long as possible. But, clearly enough, ultimate identification was what the murderer aimed at, and then it was to be beyond dispute. What does that suggest?"

"An insurance policy," said Standish, spoiling The Counsellor's merely rhetorical pause.

"Right! And there was an insurance policy in the background, for £15,000—as came out at the inquest. And there was another policy as well, for £10,000. The first was payable to Sydney Barrington. If Hawkstone died, Barrington had to pay Mrs. Hawkstone back the £15,000 that Hawkstone paid for his partnership. The £15,000 policy was to cover that risk. The £10,000 policy was payable to Mrs. Hawkstone."

"So by her husband's death she stood to gain £25,000," commented Standish. "And from all I've heard, she didn't lose much when she lost Hawkstone. Very nice."

"The money could only be collected when Hawkstone's death was clearly established," The Counsellor pointed out. "Hence the necessity for a definite identification eventually. And so the next thing is the discovery of the motor number-plates very poorly hidden at a short distance from the burned-out car. That identifies the car as Hawkstone's, and then in comes the damaged signet-ring to make the thing a cert."

"And once the Coroner's jury had given their verdict on Hawkstone's body, the cash would have been collectable, obviously," said Standish. "I'll admit you're making some sort of case, Mark."

"Most encouraging," said The Counsellor ironically. "Try a new line. Remember the decayed tooth found amongst the car débris? Recall that it fitted nicely into the blank space in the corpse's jaw. You can't forge that kind of thing. *Ergo*, that tooth belonged to that corpse. But there's no evidence of any struggle in which that tooth might have been knocked out. Not in the car, anyhow. It was a premolar tooth on the right-hand side. Imagine yourself sitting in the driver's seat of your own car and ask yourself how anyone either inside or outside the car could hit you so as to knock out a tooth in that position. Difficult to see it. And there's no other evidence of a struggle in the car."

"There might have been a struggle before Hawkstone got into the car, and the tooth might have been picked up and dropped into the car," said Standish. "You're making your murderer so attentive to details, Mark, that a touch like that wouldn't be beyond him."

"He did drop the tooth into the car," conceded The Counsellor, rather to Standish's surprise. "And he dropped something else as well. We'll come to that shortly. Meanwhile, I'll give you my musings on that tooth, as made at the time. At first sight, that tooth didn't seem to make sense, if you see what I mean. A knocked-out tooth implies—so I thought—some sort of struggle between two parties. The Inspector here tried an experiment and convinced himself, if not the Coroner, that it couldn't have been knocked out by the man banging his head against the steering-wheel in the agonies of the fire. But that implied the presence of a second party on the scene. And yet the whole affair was faked so as to make it look, at first sight, like a case of suicide. If that first line of defence held good, then the murderer was safe. If Frobisher had got his way, it would have held good."

The Inspector indicated his approval with something like a snort, but he refrained from articulate sounds.

"But suppose the suicide fake didn't pass muster,"

continued The Counsellor. "Suppose the murderer was tracked down. He pleads an alibi. What then?"

"He'd be hanged, one hopes," said Standish, with a smile to the Inspector.

"Touch of the Queen of Hearts in *Alice* about you, Wolf," said The Counsellor blandly. " 'Off with his head,' eh? No nonsense about a trial and all that sort of thing."

"Oh, I suppose he'd be tried," admitted Standish.

"On an indictment, presumably?" queried The Counsellor, with ominous suavity. "What would he be charged with, by your way of it?"

"Murdering Hawkstone, presumably."

"Quite so. I managed to push my reasoning as far as that myself. And still that tooth didn't fit in, somehow. So then, in what I may modestly describe as a flash of genius, I asked myself: 'What proof is there that this tooth ever belonged to Hawkstone?' And, without the flash of genius, you will be able to reply: 'None!' "

"And suppose I do say: 'None'?" demanded Standish.

"Then I'll tell you what I think was the murderer's third line of defence," said The Counsellor. "If he was indicted for murdering Hawkstone—on the assumption that the body in the car was Hawkstone's—all he had to do was to let the prosecution do their worst. Then, in his defence, he'd establish conclusively that it wasn't Hawkstone's body at all. The tooth was, so to speak, the keystone of that little dodge."

When put to it, Standish could think rapidly enough.

"O-o-oh!" he drawled. "Now I begin to remember something. You mentioned once about Earlswood dying of antrum trouble. Antrum trouble means the extraction of a tooth and drilling a hole up into the bone. I remember your mentioning that in one of your wild hypotheses about this business. And I suppose you're banking on the body in the car being Earlswood's body and the tooth being his tooth."

"Right!" said The Counsellor in a tone exasperatingly like that of a teacher commending a pupil. "And I remember something about that talk myself. I was just going to explain about the Dunecht mystery when you cut me short. That was a case of body-snatching, Wolf, in quite recent times; which showed me that the thing wasn't impossible even nowadays. So I went on that basis and established that Earlswood's body has disappeared from its coffin. Before long, with the kind permission of the Home Secretary, the Inspector here will be able to prove conclusively that the body in the car was Earlswood's and not Hawkstone's at all. And that brings me to the murderer's fourth and last line of defence. If he managed to upset the prosecution over the identity of the body, he'd be acquitted, since the whole case against him would obviously be based on false premises. And after that, if they tried to get him again, he could plead *autrefois acquit* and stifle the case."

"I know. If you've been charged with murder and got off, you can't be charged again with the same crime."

"You can't even be charged with manslaughter if you've been acquitted of murder. So that was the murderer's final stopper on the possible Crown case against him. Four lines of defence, and the last one absolutely impregnable, if he came to occupy it."

"Neat enough," Standish admitted. "He must be an uncommonly clever cove to have thought out all that. But it seems a big superstructure to build up on a single tooth. Had you nothing else?"

"Of course I had," said The Counsellor. "When I heard the evidence at the inquest, I was struck by the complete absence of any buttons from the underclothing of the body. True, he might have been wearing the buttonless brand. But there wasn't a mention of any charred underclothing being noticed, although the cloth of the dress trousers at the seat had escaped the fire. If it hadn't been burned, how came it that the pants underneath it had been burned away? It seemed rum, no matter how one looked at it. So I made a small bet with the Inspector here"—The Counsellor grinned openly as he confessed this—"and he kindly furnished me with the addresses of Hawkstone's usual outfitters and also his laundry."

"Oh, *that* was what you wanted them for, was it?" interjected Hartwell vexedly.

"It was. And I paid calls on these people. And I learned that Hawkstone had buttons on all his known pants and vests. So that was that. And, on the face of it, that body had been wearing all the visible articles of evening dress, but no underclothing. Well, a corpse doesn't wear underclothing. So that reinforces the tooth, as evidence."

"I see. The murderer stole Earlswood's body and dressed it up in Hawkstone's clothes that night. Admit that. What next?"

"Would you use your dining-room table for a job of that kind?" asked The Counsellor. "Or invite your friends to see you do it? No. You'd rent some nice quiet lock-up place to serve as dressing-room. And, what's more, if you had any sense you wouldn't plan to steal a body and murder a man on the same evening. Too much of a busy time, that. For me, at least. Much easier to steal the body one night; keep it in storage in a quiet place; and do your murder some other evening. That's how I saw it. So I asked myself what sort of quiet place I'd choose, if I'd been in that fix. And the answer is: a garage. So I enquired over the wireless about garages which had recently been hired; and the Inspector here put out his feelers in the same direction. We heard of a number between us, but most of them had windows or other holes through which people might have looked inside and naturally we passed them by. But we did find a windowless garage which had been let as the result of an advertisement inserted in a local newspaper on April 7th. Just note that this was before Earlswood's death; but by April 7th it was pretty certain that he was going to die from this antrum trouble."

"Gruesome bit of premeditation, that," commented Standish with a shrug of disgust.

"To continue," pursued The Counsellor. "Mr. Hartwell and I had a look round this garage. The owner hadn't seen her tenant. He'd paid a week's rent in advance by a postal order, giving no address but asking that the place should be left open for him. That looked a bit funny in itself. He'd put a new padlock on the door, so that there was no chance of the owner snooping, even if she wanted to. And there were no windows in the garage, so that no one could look in and watch any proceedings he chose to carry out inside. We learned that a car came to the garage on the night of Earlswood's funeral. Next day, a girl peered into the garage through a crack in the door. There was no car there, but she saw a long bundle tied up in sacking."

"Earlswood's body, I suppose, by your way of it?"

"Right! And a car came to the garage early in the morning of the 14th. An hour or so before the blaze-up at the Cross Roads. And the last two figures on the number-plate of that car were 56, whilst the number of the burned car was XYZ6756. Hawkstone's own car, that was, you may remember."

"That trip was to take the body away, then, after putting on the dress suit in the garage?"

"Right!" said The Counsellor heartily. "Most encouraging to see you follow so closely, Wolf. Now when Mr. Hartwell and I examined that garage, we found one or two things on the floor. We found some clay which evidently had come in on somebody's shoe. Also some bleaching-powder corresponding to a white deposit found in the débris of the burned-out car. Likewise a bit of black sealing-wax which corresponds to the black sealing-wax used in sealing up Earlswood's coffin—he'd some funny provisions in his will about his burial arrangements. Furthermore, some oil that had dripped from the crank-case of a motor. Finally, the trace of a petrol tin having been in the garage along with the body. Remember that two petrol tins were found, pitched over the hedge near the burned-out car?"

"You seem to have been very busy," said Standish with a slight touch of admiration in his tone. "I didn't think you had such a gift for detail. But I expect you weren't without expert backing," he added with a confidential glance at the Inspector.

"I said 'we,' " The Counsellor pointed out crossly.

"A nice change," said Standish, with obvious approval. "Usually you say 'I.' And quite often, too, Mark."

"Well, here's something I don't know and the Inspector does," said The Counsellor. "Just to show you I'm not claiming the credit. What about the oil in Hawkstone's car?"

"It had no Dag in it," said the Inspector, taking his cue. "I made full enquiries."

"That simplifies things," said The Counsellor. "We'll come to that point in due course, Wolf, so don't get excited. To proceed. At that stage, the next thing was to prove that Earlswood's body had actually been removed from his family vault. We investigated. With

X-rays. The coffin was empty. And just to clinch matters, the clay we found in the garage was identical with the clay littered about the steps of the Earlswood vault. So obviously someone had gone straight from the vault to the garage. See?"

"Yes," said Standish. "But hold on a jiffy. If someone dressed Earlswood's body up in Hawkstone's evening clothes, why didn't he finish the job and add the underclothes as well?"

"Two explanations for that," said The Counsellor. "The change was done in a hurry, as you can see by comparing times. Perhaps it would have run it too fine to make the thing complete. Or perhaps the change wasn't a pleasant job. Not one I'd care for myself. So it may have been scamped through natural aversion. After all, the easily identifiable things were what counted: the signet-ring and the cloth of the evening suit."

"Still, it was a blunder," Standish commented.

"Of course it was. But a murderer who made *no* blunder would never be spotted. We hope to spot this one."

"The bleaching-powder was used as a preservative of sorts?"

"No doubt. But to continue. Question was, at that stage, whether this was a murder or only an attempt to defraud an insurance company by pretending Hawkstone was dead, when actually he'd merely vamoosed and was waiting for his share in the loot. Both seemed equally likely, so far as the evidence went then. But you've seen Hawkstone's body, so I needn't elaborate the vanishing-man notion. I spare you that. Likewise my profound thoughts on same. Be thankful."

"Oh, I am," said Standish hastily. "No mistake about that. Go on."

"That's so nice," retorted The Counsellor sarcastically. "But to continue. About that stage in the affair, we came into possession of some cipher advertisements. They were sent to my Problem Department for solution; but the enquirer made a mistake about his name and address. My Solutionist unravelled them, and they turned out to be messages between Hawkstone and a Mrs. Campion, the dame who'd had a fracas with him in his car on the night he died. The last one of the series was an offer by her to spend a week-end with Hawkstone once Campion had gone off to America. Inspector Hartwell put the lot in front of her, translated. She began by denying everything. Then she admitted she'd inserted all but the last one. But she stuck to it that the last one was quite unknown to her. She'd never written it. I'm inclined to believe her there. There were one or two points in the ciphered message which diverged from her normal practice."

"Then someone else must have butted in?" asked Standish.

"Obviously. The Inspector managed to identify him. His name's Richard Barrington, younger brother of the lawyer. In fact, the fellow I supplied with patients while we were dragging his lake. And, further, he was the enquirer who sent these cipher ads. to my Problem Department."

"Meaning to drag the Hawkstone-Campion intrigue under your nose, I suppose?"

"Obviously."

"But how did he know about it?"

"Well, he knew his brother's partner, and he'd got acquainted with Mrs. Campion also. She was pretty facile in that way. Any man could pick her up. I don't suppose Barrington had much difficulty in the matter. She gave him one of her cipher ads. and asked him to hand it in at the newspaper office counter. He has a turn for ciphers. So his brother told me. Curiosity might make him decipher the ad. No doubt he looked up the rest of the correspondence in the newspaper files. No harm in that. Anyone's entitled to solve a published cipher if they can."

"And he was the author of the faked ad. about the week-end?"

"Obviously, I think."

"What's the point?" demanded Standish. "I don't quite see it."

" 'Merely corroborative detail, intended to give artistic verisimilitude to a bald and unconvincing narrative,' " quoted The Counsellor. "You see, Wolf, all the rest of the ads. might have been construed as referring to a mere silly bit of flirtation. The faked ad. put a nastier complexion on the business. Obviously Mr. Richard Barrington had some object in making the Hawkstone-Campion affair look more serious than it may actually have been."

"Possibly," admitted Standish. "But why?"

"We now bring in a fresh character. You met him lately. One Campion. A sort of vest-pocket edition of Othello, if all tales be true. Haunted by the green-eyed monster, the hydra of calamities, the ugliest fiend of Hell, in fact: jealousy. Not the right sort of husband for Mrs. Campion. Still, he married her and suffered accordingly. You saw the remains of him. He disappeared on the same night as Hawkstone did."

"I don't follow that," Standish confessed frankly.

"No hurry," The Counsellor assured him benignly. "All will become crystal-clear before I've done. We now come to an interview which Sydney Barrington, the solicitor, forced upon me. The Inspector here doesn't know this part yet."

Hartwell looked up with an undisguised frown when he heard this, but The Counsellor waved aside any possible complaint.

"He took me into his confidence," he explained, "and more or less asked me to keep my mouth shut. So I did. Up to a point. Until I knew exactly where I stood, in fact. But things are a bit too serious now for gentlemen's agreements of that sort to be binding. I went to see him. He explained to me that Mrs. Hawkstone had grown tired of being the wife of a fly-by-night, a spreester, and a man of pleasure in a sordid way. In fact, some time earlier, she'd made up her mind to divorce Hawkstone, making Mrs. Campion the co-respondent. Through Mr. Richard Barrington, they'd fished out a good deal of information about the Hawkstone-Campion goings-on, including the cipher ads. Barrington senior told me that he'd warned Campion of what was in the wind. He'd met him once or twice at the house of an old servant—which is corroborated by Mr. Hartwell, who looked into the matter. At these meetings, he showed Campion the cipher ads. Othello Campion wasn't pleased. Far from it. He entered up his feelings in his own cipher diary, which I've seen. Peevish is hardly the word. Barrington's evidence, including the faked ad., quite convinced him that his wife had gone off the rails completely."

"Why did Barrington see him at all?" interjected Standish.

"Humanitarian reasons, he said. Not wishing to burst the situation on him when he was a stranger in a strange land—America, to wit. Another possible explanation—which he did not give me—was that if Campion started a divorce case on his own with Hawkstone as co-respondent, it might make Mrs. Hawkstone's case against her husband all the stronger if she deferred it for a while. Anyhow, there it was."

"Why haven't we heard about this projected divorce case, then?" demanded Standish.

"Because Hawkstone's death made it unnecessary, obviously; and there was no use washing the dirty horse after the stable was stolen. H'm! I don't seem to have got that quite right. But you know what I mean. Dirty linen in public was what I was after, really."

"Thanks," said Standish. "I see what you mean and I hope Mr. Hartwell does, too. It didn't seem to make sense at first."

"Oh, that's by the way," said The Counsellor, airily. "To proceed. It appears, and I've no reason to doubt it, that Barrington senior let drop to Campion the news that Hawkstone would be coming to see Barrington on the night of the Friday. The burning car was found in the small hours, after that, you remember."

"Yes. Go on."

"Barrington senior told me that he had actually arranged that Hawkstone was to come and see him that night. Reason given: to discuss this pending divorce business and its bearing on their partnership. Barrington made no bones about it to me. He meant to use the divorce case as a ground for pitching Hawkstone out of the firm and sticking to the £15,000 which Hawkstone had invested. Shove him out into the cold world with no wife and not much in the way of assets, in fact. Quite stony-hearted about it. Well, to proceed, Barrington explained that Hawkstone arrived, fresh from some trouble with Mrs. Campion and in a somewhat perturbed condition. He was further perturbed by Barrington's news about the divorce case and the kick-out. Barrington says there was a bit of a scene, promises of amendment, etc. But all Barrington would do for him was to give him a stiff drink—though he'd had more than enough already—and kick him out of the house. Barrington says he was feeling very groggy himself that evening; and Mr. Hartwell and I heard the evidence about his being sick and calling in a doctor."

"That's quite true," the Inspector interjected. "We checked it, of course."

"But why didn't he tell the whole story at the inquest?" asked Standish. "If I remember right, nothing came out about this divorce business. In Barrington's evidence, I mean."

"Right! He told me he suppressed it on account of Mrs. Hawkstone, since it didn't seem to him to throw any light on the matter before the Coroner and the jury. Nor did it, as a matter of fact."

The Inspector made a movement of dissent, but The Counsellor ignored it and continued:

"Barrington asked me not to bother Mrs. Hawkstone with any questions about the affair. In fact, he said that he'd told me the whole tale simply because he was afraid I was coming near it in any case, and my next move might drag her in. Hence the tale, and a paws-off request at the end of it. I promised not to bother her with any questions. I'm not going to."

The Inspector glanced up and then made a jotting in the notebook which rested on his knee. Obviously he felt that there was no need for him to refrain from pushing his enquiries into this fresh field.

"Well," continued The Counsellor, "Barrington had been quite frank in his statement to me. Still, it seemed worth checking him. So my next move was to wile Campion's diary out of Mrs. Campion's hands. Barrington, of course, had seen it; and he told me it was written in the rail-fence cipher. Mrs. Campion has no interest in ciphers and couldn't read it. But when I got hold of it, I had no difficulty. It confirmed what Barrington had said about his meetings with Campion. And there was vest-pocket Othello written all over it. Campion had swallowed the final cipher ad. along with the rest and was blazing with rage against Hawkstone. You see, he still loved his wife, even when he thought the worst of her, and that made it extra hard for the poor devil. . . ."

He paused for a moment or two, as though reflecting on this tragedy. Then he continued:

"It was after that that I got the X-ray to work on Earlswood's coffin. The Inspector here was left out of the preliminary work because he was one of the people mixed up in Earlswood's will, so it was better that he shouldn't have a finger in the pie till the job was done. I managed to . . . h'm! . . . persuade the executors that they had better consent to the proceedings. As I told you, we found there was no body in the coffin. That convinced me that we'd got the right end of the stick, so far. The body in the burned-out car was Earlswood's, right enough, on the face of things."

"And I suppose you're going to establish that definitely by examining the skull for the hole drilled up into the antrum?" asked Standish, turning to the Inspector, who nodded in confirmation.

"Now we go back a few moves," resumed The Counsellor, "to pick up a fact or two which came out earlier, but didn't seem important then. Barrington and Hawkstone have charge of an empty house for one of their clients. It was broken into, a while ago, and a lot of lead piping was stolen from the premises. Not an uncommon affair. But the police failed to nail the thief. I don't wonder at that myself."

Hartwell glanced up with a frown at what he took to

be an aspersion on his efficiency, but The Counsellor soothed him with a gesture.

"No, no," he said apologetically. "I don't mean that. No insinuations, Inspector. You'll see why by and by. The next bit of disjointed information was the news that on the night before Earlswood's death, Hawkstone, Wyndcliffe—who's the surgeon who operated on Earlswood and also Earlswood's heir to a large extent —and one Jelf were at the Barrington's house, playing bridge. Hawkstone's car went wrong that evening and he had to leave it and get a lift home from Wyndcliffe. Then yet another bit of stray information we picked up was that Richard Barrington is a keen fisherman. What's more, he and his brother are something epicurean in the fish-diet line. Very keen on it. Then Mr. Hartwell discovered that a maidservant next door to the Barrington's had heard rummy noises in the night of April 9th. And, last bit of news in this series, the Barringtons have gone clean off fish as a diet recently. You must remember that these tit-bits came to us quite independently of each other. Put together, as I've strung them, and coupled with what you've seen, I expect you'll spot what they imply easily enough."

"One can but try," said Standish, rather doubtfully. "It's plain enough that you mean Hawkstone's car was left in the Barrington garage that night it broke down and somebody took the opportunity of filing off the engine and chassis numbers. Is that it? A very convenient breakdown, surely?"

"Anyone can pour a little water into a man's carburettor," The Counsellor pointed out. "And if your car sticks in consequence, it's natural enough to get a lift home in some other guest's car."

"It sounds plausible enough," Standish admitted. "As to the sudden distaste for fish diet, that's easy, after what I've seen. I don't know that I'd care to eat fish caught in that lake—not at present, certainly. I suppose that's what you mean."

"Right!" confirmed The Counsellor. "Two corpses in the water would be enough to put most ichthyophagists off their feed I guess."

"And the lead piping was used to wrap round the bodies to make sure they sank, obviously. You seem to be making out a fairly clear case that the Barringtons were in the business up to their necks."

"Think so?" retorted The Counsellor. "Then how do you fit Campion's death into the jigsaw, since you're so good at seeing things when they're all laid out in a row for you? Have a snap at that, Wolf. It's got to fit in somehow."

Standish pondered for a while and then shook his head, as though giving the problem up.

"No, it doesn't fit," he admitted. "What sticks me is your story that Sydney Barrington warned Campion off coming to see him on the night that he was going to square up things with Hawkstone. Campion wanted to come and see him that evening, and Barrington told you he'd put him off. Ah! Perhaps he was diddling you when he said that."

"No, I don't think so," The Counsellor declared. "In fact, I'm pretty sure that part of his yarn was true, even if he took a few liberties with the truth in the rest of it. But we'll come to that later on. There are one or two bits left which have got to be fixed in place yet, before the job's done. Consider the Barringtons on the night of the murder. Who burned that car? It wasn't Sydney Barrington. The car went ablaze at 2.30 a.m. But from 2.15 a.m. onwards Sydney Barrington was in the hands of Dr. Arkwright. So unless his astral body was at the Cross Roads while his physical body was in bed at his house, he can't have been the fellow who lit the funeral pyre. I'm not strong on astral bodies myself. It's easier to assume that Sydney Barrington's alibi is sound, since it's supported by three credible witnesses. What about dear Richard? He was down at his bungalow, giving his well-known imitation of Izaak Walton. And his car was in the local garage there, getting some tinkering done to it. Both of them, you see, quite clear of suspicion. So where are you?"

"There was that bicycle..." said Standish, cautiously.

"Yes. Easy enough to say that after the thing's been jammed under your nose," said The Counsellor scornfully. "But no one took that trouble to help the Inspector and me. We had to infer it from three things which came out at the inquest: the inflator, the tyre mark in the mud and a scrape of paint on a gate where the cycle had slipped. By the way, Mr. Hartwell, what about the tyre-pattern?"

"That's all right, sir," the Inspector assured him. "I've compared the tyre with the cast of the pattern I took when I spotted the track and they fit precisely. There's a chip in the rubber of the tyre which matches a defect in the cast exactly; so it's not merely a case of two tyres of the same make. The cycle from the lake was the one that left the track in the mud near where the car number-plates were found. That's beyond argument. But do you think this microchemist is likely to make much of the paint left on the scrape when the cycle slipped? There doesn't seem much to go on."

"I didn't expect much," The Counsellor confessed. "But things are better than I'd hoped. You saw me scrape the black paint on the cycle and find aluminium underneath? The scrape ought to contain the ingredients of both paints, and that's not a common mixture. It looks as if that cycle had been bought second-hand

and repainted by an amateur to make it look less conspicuous than a grey machine might be."

"Second-hand aluminium-painted cycle," Hartwell noted in his book. "See if sale can be traced. I'll look into it; though, except for the unusual colour, it's a pure chance of finding the seller. Perhaps you could help us over the wireless, sir?"

"I'll ask my listeners, anyhow," The Counsellor assured him. "No use leaving any stone unturned. But even if we both draw blank, there's enough to make a jury fairly sure in their minds, I think. Now let's see. . . . Oh, yes, there's another point. When Mr. Hartwell and I inspected the garage where Earlswood's body had been stored, we found a fairly fresh oil-drip on the floor, evidently from the crank-case of a car. The old dame who owned the garage told us that she'd given the garage floor a wash and brush-up before her tenant came in. Obviously this oil-drip was later than that. Now she'd seen a car come into the garage in the early hours of Saturday, just before the blaze-up at the Cross Roads. It was a Hernshaw-Davies. She recognised the radiator type and the mascot, and she spotted the last two figures of the number, as I told you. That was Hawkstone's car. Had it left the drip? Or was the drip from a second car? A car had come to the garage on the night of Wednesday, April 12th—the day when Earlswood was buried in his family vault. So the old dame's daughter told us. She'd heard it, but couldn't identify it for us."

"This is getting a bit complicated," protested Standish.

"Wait a moment," said The Counsellor. "That oil on the floor had Dag in it—colloidal graphite. Mr. Hartwell's been enquiring and he finds that Hawkstone's car had no Dag in its engine. Therefore that oil wasn't left by it, but must have been left by the other car, the one that came to the garage on the night of the funeral."

"Bringing the body from the cemetery?"

"Obviously. Because next day the girl saw that long bundle in the garage, wrapped up in sacking. To cut the tale short, the Inspector here made a search for a Dag-containing engine amongst all the likely cars—and some unlikely ones, too, just to be fair. What's the result? He'll tell us."

"Mrs. Campion's car has a heavy oil-drip, but no Dag in the sump," explained Hartwell. "Mr. Jelf's car had a heavy drip, and he used Dag in his engine; but his car was under repair at the critical time. Mr. Richard Barrington's car is an old one with a bad drip, and he uses Dag. The Coroner's car has no Dag in it. Mr. Wyndcliffe has a new car with no drip and no Dag. Ditto, Miss Glenarm."

"Whence we infer," said The Counsellor, "that Richard Barrington's car *may* have been the one that came to the garage with Earlswood's body that night. It fulfils the conditions, anyhow."

Standish reflected for a moment and then raised a criticism.

"I seem to find two points lacking in your discourse, long as it has been. You've supplied no motive for this orgy of crime; and you haven't accounted for Campion's death. Both seem fairly important matters. What about them?"

In turn, The Counsellor pondered for a few moments.

"Motive?" he said, at last, in a reflective tone. "You don't need to *establish* motive in prosecuting a man for murder. Motive needn't come into the story at all. But if you're hungering for one, Wolf, I'll throw out a hint. There's a mutual affection between the Barrington brothers. Richard seems to have been an expensive sort of relation. Got into one bad scrape at least, I'm told. Cost his brother a fair number of doubloons or *moidores* to square it up. Also he cost something to set up in the business of fang-pulling. Sydney had to fork that out. Told me so himself. So Richard owed his brother a good turn of service if it happened to be needed. Richard, I may add, is a wholly amoral personage, so far as I'm a judge. So the service need not have been one of a high ethical nature.

"Now, observe this carefully. The whole of this carefully-staged affair seems to centre round Earlswood's illness. It only got into its swing when it was plain that the antrum trouble was likely to turn out fatal. And, at once, things began to move: you get the hiring of that garage, the scheme for getting Hawkstone's car numbers filed off, the supplementary cipher ad. inserted. . . ."

"How could they know the antrum trouble was going to be fatal?" demanded Standish, alertly.

"Wyndcliffe probably gave them his view about it. Remember that the dentist on that job was Richard B. and Sydney B. was Earlswood's friend and solicitor. They could show interest without raising any suspicion. And if Earlswood pulled through, they'd done nothing that would attract attention. They could just drop the scheme at that point. But as soon as Earlswood was dead, they got to work on the Campion affair, because they felt sure of their ground then."

"M'yes," said Standish, rather doubtfully. "Plausible, perhaps. I suppose it stands the test of dates. But where's the motive for it all?"

"In the Earlswood estate finances or I'm a Dutchman," declared The Counsellor, confidently. "Earlswood's death means an overhaul of the estate accounts. Sydney Barrington's firm has had charge of them for a generation. Assume he's been helping himself to the funds. Quite O.K., no doubt, so long as Earlswood lived. Sydney B. was an old friend, and Earlswood wasn't likely to demand an auditor's report from him. But when Earlswood's death threatens, like a bolt from the blue, then the missing cash had to be replaced almost at a moment's notice, to put things square for the auditors who were sure to be called in. Where was it to come from? Obvious source: the Hawkstone insurance."

"But even if Barrington collected that £15,000, he might have to pay it over to Mrs. Hawkstone under the partnership agreement," objected Standish. "He'd be no better off."

" 'He needs must go, whom the devil drives,' " retorted The Counsellor. "Shakespeare, that is. And Rabelais says: 'Necessity has no law.' Are you going to set yourself up against the Swan of Avon and the Curé of Meudon? They knew what they were talking about. No doubt he counted on his old friendship with Mrs. Hawkstone. She wouldn't press for the money immediately if he asked her to take an income instead, temporarily. Mere hypothesis, sez you? Maybe. But the man's a wrong 'un, convicted out of his own mouth on oath. That evidence he gave at the inquest was full of half-truths plus plain suppressions of facts. And, if you want my opinion, all that tale he told me about Mrs. Hawkstone planning a divorce was just a brilliant effort of his imagination. He'd pulled it off when he used it on Campion; and he thought it would pass muster with me when he made his gentlemen's agreement that I wasn't to bother Mrs. Hawkstone with questions about it. Sleeping dogs were to lie—like Barrington himself. See?"

The Inspector said nothing, but he made another

jotting in his notebook. The Counsellor smiled as he saw this. Hartwell obviously intended to follow up that hint about the Earlswood estate funds.

"You haven't dealt with Campion's death yet," Standish pointed out. "I'm still curious about it."

"The Campion affair is a side-issue," declared The Counsellor. "I believe Campion came by his end almost inadvertently, by mischance rather than according to plan. There's no need to produce irrefragable proof that he was murdered, so long as the Hawkstone murder case yields a conviction. You can't hang a man twice, so one conviction's enough."

Standish shrugged his shoulders, evidently unsatisfied with The Counsellor's recital of his views.

"You've given us a mere gallimaufry of stuff," he said critically. "What I'm still waiting for is a plain tale in proper sequence. Title: 'How it happened.' Have a dash at that, Mark."

"Gallimaufry's a good word," said The Counsellor. "I didn't know it was in your vocabulary, Wolf. Congratulations. And perhaps you're right. I've given you the facts and it seems you haven't been able to sort them out. Your fault, of course. I'll now proceed to remedy your deficiencies. Give you a straight tale from the start, in simple language and proper order, missing out proofs already supplied."

Chapter XVIII

THE SEQUENCE OF EVENTS

"THIS is how it was," began The Counsellor, with a slight variation in one of his favourite clichés. "I pass over the embezzlements of Barrington senior and the misdeeds of Barrington junior in times of yore and years long gone before, as it says in Burton's *Arabian Nights*. I've explained that they'd only come in if you want to prove motive, whereas there's no need to prove the existence of a motive when a man's tried for murder. So we begin with Earlswood feeling a pain in his upper jaw and visiting his dentist, who was Barrington junior. Barrington junior extracts the premolar tooth which seems to be the cause of the trouble.

"Now Richard Barrington, as he explained to me, has an ambition to make a name as an authority on odontology—or, in plainer English, he wants to write a book about fangs and their failings. And on this account he preserves all the defective grinders he removes from his patients and keeps them, carefully labelled no doubt, for reference. So there you have Earlswood minus one premolar and Richard Barrington in possession of this rather deteriorated article, which he adds to his collection with proper pride, no doubt.

"Next stage. Earlswood finds his jaw no better, and returns to his dentist. Richard Barrington then spots trouble in his patient's antrum. It's easy enough. Take patient into a dark room. Shove a small electric bulb into his mouth. Healthy side of the jaw shows up from outside as a sort of translucent red, whereas the pus on the diseased side appears as a dark shadow. Or you can do it by X-rays. What I mean is: that it's a simple business, quite within the scope of even Mr. Richard Barrington's technical outfit. An operation is required, within twenty-four hours. Wyndcliffe is called in. He drills a hole up into the antrum, via the socket of the extracted tooth, so as to drain the antrum, which is a natural cavity in the bone of the upper jaw, I may say. After the operation, Earlswood doesn't improve. A bit abnormal, that, for usually the operation is a complete success. Still, very occasionally things go wrong. Operation too late, or what not. The inflammation in Earlswood's antrum increases instead of subsiding. Wyndcliffe realises that it's going to be a case of a death certificate. He mentions this to Richard Barrington.

"Up to that stage, all's fair and above-board. But Richard passes the news on to brother Sydney, whom it shocks markedly owing to the likelihood of his little help-yourself methods coming to light if Earlswood dies. Most people admit that past events have led up to the present. Sydney Barrington probably wished that they didn't. But I once read a book by one Benjamin Kidd. His notion was that the future also controlled the present, because people do their best to ensure happiness in their future by taking pains with their present conduct. Whether Sydney Barrington had read Kidd or not, he acted like a true disciple He saw penal servitude in the future if he didn't mould his present doings properly. So he started in to mould 'em in quick time. He must have been a swift thinker, I imagine.

"Obviously, he and his brother between them hit

on the notion of collecting Hawkstone's insurance money: the handiest bit of substantial cash in sight. Then one of them—I suspect the legal brain—got the brilliant idea of substituting one body for another, and so piling up line upon line of defences, in case things went wrong. So the next move was the hiring of that garage in such a way that the identity of the hirer didn't transpire. 'Transpire' is correctly used there," said The Counsellor, with modest pride.

"At the same time, a second idea cropped up. Richard's this time, I guess, since it wasn't so clever as the first one. Richard knew all about the Hawkstone-Campion goings-on; and he couldn't have been ten minutes in Mrs. Campion's company without hearing how jealous her husband was. Why not drag Campion and his green-eyed monster across the trail, just to thicken things up a bit? So in went that faked cipher ad. about the week-end, just to provide ammunition if required.

"The next move was to get possession of Hawkstone's car for a night, and file off the engine and chassis numbers at leisure. As you know, they invited him to bridge. While Brother Sydney was at the card-table with his friends, Brother Richard went out into the garden and poured some water into Hawkstone's carburettor. So I suppose, anyway. It's what I'd do myself in such circs. So Hawkstone found his car wouldn't start and got a lift from Wyndcliffe. And the two brothers spent a happy hour or two with files, removing those numbers.

"And just in time, too. That very night, Wyndcliffe's prognosis came true. Earlswood got thrombosis and shortly afterwards departed this life. Then things began to move. Sydney Barrington got into touch with Campion and arranged a meeting with him. Next day came Earlswood's funeral. Sydney Barrington was Earlswood's solicitor, so obviously he must have known all about these curious provisions in the will which prevented the vault from being sealed up for a calendar month, on account of Earlswood's fear of premature burial.

"In the evening, after the funeral, Sydney met Campion and told him a few circumstantial lies about a projected Hawkstone divorce suit, with Mrs. Campion as co-respondent, backed up, of course, by the faked cipher ad. as conclusive *pièce de conviction*. And, in the small hours, either he or Richard paid a visit to the hired garage and screwed a fresh fastening on to its door. No doubt an examination of the premises was satisfactory. And the car left an oil drip.

"The next evening they had to work double tides. In the early part of it, Brother Sydney had to meet Campion and instil a few more suspicions into the poor devil's mind. Then, late at night, he had to make a trip with his brother to the cemetery. I assume they were both there, for body-snatching's a two-handed job at the least.

"As to the details of that affair, it was a sitter for two gentlemen like the Barringtons, with no scruples and few nerves. The caretaker of the cemetery—as I ascertained—never bothered to patrol the place after dark. They'd take their car to the church gate, which was a long way from the caretaker's cottage at the main cemetery gate. Sydney Barrington, as solicitor for the Earlswood estate, had the keys of the locks on the door of the vault, and also the seal used to put a guard on the coffin lid. He knew all about the electric warning gadget and how to put it out of action by disconnecting the wires from the binding-screws on the coffin. So they got poor Earlswood's body away easily enough, wrapped up in sacking, and dumped the bundle in the hired garage, where a girl saw it through a crack in the door next day. They probably put some bleaching-powder in the bundle for obvious reasons; and they brought two tins of petrol with them, which they left in the garage that night, ready for the bonfire. Probably they used Richard's car and left more oil drips in that garage.

"Now we come to the murder, which occurred on the following evening. Richard Barrington had gone down to his bungalow to establish some sort of alibi. Tried to strengthen it by leaving his car at the local garage to be fixed up. His alternative means of transit was that old bicycle which we fished up out of his lake to-day. No doubt he bought it second-hand from some dealer well out in the country; and as it was aluminium-painted, he re-enamelled it black to make it less conspicuous. Astride this destrier, he pedalled up to the Cross Roads, arriving at dusk, or later, and concealed his machine where the Inspector found the tyre-marks in the mud. Then he set off as an undistinguished pedestrian and made for his town house.

"Meanwhile, Brother Sydney had been doing his turn. He'd got hold of Hawkstone just when the office closed down. Or so I assume. And he'd made some excuse for seeing Hawkstone late that evening. Easy enough to fake up some urgent business, coupled with a tale of some engagement which would prevent him seeing Hawkstone till late in the evening at his house. I don't think he said anything then to make Hawkstone uneasy. Otherwise Hawkstone would hardly have spent his last evening in a spree of sorts with Mrs. Campion. Anyhow, on some excuse or other, Sydney lured Hawk-stone to the house in Avon Drive; and the Brothers Grimm, so to speak, were waiting for him when he turned up. The rest was pretty simple. Hawkstone already had one over the eight, and wouldn't mind taking another to put it into double figures. Richard was a dentist. He'd have novocaine in stock. You can call it procaine, if you don't like the other name. Put enough of it into a whisky-and-splash and the job's done, quietly, effectively, and with no fuss. I don't pin myself to novocaine. Any quick-acting painless poison would do. But they had novocaine handy. And so, exit Hawkstone.

"The fact that the body would have poison in its stomach didn't worry them; because they didn't mean *that* body to be found. They stripped off the outer clothes. Then they wrapped it round with plenty of lead piping which they'd secured in advance by that supposed house-breaking. They didn't need to break into that house. Brother Sydney had the keys, and why shouldn't a solicitor go and look over his client's property, thus showing zeal? No doubt they faked things to look as if a housebreaker had got in and stolen a lot of lead. But one can't blame the police for not catching *that* particular thief. Of course, before putting on the sinker, they must have gone through Hawkstone's pockets and removed anything likely to give away his identity at a glance. Most likely they found his key-ring with the insurance tag on it. Sydney would pouch that—and 'find' it next day at his office as he swore he did. They must also have mutilated the stone in the signet-ring, to suit their purposes.

"'First thing to do is to get rid of the body,' as Mr. W. W. Jacobs sagely remarks. So I expect they took it out and put it into Hawkstone's car as quick as they could. And here's a point where I offer two alternatives to you. One of their possible defences was that Campion had murdered Hawkstone and cleared out, leaving no trail. If they hit on this idea in advance, then Sydney Barrington's hint to Campion about Hawkstone visiting Avon Drive that night was intentional, and meant to lure the poor devil there. But possibly Brother Sydney made a mere mistake when he blurted that out; and that line of defence was an afterthought. If so, they must have been distinctly peevish when Campion discovered them shoving the body into the car. On this basis, he must have been hanging around the house, knowing that Hawkstone was coming and meaning to give him a thrashing when he could lay hands on him. The important point is that here was a witness who'd have to be silenced. No great difficulty in that. Our plausible friend Sydney would say a few words and get Campion to go into the house for further explanations. A drink and novocaine as before, and there was a second corpse on their hands. This time they didn't need the clothes. All they had to do was to wrap some more of the lead piping round the body and take it out to Hawkstone's car. They could pack both bodies into the back seat space and cover them up with a rug. And then Brother Richard would drive off, *en route* for that hired garage. If anyone heard the car, explanation was easy. That was Hawkstone going away after his visit.

"Now for Brother Sydney's alibi. A good dose of ipecac. or some other safe emetic was all he needed. A G.P., called in the middle of the night, would never think of the sickness as self-induced. And no doubt Sydney had been wise enough to order some indigestible dish in his dinner menu which he could blame for his sad state. So there he was, fitted out with a perfect alibi for the coming dirty work at the Cross Roads.

"Brother Richard had the hard end of the stick. He drove to the hired garage, where he unloaded the two bodies. Then he dressed Earlswood's body in Hawk-stone's evening clothes, including the dress shirt, on account of the links and studs. After that, he put Earlswood's body in Hawkstone's car, along with the two petrol tins which he'd stored in the garage, ready; then he locked up the garage with the two bodies in it and hared off for the Cross Roads. Arrived there, he took off the number plates and threw them away. Probably he'd unscrewed the bolts of them most of the way in the garage, so that no time would be wasted at the Cross Roads in getting them free. He'd also put Hawkstone's ring on the finger of Earlswood's body. *And* he was careful to drop Earlswood's tooth on to the floor by the driving seat. Why? Because Hawkstone had a complete set of snappers and Earlswood was one short. If there was a tooth in the car that fitted the gap in the set, nobody would be inclined to look further. They'd think it had got knocked out in a struggle or by accident. But if no tooth had been there, they might have begun examining the jaw and then they'd have found the hole drilled up into the antrum. See?

"The rest of the work there was easy. Richard emptied the two petrol tins into the car, mostly over the body, and threw the empty tins over the hedge. Then he took out the blue glass bottle which he had in his pocket and poured the solution of phosphorus in carbon disulphide over some dry place in the car, dropping the empty bottle alongside the body. And then he cleared out, unseen. In a few minutes at most, the stuff would evaporate; the phosphorus would catch fire; and off would go the petrol.

"The dancing-party must have bothered him a bit; but he would be over the hedge before they came up, and they didn't spot him. He recovered the bicycle, not noticing that the inflator was missing. It had got knocked off when the bicycle slipped as he leant it up against that gate so as to have his hands free to open the fastening. And so back to Avon Drive, where he'd hang about until he was sure the doctor had gone and the house was quiet again. Doubtless Brother Sydney hung out some signal that the coast was clear; a reading-lamp on or off in his bedroom, likely. Brother Richard could then go into the garage. No doubt they'd left the door open so as to avoid noise. He'd leave his bicycle there. Probably he shoved the car out on to the road by hand, lest the maids heard the self-starter going in the garage. And so off again to the hired garage to get the two weighted bodies aboard, drive them down to his bungalow, and sink them where we found them. Then back again in his brother's car, hell for leather because time was getting on. Then manhandle the car into the garage to save noise, get astride his bicycle, and off again to his bungalow. Probably he sent the bicycle to follow the bodies as soon as he got there. And so to bed, as Pepys remarked. You may have heard him called Pepps, and Peppis; but I assure you that Peeps is the true pronunciation. You'll find evidence of it in the parish records of Ashtead, if you doubt my word.

"And there I leave the pair of them, firmly entrenched behind four separate lines of defence, and no doubt as pleased as possible with the night's work.

"Explicit!"

>>> If you've enjoyed this book and would like to discover more great vintage crime and thriller titles, as well as the most exciting crime and thriller authors writing today, visit: >>>

The Murder Room
Where Criminal Minds Meet

themurderroom.com